I0563242

Down to Earth

by

Tammy D. Walker

The Daw County Sisters Mysteries,
Book Two

Down to Earth

Cover Art by *The Wild Rose Press, Inc.*

The Wild Rose Press, Inc.
PO Box 708
Adams Basin, NY 14410-0708
Visit us at www.thewildrosepress.com

Publishing History
First Edition, 2024
Trade Paperback ISBN 978-1-5092-5671-6
Digital ISBN 978-1-5092-5672-3

The Daw County Sisters Mysteries, Book Two
Published in the United States of America

Dedication

For all my fellow women in STEM

Chapter One

As thunder shook the old beams that held the Hengesbach farmhouse upright, Stacey Hengesbach shook her head at her daughter. The lights flickered. "Addie, I'm sorry," Stacey said. Lightning struck again, this time closer than the last. "We're not paying for you to drop out of school. You have two more years. Be patient." Which was, if she remembered right what being sixteen was like, just about as good as telling Addie she had another million years left before she could leave tiny Dawville, Texas for anywhere else.

"It's not dropping out, Mom." Addie grabbed a mug and filled it with the last of the coffee. "It's finishing my coursework early. I'll graduate. And I need to do this now."

"But you won't walk with your friends at graduation," Stacey said. She thought better of telling Addie not to drink so much caffeine. One argument at a time. "And there's junior prom, two homecoming dances you'll miss, and senior prom. You'll regret it."

Addie spooned sugar into her coffee. "No, Mom, you'll regret me missing all those dances." She hit the sides of the mug with the spoon as she stirred, sending dark brown splashes onto the counter. "I wouldn't have missed them in Germany if you'd have let me go this year."

"I don't think they have homecoming dances in

Germany, Addie." Stacey wiped up the spots of coffee off the counter. "At least they don't have homecoming mums, anyway."

"I'm not going to homecoming with a date this year."

Another flash brought Stacey's eye to the green apple clock on the kitchen wall. It had been Rick's grandmother's clock, one that had stopped not long after they were married. Rick took it off his grandmother's wall those decades ago. She'd told him if he could fix it, he could have it. He tinkered with it in the slow, careful way he tinkered with just about everything. One afternoon, he hung it up in their kitchen. The apple had ticked along cheerfully ever since. "It's time we took you to school."

"We?" Addie gulped down the rest of her coffee and set the mug down hard. "Are you not letting me drive myself to school now, too?"

"There's a nasty storm out, baby girl. That's all."

Addie grabbed the keys to her pickup, an old hand-me-down that had seen better days as the high school vehicle to all four of Stacey and Rick's kids. As the baby, Addie got the most run-down of things, but she never complained about it. "I'm going."

"Take the SUV," Stacey said. "If you're going out in the rain, at least take something more reliable."

"But you have errands to run today, Mom."

"I don't want to add pulling you out of the mud to the top of that list."

Addie put down the pickup keys and took the keyring with the SUV's remote dangling off it. "Fine," she said. Addie looked back at Stacey. She couldn't help but see her little girl in those big hazel eyes of hers, even if they were framed by purple hair. "I'll be back right after school to help with the trunk shakers."

"If the storm keeps up, we'll have to put off the harvest for a bit. Much as I don't want to do that." Stacey sighed, not wanting to think about how putting the pecan harvest off would mean putting off dozens of other time-sensitive tasks.

"See?" Addie smiled at Stacey for the first time that week. "You don't like waiting, either, do you?"

****

Stacey watched as long as she could as Addie drove off into the storm. Addie, like her other kids, had been driving farm trucks since she was big enough to see over the steering wheel. She'd jumped into a UTV at eight years old and hadn't looked back. Like Rick, Addie was practical about things. It wasn't Addie she was worried about. It was the other drivers, the other kids Addie's age that didn't have her experience behind the wheel and elsewhere. Another bolt of lightning flashed. Thunder shook the kitchen. Rick had gone to town for a bit to get a new tire for their old tractor, and Stacey felt the weight of her own solitude like she wouldn't be able to hold up too much longer underneath it.

She sat down at the kitchen table with her laptop and a cup of coffee. At least getting the documents ready for their next round of taxes would keep her mind off Addie for a while until the storm raged on.

Her phone buzzed with a message from Addie.

—*Got here okay.*—

Which was another reason she and Rick ought to have let Addie go to Germany her junior year as she'd wanted to do since passing the language test her freshman year. They'd driven down to Houston together as a family, Stacey, Rick, Addie, and Ethan, the kids taking their German exams at the Goethe Center while Stacey and Rick waited. Stacey's grandparents were fluent, and Rick's mother, too, though the Texas dialect they'd spoken wasn't quite the same as what the kids had learned in class. Still, it connected them to family, didn't it? Even if it wasn't a language Stacey or Rick understood at all.

Addie had begun to collect brochures and catalogs, travel magazines and pamphlets all aimed at studying in Germany. Stacey never asked Addie why. She knew the lure of somewhere else was strong enough when she'd lived in this one small Texas town her entire life.

Sun filtered in through the althea bush that grew too close to the house. She couldn't use the storm as an excuse anymore, and she needed to run a few errands. A pecan cake she'd baked yesterday waited in a cake taker for her first errand. Stacey had been tasked by the Dawville Lutheran Ladies' League to welcome a newcomer who'd just bought the fifteen acre plot of land once owned by the mother of their neighbor, Harold Dutton. Just how the newcomer had managed to get Harold to part with it was a mystery, one no one in Dawville had managed to solve yet. No one had managed to make any real contact with her, the woman with the designer pant suits who hadn't done much shopping around town except for a few quick trips into the grocery store for produce. Her car was always there, so the DLLL figured she was either an early retiree or she worked from home. A friendly visit from a Dawville Lutheran Lady might break her from her silence. As her nearest neighbor, Stacey had been assigned the job.

****

Stacey bumped the truck over the gravel drive that led to the newly paved county road. If anything, Stacey should have been excited about the paving. That and the two-lane highway that had finally been completed as a four lane with a bridge over the railroad crossing. Between the winery boom and the vineyards taking off, Dawville had been named one of the most exciting small towns to relocate to by more than one big city publication. Even for all the road updates and the new shops and cottages going in where farmland once was, though, Dawville was still the small town she'd grown up in, the one her kids had grown up in. The cake shifted in the pickup's front seat as she waited at a red light to turn from the county road onto the highway.

Sunlight glittered off the signs in the shopping center. A bucket truck parked in front of the Bluet Café. A worker in the bucket was taking down the old wooden sign and putting up the new lighted sign with the little blue flowers each done in glass surrounding the café's name. Stephanie, her best friend since second grade, had beamed when she showed Stacey the designs for it a month ago. Stacey lifted a hand to wave to Stephanie overseeing the light's installation, but no way her friend could see Stacey from here. The light turned green, and Stacey pulled onto the highway.

Fifteen minutes later, Stacey arrived at the acreage that had belonged to Harold Dutton's late mother. The place, mostly scrub surrounding an old wooden cottage, hadn't been well kept in the last decade or so the old woman had lived there, and Harold had done just about nothing to it after she moved into the nursing home the last few years of her life. No one had heard about the place going on the market, which was only a little surprising, given how fast farms had been cut up and sold to folks moving in from California, Oregon, or New York. Some places had barely shown up on real estate listings before they were listed as "pending," "under contract," then "sold." She and Rick had thought about selling off part of their grazing land earlier when drought had threatened their pecan crop, but they'd thought better of it. The farm had been in the Hengesbach family for four generations. She and Rick couldn't sell any of it, or that would feel like failure.

Stacey pulled her old truck toward the house over the trim new concrete driveway. So that was what all those concrete trucks had been about. A fleet of pickups flanked the driveway, all filled with tools and lumber. The house stood about a quarter of the way in from the edge of the fifteen acre lot. About twenty yards behind the old cottage, a frame for a much larger building stood. Workers emerged from their trucks into the yard.

"You looking for Ms. Clarke?" The foreman, someone Stacey didn't recognize, pointed to the cottage. He continued tapping at a tablet. The folks around here in construction couldn't keep up, so it was just as well Tess Clarke had brought someone in from wherever she'd come from. "She's in there."

The cake looked as though it hadn't fared well, but Stacey brought it with her anyway. The cottage had been painted and the windows replaced. At least that meant the newcomer wasn't planning to knock down Mrs. Dutton's cottage. Stacey balanced the cake taker in one hand as she pushed the button beneath the doorbell camera. How much had that cost, getting internet access all the way out here? No one answered after a few moments, so Stacey tried again.

"Yes?" came a clipped voice from the speaker. "Are you with the workers? I've asked that all communication go through Mr. Lane, the foreman, particularly when I'm working."

"Sorry to bother you, ma'am." Stacey shifted the cake taker, angling it toward the camera. "I'm not with the workers. I'm with the Dawville Lutheran Ladies' League. Mrs. Muller, the pastor's wife, said she'd asked if this would be a good time to drop by."

"Well." The intercom buzzed for a moment and went silent. After a few moments, the door opened. A tall woman with sharply cut hair around her angled face looked out from behind it. "Come in, then. I'm Tess Clarke."

Stacey wiped her boots on the mat and followed the woman inside. Much work had been done on the inside of the cottage as well. Gone were the quilts and ditsy prints, the doilies and lace curtains Stacey remembered from her time as a younger member of the DLLL sitting with the dour widow. And long before that, too. Arranged between stark white walls were a modern teal sofa and two imposingly straight-backed chairs. Three black canvases hung opposite the windows, which were covered with black curtains. A metal light fixture hung down from the ceiling. It had blades, so it must have been a fan. The new owner spoke a few words at no one in particular, and the lights came up. Stacey could see now that there was a sort of texture to the black canvases, something you had to look hard to see. "Please, sit. Would you like tea?"

"That sounds nice, thanks," Stacey said. "May I bring this to the kitchen?"

"Is it another cake?"

"Another?"

"The Catholics brought one yesterday," she said curtly. "And the day before that, Mrs. Dutton."

"Mrs. Dutton?"

"Not the dead one, of course."

Stacey laughed. "Not the dead one, right. It's just that we don't see the living Mrs. Dutton around Dawville all that much either."

"Better the living one than the dead one." Tess Clarke motioned to the coffee table, which held a couple black and white photography books. "I'll have the tea out in a moment and plates for the cake. The Catholic woman didn't stay long over the hummingbird cake she'd brought, but Mrs. Dutton lingered."

Stacey nodded, but she stopped herself from saying more. She didn't like to gossip. Even if this was exactly the sort of posh place the younger Mrs. Dutton had bragged about frequenting before. In the brighter light of the fixture overhead and a couple metal lamps that could have been made out of angled scraps Rick kept just in case they'd ever be useful, Stacey took a closer look around. She wasn't sure what she was looking for, exactly. Stacey had met a fair number of women like Tess Clarke who had recently moved to Dawville. Women who were somewhere between forty and sixty, active, stylish, sharp. For the most part, they'd kept to themselves at first, but ultimately, they joined either the Lutherans or the Catholics, and they settled in as best as they could while maintaining what ties they had to bigger cities. Remote workers themselves or wives of remote workers, they could live the small town life without needing the small town the way she and Rick needed the land or Stephanie needed the café and the people who worked in it. Stacey hadn't yet figured out how she felt about so many new people moving in all at once. It was hard to untangle how she felt about them and how she felt about the wine industry and how Dawville itself was moving forward, unable to resist change entirely.

Tess Clarke pushed a small cart on which was a sleek modern tea set with matching cups, saucers, and plates for cake. Tea steamed in the pot. "The tea is Assam, which is quite strong, and what I prefer. Fortunately, it's easily shipped in from the shop I used to go to in Houston. The tea grows in one area in India, which is rather like Champagne or Bordeaux, only more accessible, but it's not as fussy as Darjeeling. Does this area have a designation for its wines?"

"What?"

"For the wines. As they do in France. Brilliant marketing, that. Trademark the name of a place and its associated wines. There's a long German heritage here, so there's that, but the climate of Central Texas and Germany are so different, the grapes you might grow here wouldn't be analogous to those a vintner in Germany might grow." Tess poured tea and offered Stacey the cream and sugar. The tea was hot and smelled strong, like the smell of dead branches in fall.

"We don't grow grapes," Stacey said. "We grow pecans."

"We who?" Tess opened the cake taker. "Oh, pecan cake. Do pecans have terroir, like wines?"

"We, my husband Rick and I," Stacey said. "And our kids."

"I never married," Tess said. She cut an exact piece of cake and set it on a plate for Stacey. She cut herself another, nearly the same, cutting through the pecans cleanly. A sharp knife, one hardly used, or newly sharpened anyway. "And no children. Which must set me apart from women in Dawville."

"Maybe before things changed," Stacey said. The tea was still far too hot. She broke off a small piece of pecan cake with the awkwardly thick tines of the squared off fork. Something industrial about that too. The cake, though, the cake was as good as she'd hoped it would be. A recipe handed down from her great-grandmother, though improved over time as the generations got access to different ingredients. But the spirit of the cake remained. The generosity of it, the act of welcome and friendship.

"Well, then," Tess said. "Let's get down to why you're here."

Stacey swallowed her bite of cake. If the tea hadn't been too hot, she might have taken a sip or two to stall. Why was she here? Community building, there's that. Welcoming a new member to the area. Maybe it had been a mistake to volunteer. They should have sent Tiffany, the librarian who'd grown up in suburban Austin. They should have sent any number of the women who'd moved to Dawville not long ago from their upper crust Dallas neighborhoods, and who'd settled in right away to small town life. Or those who'd built a weekend home here and still worked in their Houston interior design firms or advertising agencies. Or, if she'd deign to listen to the DLLL's request, Minty Sanders, the wife of the retired Daw County judge and heiress to her grandfather's oil wealth. Anyone but Stacey. Tess had bought up so much acreage, they'd all thought she must have been at least a hobby farmer. Not from the looks of it. "Just to drop by and welcome you to Dawville."

"And ask me to attend church services?" Tess sipped at her tea. Maybe if you drank boiling water all the time, you got used to it, the way Stacey had gotten used to making coffee then getting too busy to drink it until it had cooled. "You said you were from the Lutheran women's something or another?"

"If you're interested," Stacey said. "We have an active group there."

"Sorry, no," Tess said. "Never much interested me. Do you have a botanical society?"

"At the church?"

A knock at the door. Tess stood up and excused herself. Stacey looked down at her jeans against the crisp teal upholstery, her boots on the black rug. Obviously, Tess Clarke would not be interested in her homey pecan cake and her church ladies' group. Stacey looked down at the photography books that Tess had slid over to make room for the boxy tea service. One showed the artwork of someone Stacey had never heard of, someone modern and hard to understand. The other was skyscrapers at odd angles. Why, Stacey wondered, did people move here if they just wanted to go to the city anyway? Why bring the city here when the city had enough land and people as it was?

"Of course, not at the church," Tess said, picking up the conversation where it had left off, as if there had been no knock at the door. "Though if you must mix up biology and religion, I suppose the church is where that will take place."

Stacey shook her head. "Faith is a matter of the heart," she said. "And we do go to church for that. As for farming, we're pretty keen on the science that comes out of the county extension office." She finished her last bite of the pecan cake, regretting that such a good one should be left for someone who wouldn't appreciate the fact that the pecans had come from her family's farm. "I should go if you need to talk to your construction crew."

"I don't," Tess said. "Not a construction matter. Harold Dutton wanted to see me. Yet again. I asked the foreman not to let Mr. Dutton onto the property, or else I'll be forced to call the police and report him as a trespasser. His wife was cordial enough. Even if she talked at me for the better part of an hour when she dropped off that lovely opera cake from the Bluet Café. It was, until Mr. Dutton came threatening me and accusing me of stealing the land from him. Stealing, as if I'd steal anything. I paid the sale price his agent asked for. Lucky timing, that. I was first in line, for once." Tess looked coldly at the covered windows. "You move out to the countryside for some peace and quiet, and then people come parading in at all hours. I do have work to do, you know."

"There must have been some misunderstanding, then," Stacey said. She picked up her battered old bag and stood up. "Mrs. Muller said she'd arranged a time with you."

"She did ask if I would be free this morning," Tess said. "I said that I could be free if needed."

Mrs. Muller had made no mention of Tess's wording. Stacey stuck out her hand. "I won't keep you then," she said. "It was nice to meet you."

Tess turned and walked to the door to open it. "I do need to call my lawyer again, to document the further attempted harassment by Mr. Dutton."

Stacey dropped her hand. "He might be grieving, you know," she said. She went to the doorway.

Somewhere behind them, a table saw shrieked as it ripped into a piece of lumber. "This is the house he grew up in, and it's the house his mother lived in for all but the last few years of her life. Maybe he regrets selling it."

"He claims not to have sold it," Tess said. "I've offered to show him the documents."

"Documents don't do a thing for grief, Ms. Clarke."

"They do prove that I'm in the right, however. Good day, Mrs. Hengesbach."

Chapter Two

Stacey drove carefully out of the old Dutton place. She knew she shouldn't call it that any more, but Tess Clarke's attitude proved all the more that this is what it was. And nails in tires were always a possibility. She put it out of her mind and focused on her next errands. She had paperwork to drop off at the winery association for the upcoming Wine and Pecan Festival. She looked down at her jeans and boots. Jenna Bailey, who'd lived here for the better part of a decade now, had been a welcome part of their community almost on her arrival with her family. But something about the meeting with Tess Clarke unnerved Stacey. She'd have time to go home and change even if she stopped in at the Bluet Café and had a cup of coffee. That would be welcome after the Assam tea she couldn't drink.

As she came to the light, she pulled up to a stop just behind the newly painted crosswalks. Though she hadn't been pulled over, she'd heard too many stories of trucks nosed a few inches past where they should have been and then getting citations from Sheriff Williams and his crew who focused a little too much on traffic violations now that the money for his department came from taxing the newcomers. Somehow, he had gotten himself on the good side of both the newcomers and the long-time residents, and he had an election coming up soon to think about. No one walked here, or not that anyone she knew of or saw walked. Mostly newcomers drove pickups that were too shiny and clean to have done any sort of work. Maybe she was a little jealous. The pickup idled a little rough, and maybe it was time to retire it to the field. Something to worry about later. The light changed, and Stacey pulled out into the intersection. A ping echoed though the truck's cab, then the tell-tale roughness of her rim against the new pavement. Stacey whispered a few choice words to herself, turned on her hazard lights, then looked for a way to pull over fast. Fortunately, a tractor going about as slow as she was let her into the right lane, and she made her way from there to the parking lot of the Bluet Café.

She bumped carefully as she could to an open area in the parking lot. Something flashed in her rear-view mirror, and she came to a stop in the middle of a few open spaces. That would give her enough room to change the tire. The door squealed open. Behind her, the back driver's side tire was starting to shred. Stacey cursed the new construction making Dawville shiny and clean as a toy pickup. She pulled the metal from what was left of her tire and tossed it into the toolbox in the back of the truck's bed. Whatever it was looked vaguely like a small horseshoe with pointed ends like a goat's hoof.

"Saw you had some trouble there, sweetheart."

Stacey breathed in hard, like coming up from under the water too long. "Just some metal in a tire," she said to the sheriff. "Got a spare in the back. I'm good."

"Naw, let me help you." Sheriff Les Williams, Jr., put his hand on the side of his uniform-covered paunch. "Ain't right if I don't help a lady in trouble."

"Oh, it's no trouble," Stacey said. She pulled on her leather work gloves then reached into the truck bed to get the spare and tools to change the tire. "I've been changing tires since before I could drive."

Sheriff Williams grabbed her shoulders and led her away from the truck. "Why don't you get yourself a cup of coffee while I take care of this tire?"

"Because it's my truck, my tire, and my tools," Stacey said. "The jack's a little crooked, and the underside of the truck took a piece of lumber the wrong way ages ago. I know this truck and my tools. I can fix it."

A smirk pinched the sheriff's face. He grabbed the spare tire and dropped it to the ground. Instead of landing flat, the tire bounced and rolled toward the highway. Stacey thanked her boots and dashed after it. The tire rolled through the lot and sailed into the grassy ditch between the shopping center and the busy road beyond. Just in time, Stacey kicked the tire on its side. She grabbed it and ran back to her truck.

"If you don't mind," Stacey said, "I appreciate your offer to help, but I can do this. And I have to get home soon to see to the trunk shakers." Stacey laid the tire flat, then grabbed the tools.

Sheriff Williams made a sort of grunt she could just barely hear over the passing cars. "You changed lanes without signaling. I could give you a citation for that."

"I didn't signal because I had my hazards on," she said. Stacey pulled the hub cap off and began to undo the bolts that held the wheel to the truck. "Besides, I waved to the tractor driver, and he let me over. I did signal my intent to get off the highway."

"You're having a lucky day, aren't you? I won't cite you because you were doing the best you could," he said. "You give me a call if you need something."

"That's generous of you," Stacey said. She wiped grease and dirt onto the knee of her jeans. "I appreciate that."

"As long as you do." Sheriff Williams got back into his patrol car and pulled back onto the highway.

At least Stacey had the good fortune of stopping just in front of the Bluet Café. She could use a good cup of coffee right about now.

Even at mid-morning, the café was half full. Mostly the couples who came here to retire or the groups of wives who had no outside work, or, for that matter, no inside work in their homes either. Stephanie had a good eye for business, taking the Bluet Café from a breakfast and lunch place locals would come to for a hot meal and to catch up on the local news to a boutique coffee and pastry shop with extended hours for afternoon tea. Stephanie was Dawville through and through still. She kept local favorites on the menu, the hearty bacon and eggs plates and homey pecan pies alongside quiches and croissants. She even served Darjeeling tea.

No one would know by looking at her that she'd had it as hard as she did. Worked her way through community college, then got pregnant with her daughter before she could graduate with her bookkeeping certificate. She had a nice, small wedding—Stacey was her matron of honor—and she and her new husband moved into a little trailer next to the shop where he worked. They both had big ideas about life, so he left her at home with her mother-in-law and a toddler and went to work on an oil rig in the Gulf of Mexico. The money was good, much better than he'd brought in working in Dawville. And he could come home for a week after being away for a while and just spend time with his young family. Something wrong happened one time on the rig, and for a while, Stephanie just froze up, doing what she needed to do to take care of her daughter and her grieving mother-in-law. Stacey and their other friends did what they could, taking the baby for afternoons and bringing dinners over. When she finally came out of her shock, she took the insurance check from the oil company and bought out the Gruene Family Diner when the last of the Gruenes who still lived in Dawville wanted to retire.

Everyone said she should have put the money away for her daughter, that she blew it on this failing business. It was February, and maybe because these little star-shaped flowers were everywhere underfoot, Stephanie renamed the diner the Bluet Café, and, with the help of her mother-in-law, she turned the place into a success.

The Bluet was even successful enough for the likes of Minty Sanders and her crowd. Mrs. Sanders opened the door to the café. She stepped out with such grace in her heels that Stacey wondered whether the boarding school she's gone to as a girl had taught her that walk. From a tiny bag, she slipped a pair of oversized sunglasses and settled them over the perfect arcs of her eyebrows.

"Good morning, Mrs. Sanders." A rock that must have wedged itself in the tread of her boot pushed up into Stacey's foot. She shifted.

"Isn't it." Mrs. Sanders unlocked her Mercedes with a remote. "If you'll excuse me."

Stacey nodded and stepped out of the way, though Mrs. Sanders was headed the other direction.

The bells rung on the door as Stacey opened it. Over the hum of the crowd, Stephanie called out to Stacey.

Stacey stomped any mud she might have had on her boots from the old Dutton place onto the mat outside and went in. At the corner of the tidy bar beside the case that showed off cakes and pies and all kinds of delicate pastries, Stephanie sat a cup of pecan coffee and a little pitcher of creamer. "You look like you could use about three of these," Stephanie said.

Stacey breathed in the coffee's nutty aroma. Coffee brewed with 100% local pecans grown at the Hengesbach Family Farm. She poured in the cream and watched it swirl around the surface. "It's been a morning," Stacey said. "Been out to the old Dutton place. Ms. Tess Clarke is a piece of work."

"Weekender?"

"Worse, I think," Stacey said. She sipped the coffee, smooth and comforting. "She's building a new house behind Mrs. Dutton's cottage."

"She's not tearing down the cottage, is she?" Stephanie folded her arms over her apron, hand-embroidered with tiny four-pointed bluets by a local shop. "Such a sweet little house. It's part of Dawville history."

"Not sure what she's doing," Stacey said. "I took off after she had to deal with Harold Dutton wanting to speak to her. She didn't want to speak to him."

"Who would want to speak to him?" Stephanie smirked and shook her head. "Latest gossip around the pastry case is that Judy finally got fed up with him and found herself a nice apartment somewhere in Houston."

"Judy's been fed up with him for ages, though." Stacey took another sip of her coffee. The warmth of it settled her. "I'm not surprised, anyway."

"Apparently, Harold was. How can you be married

to someone for ten years and be that unaware of what's going on in your own marriage?" Stephanie looked over toward the door. Her own marriage was too short, hadn't it been? At least a dozen men had tried and failed to get Stephanie back down the aisle over the past twenty years. Anyway, Stacey did have an idea about how someone could be that unaware of what's going on in their own marriage, but she didn't want to say so.

"If it makes her happy. Couldn't have been good with Harold being as tight-fisted as he is the whole time." Stacey shrugged. "Tess Clarke said she brought over a cake from the café. Judy must have been in a good mood then. Or got some cash."

Stephanie nodded. "Special order. She asked for the nicest cake I could make. Told her I wanted to try a recipe for a chocolate opera cake. She didn't even flinch at the price. I made two, and it was divine. Mom and I split a piece, and the rest sold out in ten minutes."

"Save a piece for me next time, will you?"

"If Judy Dutton needs to get something out of Tess Clarke, I sure will."

Stacey followed Stephanie's gaze over to the door. As the bells rang out, Vanessa Dumont pushed her way through with what must have been dozens of freshman writing essays to grade. Something passed over Vanessa's face when she saw Stacey and Stephanie watching her, then Stacey saw why. Through the door came Addie, red faced and wiping her nose with a tissue.

"Oh, good grief," Stacey said. She started to get up, but Stephanie put a hand on her arm. She wanted to push her friend away, remembering the way Sheriff Williams had tried to move her away from her own truck. But she looked at Stephanie instead.

"Cheryl went through the same thing at this age," Stephanie said. Cheryl, Stephanie's daughter, was majoring in accounting, on scholarship at college. Stacey remembered Cheryl's more rebellious days, but still it felt like a punch seeing her own daughter with Vanessa, someone who'd been trying to make friends with Stacey since she'd moved to Dawville seven years ago to head the English department at Daw County Community College. "Let Addie have some space."

"Some space?"

One of the waitresses led Vanessa and Addie to the professor's usual booth in back where she often set up for hours to grade papers. If Addie had seen Stacey, she showed no signs of it.

"She just needs to push against you to figure out who she is," Stephanie said. "You know this. You've been here three times before."

"It's different," Stacey said. "She's my youngest." She drank down the rest of her coffee. "She sent me a text this morning telling me she got to school okay."

"Don't you remember what it was like being sixteen?"

"I do." Stacey remembered a little too well. She hadn't been rebellious, exactly, but she did have her moments. Drinking at the lake with her friends when she'd told her parents she'd gone to Stephanie's house to spend the night. Ditching gym class to sit under the bleachers and trash talk their teachers. And then there was Dale Hillegeist. Stacey and Rick started going out their freshman year after they started talking during an FFA meeting after school that fall. During the summer between their sophomore and junior years, Rick declared they needed to take a break until fall. She never did ask him what he did that summer. And she couldn't figure out whether she felt what she'd done with Dale was something to bad to confess or just something exciting to remember. They'd gone around town together for weeks, sometimes parking under the stars and making out in the back of his half-rusted out Camaro. The night before school started, she let Dale, briefly, get to third base with her before stopping his hands. Stacey had been having fun with Dale, but Rick still had her heart. She knew if she and Dale went too far, then she'd risk not getting Rick back. They did get back together, and, a couple years later, Rick proposed to her on the night of the Senior Prom. "Unfortunately, I do. Remember, I mean."

"Be easy on her," Stephanie said. "Don't push her further away."

Stacey sighed. "Thank you." She put down her empty coffee cup. "For the coffee. And the advice."

Addie had been crying. She could never hide that, not from Stacey. Vanessa had set her box of essays on the seat of the extra chair at their table, and she had her arm around Addie. They were huddled together, as if they were sharing some secret Stacey couldn't fathom.

"Made it?" Stacey said. She started to pull out the fourth chair around the table but stopped when Addie shot her a look. "Don't say you didn't lie to me because you didn't specifically say you'd made it to school."

"Mom—" Stacey wanted to move Vanessa out of the way, put her arm around her daughter, but she was also madder than she'd been in a while. Skipping school was, as far as she knew, new for Addie. "I can explain." Addie took in a long shuddering breath and looked up with those big hazel eyes of hers. Must have been looking at the ceiling, trying to stop crying?

"You can explain skipping school?"

Vanessa motioned to the free chair. "Stacey, sit, please. I'm glad you're here too. I found Addie looking upset when I went over to the high school." Vanessa taught one class there, a senior English class that gave students credit for that course as well as for their freshman writing classes at Daw County Community College.

"I think it's best I don't sit," Stacey said. Though she was something of a newcomer, Vanessa Dumont had made it a point to show up at just about all the local festivals and events, even to the point of becoming secretary of the Daw County Lutheran Ladies' League and historian of the Friends of the Daw County Library. More Amy's friend than Stacey's, which made sense since her sister had been one of the two librarians at the Daw County Public Library for the past twenty years until she left Dawville to work as a librarian on some luxury cruise ship. Years ago, Addie had confided in Stacey that Vanessa was someone she wanted to be like when she grew up, though Addie couldn't explain quite why at the time. Stacey knew. Stacey saw in Vanessa what Addie must have seen: some glimpse into another life, another world. Vanessa wrote poetry. And she read it to the good people of Daw County, who politely smiled and nodded, though she might as well have been speaking another language. Maybe a language Addie was beginning to understand? "I think it best that I take my daughter back to the high school."

"It's lunch time, Mom," Addie said. She gasped between sniffles. "My weird early lunch time, and I'm allowed to be off campus for another fifteen minutes. And if I'm late, I'm just missing study hall."

"That's not the point, Addie," Stacey said. "Vanessa took you from campus without my permission."

"Mom, that's not true," Addie said. Her eyes had begun to water again, and her mascara made long trails down her cheeks. Vanessa handed her a small packet of tissues. "I asked Vanessa if I could talk to her away from everyone else at school, and she said she'd take me here."

"Was she going to drop you off at school again?"

"Yes," Vanessa said. "Of course."

Stacey pointed to the pile of essays. "You brought an awful lot of work with you for just a quick cup of coffee and a pep talk."

"I meet the rest of my department here Thursdays for lunch," Vanessa said. "It's our departmental meeting for the week. And sometimes I stay on for a bit until I teach my afternoon classes at the college." She set her bag on the pile of papers. "And why are you interrogating me? You haven't even asked why your own daughter is so upset."

"I know why my daughter is upset, thank you," Stacey said. Even over the chatter in the café and the clanking of dishes around her, she heard a faint sound of sirens. A lot of them. "If you must know, we'd started this discussion this morning, so I am more than aware of what is upsetting my daughter, who wants to drop out of school." Stacey shook her head. For an educator, this was too much. "And you, of all people, are taking her away from school, probably telling her, oh, sure, it's fine to drop out. Go have an adventure and don't think about your future."

"No, Mom," Addie started. She hiccupped.

Red and blue lights strobed into the big picture

windows of the café. The dining area got quiet really fast, everyone stopping mid-bite and craning their necks to see where the lights were coming from and where they were going. A fire truck was followed by an ambulance and two of the county sheriff's office's big SUVs, all screaming down the highway back down the way she'd just come from Tess Clarke's, from the Duttons' place that sprawled just behind it.

For a moment, Stacey wondered whether something had gone wrong at the construction site. Some accident, or something on fire. Wouldn't that make things worse for Ms. Clarke. Stacey shouldn't think things like that. She was just mad, just burning mad, from folks like Tess Clarke changing Dawville. Folks like Vanessa. And, to tell the truth, she was mostly just mad about them setting things up so that Addie thought it would be okay to miss out on her last two years in Dawville.

Traffic must have been stopped somewhere, since there was a gap even after the trucks had blown by. After the pause, in dramatic fashion, a Camaro blew by, lights and sirens letting everyone know. "Oh," Stephanie said into the silence after the changing tones of his siren had faded. "Wasn't that Sheriff Williams?"

"Must be a damsel in distress somewhere," Stacey said. "It is election season."

About half the folks in the café chuckled. Across the highway from the café was the smiling face of Sheriff Williams himself, looking sternly from his campaign billboard that reminded everyone to vote for him in November.

"You don't think he could be following the rest of the emergency vehicles?" Vanessa was still looking sympathetically at Addie. "Going wherever they were?"

"Maybe," Stacey said. "Looks like the sheriff's office already had two trucks on their way. But maybe you missed seeing that? Unless it was something that bad, I don't think they'd need the great sheriff himself." Addie had gone pale under her red cheeks and nose. "We need to get you back to school, young lady."

"I can take her," Vanessa said. "Laura and Jae are here." She nodded out the window. The other two members of the Daw County Community College English Department were coming out of a parked car. "They can watch the table for a few minutes."

"Of course not," Stacey said. "Get your bag, Addie. We're going back to school."

"But, Mom," Addie pleaded. "Can I go home and wash my face at least?"

Stacey shook her head at her youngest child. "Last I checked, there were bathrooms at the high school that had soap and water. You need to get to class." Addie didn't argue. They rode to the school in silence, neither one looking at the other the whole way there.

Chapter Three

The ground had been too wet to run the shakers, those machines that grabbed the trunks of their pecan trees and shook from them the ripe pecans. Early fall storms were nothing unexpected, but still, Stacey didn't like this part of her job, the uncertainty of it. She did like the rest of it though. The trees were there for them year after year. Even when they were dormant, she knew their presence, she loved the feel of their rough bark under her hand. The Hengesbachs—Rick's parents—had put in the first of the current pecan trees just before they'd brought Rick and Stacey, newly graduated with their agriculture degrees from Sam Houston State University, into the business.

In a way, the whole thing seemed too easy. Since she was a kid in her dad's tractor repair shop, she'd known she wanted to live on the land here, do what seemed like a sort of magic with the dirt and water and seeds. She and her younger sister Amy had been in 4-H since they were old enough to join. Amy had made hand-sewn things, embroidered and quilted together objects that she might have read about in those books she'd always had her nose in. Then, she switched to baking.

Stacey, however, knew from the start what project she wanted to do, which one she was certain she'd get a ribbon for. Growing things. Their grandmother's garden was a place of such comfort for her. Not just the flowers she grew, but the steady progress through the year of the vegetables and fruits she planted, of the peaches and pecans off the few trees they had in their yard. Her mother would take Stacey and Amy over on Sundays after church. Amy would sit inside, working on her projects or reading a book. Stacey would go out with her grandmother to see what was growing. She had a sharp mind for remembering what kinds of seeds came from packets or, just as likely, what came from seed her grandmother saved or had traded seed with a neighbor for. Just a patch of three acres, house, small garden, and a few chickens, but it seemed like an entire kingdom to Stacey when she was a kid. Their grandfather drove long-haul trucks, and when he came home, he'd tell them about what he'd seen along the way to where he'd been and back again. Amy could sit in wonder at her grandfather telling them about the different cities he'd passed through, or sights he'd seen along the side of the long highways he'd driven. But Stacey could feel it even then what brought him home, how good, just good, it was to sit on the porch swing with his iced tea, taking in this little world they'd created here.

She was thankful too for her dad taking her into his garage, his work, where he took things apart, figured out what was wrong, and put them back together again, good as new. Told her he wouldn't teach her how to drive until she could change a flat tire. Told her he wouldn't take her to her driver's test until she could change the oil in her truck.

Amy hadn't needed to do either. Stacey figured their mother must have talked him out of that for their less handy child. Sometimes, you had to make different rules for different kids, even if you were all part of the same family. Stacey imagined Amy would go off and settle somewhere grand and exciting, but, no, when she'd almost finished her library science degree, she met her husband Neil, a wine broker from England who'd settled on a career working with Central Texas vintners, and they came right back to Dawville.

For a while, anyway. Once Angus, their only child, graduated from high school, Neil decided he'd had enough of Daw County and its wines, and he moved to Houston to start over again. Amy took a job as a librarian on a cruise ship. And Angus went off to Texas A&M along with two of his cousins, Stacey's oldest two boys. So maybe Stacey was right about Amy. It just took her a while to fly away. Stacey wondered if Amy regretted staying in Dawville so long, but she didn't know how to ask. Or she just didn't want to find out.

Stacey tossed in bed. Rick had come home late, did the thing where he tried to shower and get in bed as quietly as he could so as not to wake her. Stacey played along and pretended to sleep. She didn't want to talk now, anyway. Addie had taken her dinner into her room, saying she had too much homework to sit at the big dining table that had once seated their family of six. Stacey took her plate to the kitchen, turned on the news, and tried to pay attention to what the anchors and reporters said about places that were beyond her.

****

Addie must have woken earlier than she usually did, or she hadn't slept. Stacey decided it must have been the latter. Dark circles haunted the girl's eyes and her shoulders slumped. She was dressed, though, and her purple hair was back in a neat, low ponytail. Her bag slumped too, waiting for her at the door. Cup of coffee in one hand and keys to the old truck in the other, Addie gestured at her mother. "I'm going."

"No, you're not," Stacey said. "You're half asleep. I'm driving you this morning."

Addie slung her bag over her shoulder. Hot coffee sloshed from the cup onto her t-shirt, but Addie didn't flinch. "I'm fine, Mom."

Stacey grabbed the truck keys from Addie. She didn't resist, but she did glower at her mother. "Truck has the spare on. I need to go get a new tire for it before you can take it again."

"I'll take the SUV, then."

"No, I need the SUV. I need to go see Jenna." Stacey grabbed the keys off the pegboard before her sluggish daughter could turn for them.

"Mom—"

A knock on the front door echoed through the house. No one used the front door, just the one that led out the back from the kitchen. Rick called out that he'd get it. Stacey was about to argue with her daughter about taking her to school when she saw the imposing figure of Les Williams come through the door.

"Morning, sheriff," Stacey called out from across the house. "You want a cup of coffee? I was just taking Addie to school, but I'd be glad to get you a cup."

Sheriff Williams waved at Addie, but she either didn't see him or ignored him altogether. "You still making that pecan coffee? That sounds nice, Stacey. Black with two sugars."

Stacey nodded and turned to the counter. One cup was left, probably a bit bitter from sitting too long in the carafe now, but she didn't care. It was the last of the plain breakfast blend she'd bought on sale, and it was going a bit off anyway. "Always."

"Mom, I need to go."

"If you've got a slice of that cake you had last time, too, that would be fine."

Stacey sighed. She put the keys to the truck and the SUV into her pocket. She was wearing her nicest suit slacks that didn't have much in the way of pockets in the first place. She probably did have a slice of peach cake from last time the sheriff had eaten some of her baked goods. He and Rick were in the local ham radio group together, a group Stacey was nominally secretary of, being one of the wives who actually had her license. She'd maintained it just for the sake of emergencies and still practiced with the local storm spotting and rescue teams, but it wasn't a hobby for her as it was for Rick. Sheriff Williams was in a good half of the social clubs in the area, so she had no idea whether he'd ever actually been on the air before. Being in groups gave him an excuse to drop in on folks, though. And sample the cakes and cookies the women brought to the meetings.

Stacey rummaged around the freezer and found a chunk of what she hoped was peach cake wrapped in about ten layers of foil and plastic. No time to defrost it properly, though. She tore off the wrapper and tossed the cake on a plate. Bits of frost clung to the crumbling edge of the cake. Too cold to cut through decently. Stacey put the plate in the microwave and cooked it on high for a minute.

"Mom, can I have the keys to something?"

Over the hum of the microwave, Stacey studied her daughter. "I will take you as soon as this cake is out of the microwave."

Addie protested. Rick and Sheriff Williams talked

in their deep voices in the living room. Stacey poured a cup of coffee and dumped in too much sugar. As she stirred, she splashed the sleeve of her jacket. She'd worry about that later. The microwave dinged. The cake was rubbery, but it would do. "Here you go," she said. She set the plate and cup in front of the sheriff on the coffee table. Her pocket felt light, and she heard the kitchen door slamming. "If you'll excuse me."

Addie was weaving toward the SUV. She put the truck's keys into the SUV's door and turned back and forth. "You are in no condition to drive, young lady," Stacey said. "Come in. Are you feeling sick?"

"I'm okay," Addie said. "I just need to go."

"Let me get my papers, and I'll take you."

Addie leaned against the SUV's door. "Why isn't this working?"

Stacey held back her urge to tell her daughter to get back into the house, but that was why she probably hadn't slept. She gathered up the girl into her arms instead. "No, you're going back in. And you're going to bed. What's going on?"

"I think I left my backpack."

"Yes, you left your backpack," Stacey said. "It's okay. I'll call the school. Tell them you're not feeling well today."

"No, I want to go to school, Mom."

Which isn't what she'd said yesterday, but Stacey didn't argue. Gently, she guided her back in through the kitchen door. Addie wobbled to the stairway at the back of the kitchen up to her room. "Wake me up in fifteen minutes so I don't miss school."

"I'll check in on you soon, baby girl," Stacey said.

****

Stacey picked up the sheriff's plate from the side table in the living room. She swept the crumbs around it into the plate. They stuck to her hands. She set the coffee cup, which had left a ring beneath it, onto the plate and walked them to the kitchen.

"Social call?"

Rick spun around. The freezer door closed behind him loudly. "You could say."

Stacey set the dishes into the sink. "Addie had a hard night. Any idea what that was about?"

"I didn't hear her up last night when I got in." Rick tapped the freezer door. "I tried to be quiet."

Stacey kissed her husband on the cheek. After decades of marriage, she still loved the plain scent of his skin. He'd shaved yesterday for his meeting, but not this morning. He said it was laziness, but Stacey wondered if he knew that she liked that sense of her lips not meeting the same texture each time she kissed him. "Thank you for that," she said. "What did the sheriff want?"

Rick shook his head. "You won't believe this," he said. "You know that new tower Harold Dutton put up not long after his momma's place sold?"

No one in the ham club could believe it either. Harold wasn't a regular, but he did join them now and again, particularly when he could boost his score on some contest or another. Stacey snorted out a laugh. "Don't tell me it fell over?"

"It fell over. Right over that new owner's fence," Rick said. He eyed the freezer. "Smashed a number of trees going down and crashed into the building foreman's truck."

"Serves him right," Stacey said. "You want some of that cake I served up?"

"Bad news is that Harold was on it."

"Is he—?"

"He wasn't all the way up, so he's alive," Rick said. "But he's pretty banged up. He'll be in the hospital for a while, Les says. He's not conscious for the moment, so they can't interview him. See what went wrong."

"Harold Dutton was what went wrong on that tower," Stacey said. "Is it true that he hadn't put a light on top?"

"Something like that."

"What did the sheriff want to talk to you about?" Stacey needed to leave soon if she was going to make her meeting with Jenna on time. "Harold didn't mention anything about his tower at the last couple meetings he was at, or at least I didn't hear him." Although she was a ham herself and secretary of the club, Stacey was often tasked doing double duty, setting out refreshments and making sure the wives of the older members had plenty of iced tea and cookies.

"That," Rick said. He coughed. "He also wanted to ask about your visit with Ms. Clarke yesterday just before the tower fell down. He said the foreman told him that you'd just been over there talking with her not long before the accident."

"Why didn't he ask me himself?"

Rick sighed. "Beats me," he said. "I said you were there, but he told me he didn't want to interfere with the ladies." He squinted for a moment. "You and Addie?"

"That young lady needs to get her head in the present moment," Stacey said. "Stop daydreaming so much about escaping elsewhere. Why is she staying up all night now? If she weren't in such a sad state this morning, I'd have told her what's what."

"I trust you on this one," Rick started. "Addie's always been one to have big dreams, so if you think that's all that's going on, then I'll stand behind what you think is best here. I never wanted to run off like she seems to want to do."

"Neither did I."

"Maybe she gets it from Amy," he said with a shrug.

Stacey could have argued that it was any one of his older brothers she could have gotten it from, but she didn't have the time or the heart to argue. True, his middle brother lived in Houston now and did something managing computer systems, and he'd always been a favorite of the kids. Never married himself, so maybe that was why he treated his niece and nephews as richly as he did. Sent them postcards—one addressed to each of them—when he went around the country or overseas. There was that, but there was also Rick's oldest brother, who joined the army right out of college as a way to get out of Dawville as fast as he could. Then was killed in Iraq not long after. Stacey looked over at the apple clock. "I need to go," she said. "Will you reschedule the shaker trucks?"

"Will do," he said.

Stacey turned to go, but she heard Rick open the freezer door. "I'm sorry, honey. I gave the sheriff the last of the peach cake."

"That's a shame."

"You hungry?"

"Nah." Rick smiled. "Just wondering what exactly you did give him. Whatever it was, that was definitely not peach cake."

Stacey felt guilty for a moment. Only a moment. She grabbed the keys to the SUV and kissed Rick one more time.

****

The offices of the Daw County Wineries Association was just about as far from Tess Clarke's minimalism as they could get while still keeping the feeling that they were somewhere richer, better than most places around Dawville. Everything shone in rich golds, browns, and, of course, deep warm burgundy. The chairs in the waiting area were velvety brown. The same color as the coffee that had splashed onto her jacket sleeve. A prim young woman in a suit sat at the reception area desk taking phone calls. Across from her were a row of portraits of the festival's patrons, including a prim picture of Minty Sanders. Who was really Margaret Sanders, as noted by the gold plaque under the photograph, but no one had ever called her by her given name as far as Stacey knew.

The prim young woman looked up. She could have been a younger Minty Sanders. "Jenna will be out to meet you shortly, Mrs. Hengesbach."

Stacey thanked her. She couldn't get the tower out of her head, though. Stacey wanted to feel bad about Harold Dutton, but she had a hard time doing so. The work of this morning was to go over the final details of the Wine and Pecan Festival, an event that they'd begun working on the day after last year's Wine and Pecan Festival had concluded. She had to focus on that instead. It was the major event in Daw County, and it brought oenophiles in from across the country. For three days, they sipped wines produced in the county, tasted grapes grown either in the county or nearby, and, of course, nibbled their way through pecan cakes, pecan pies, and every manner of wild game cooked up with pecans on top or in side dishes nearby. The whole county and those surrounding it—all the hotels and B&Bs, the restaurants and gift shops and even the gas stations made more the weekend of the festival than any other during the year. Everything was, in this complex machine, in place as far as Stacey knew. She and Rick had been tapped to represent the area pecan growers, which meant, of course, that the work had fallen to Stacey. Rick was busy on the farm. Harvest time was near, after all. She looked down at her watch when she heard heels on marble tiles.

Jenna Bailey walked out with an exceedingly well dressed pair. They smiled and shook hands, and Jenna took them over to where Stacey sat. She stood up and smoothed out the creases in her slacks.

"Mr. and Mrs. Lane," Jenna said with her smile, "this is Stacey Hengesbach of Hengesbach Pecan Farm. She'll be giving our speech this year on behalf of the Pecan Grower's Association. Stacey, these are the Lanes, who are looking to start a winery in the area."

Stacey shook both of their hands. For a moment, she felt the woman's eyes on her sleeve. "Update on that, Jenna. Turns out, my husband is giving the talk," Stacey said. "The Pecan Growers thought it better that he give the speech since the farm was in his family, not mine. Works better with the theme." Stacey had bristled at the idea of that, but since the theme was "It's a Family Affair," and she could rewrite what had been her speech into something suitable for Rick to give, she quietly assented. It was, after all, a family affair.

Jenna nodded. They all exchanged pleasantries, and the couple left through the heavy oak doors. Stacey followed Jenna into her plush office.

Once the door was closed, Jenna dropped her smile.

"I can't believe it, Stacey," she said. "I loved your speech. What were the pecan growers thinking?"

"They were thinking they wanted Rick," Stacey said. She leaned back into the soft leather chair that was pulled up to the round table at which she and Jenna worked. "Rick's family owned the farm for generations. His parents put the pecan trees in starting before Rick's brothers came along. So that's what they were thinking."

"They were thinking wrong," Jenna said. "No, you should give the talk. You're the vice president of the group, Stacey."

Stacey smiled. "I'm okay with this," she said. "One more thing off my plate. Besides, I'm happy that our farm will be highlighted this year. That's an honor."

Jenna shrugged, before she opened one of the many folders containing the last of the details to hash out. The meeting went, thankfully, quickly and smoothly. Although Jenna was a newcomer, she'd settled in quickly, married the son of the congressman representing Daw County in the Texas legislature, and established herself as a force to be reckoned with. True, she struck people as a little snobbish—she'd kept her name when she'd married, after all, and she had an *au pair* to care for her twins while she worked—but Stacey could see through the surface her love of Daw County, even if she had been born and raised in a suburb of Dallas.

They finished up the last of the details. "This one should be a winner this year," Jenna said. "We need it after losing tourist dollars the past couple years. And even the parts of Daw County that don't need the money could use the morale boost."

Stacey nodded. The farmers around here hadn't taken as much of a hit as the wineries that were also restaurants and B&Bs. But they were all getting back to normal.

Jenna's cell phone rang. She picked it up off her desk, flipped it over, and set it down again. "Sorry, the twins had runny noses this morning," she said. "But that wasn't my *au pair*." She pronounced the phrase in what sounded to Stacey like perfect French.

"I remember those days," Stacey said. With four kids, runny noses were a constant.

"At least it wasn't someone threatening the festival."

"Who would do that?"

Jenna smiled. "I shouldn't have said anything. I'm just bitter."

"If they're threatening the festival, then they're threatening the good of the community, I'd say." Stacey shook her head. "Much as I love how Daw County is a family, we need to get those tourist dollars in here one way or another."

"I agree," Jenna said. "Certain people with no regard for their neighbors, however—" She trailed off and waved her beautifully manicured hand.

"Newcomers wanting to keep up the illusion that they're back in the middle of nowhere?" Stacey laughed. "We're rural, but we're in the middle of Texas, not in the middle of nowhere."

"No," Jenna said. "Definitely old timers."

Stacey was curious. "Secret's safe with me."

Jenna paused for a moment, then leaned forward. "The worst have been coming from a certain landowner who puts up towers without lights, we'll say. Jack McGraw came in here cursing after flying over said tower owner's land with a couple of major restaurateurs interested in the county's wine offerings." Jack McGraw was one of the local pilots who flew chartered flights in and out of Daw County's tiny but increasingly comfortable municipal airport. He'd probably flown in the couple Jenna had just introduced Stacey to. "No lights on his towers."

Harold Dutton. Of course. Stacey recalled the last ham radio club meeting when the subject of tower safety and FAA regulations had come up. And Harold's disregard for said regulations. "Did he report it?"

"I did," Jenna said. "As soon as Jack left. And I told Harold that it was me who contacted the authorities. Or at least I left a message for him with Judy. I can't have my contacts endangered as such."

"What happened?"

"No word yet, and Jack hasn't flown low over his land," Jenna said. "I'm waiting to hear back from Harold. Judy laughed off my concerns. But Harold left yet another long, rambling voicemail a couple days ago. Nothing concretely threatening, but worrying enough. As if he'd do something to undermine the festival. I'm waiting for today's diatribe."

Stacey glanced at the gilt mirror hanging above the small table where they worked. The office faced north, and the mirror cast the soft light of the morning back into the office, making the gold and soft browns glow on the surfaces. "You did hear about what happened to Harold Dutton yesterday?"

Jenna stacked the papers neatly and set them back into the file folder. Something for her assistant to take care of later. "No," she said. "What did he do?"

"One of his towers came down yesterday morning," Stacey said. "With him halfway up."

"He's not—"

"No, he's not dead." Stacey studied Jenna's expression, trying to read who she had concern for exactly. "He's pretty banged up though. Still unconscious in the hospital."

Whatever it was Jenna had been thinking passed. "Well," she said curtly. "That's poetic, isn't it?"

Chapter Four

Back in her SUV, Stacey turned on the radio. She needed to drown out whatever it was she didn't want to think about: Harold Dutton's threats to Jenna and the Wine and Pecan Festival and his subsequent fall from his antenna tower. A station came in under static. She looked down. 89.1MHz, not a station she was familiar with. She hadn't turned on the radio since Addie had driven, and Addie was constantly looking for new music from those big city stations that would just come in on the car radios when she was out driving. Most often, of course, she'd stream music like any kid her age, but there was something of a thrill, she'd more or less told her mother, about finding a new song before anyone else at her school did. The RDS on the radio didn't display the station's call sign. Something else to fix on one of their constantly breaking vehicles. Something like this didn't matter. And anyway, the songs were from the 1990s, her own teenage years. Nothing new here, though Stacey knew first hand how rediscovering something from the past sometimes made a sixteen year old feel, for a moment, a bit like she knew more about the world.

Her phone rang. She tapped the speaker to answer. "Stacey, good I caught you, babe." Rick must have been driving some old piece of equipment somewhere on their land judging by the growl in the background.

"Sure is, honey." Their usual back and forth.

"I mean, good I caught you before you got home." The engine of the machine in the background idled. "Boys in the ham club heard about Harold."

"Oh?" Technically, she was one of the boys, but she didn't want to argue. Her hands gripped the steering wheel.

"And they thought you might want to do something nice for Harold. Something to bring by the hospital from the club."

Stacey pulled to a stop at the red light. "They asked me?"

"Well, I said you were out anyway. Save one of their XYLs from going out."

"You did." It irked her that Rick used the good old boy lingo of the ham club. XYLs, in this case, which meant the formerly young ladies the hams were married to. But she was more irked that she'd been volunteered to run errands for another group. Again.

"You're good at this kind of thing, babe."

"I am?"

"You're a sweetheart, babe. The boys appreciate it. Need to get going. Oh, and Addie asked if you could bring home Gertie's for lunch. That sounds good to me too." Rick hung up.

Stacey turned on her blinker. Straight through the light meant going home, going to check on Addie, but if her daughter was craving a smoked kielbasa, then all must be at least somewhat right. Left meant the florist's, which was probably the quickest and easiest way out of the errand she'd been tasked with.

****

She picked up a simple bouquet and signed the card from the Daw County Amateur Radio Club. The thing

43

came in a glass vase that was dripping slightly. Fortunately, the hospital wasn't too far, and Gertie's had a drive through she could get to easily from there.

The hospital always felt cold to her. She knew they kept the air cold in here to prevent infections from spreading, but ever since her Opa came here after his stroke and her Oma after her heart gave out not too long after, she couldn't help but feeling a pang whenever she passed through the automatic doors with their reassuring seal. Before that, she'd only held good thoughts about the place where she'd gone to have her four babies, each time going home from here with a healthy child. Sure, there were accidents, emergency stitches and the time her older two managed to break their arms within a few weeks of each other. But that was childhood, parenthood.

She asked up front about Harold's room.

"Oh, he's not allowed visitors right now," the receptionist told her. The same receptionist who'd been here when her kids were born. Something reassuring in that. "But we can bring the flowers to his room."

"That would be good, thank you." She handed over the vase, and the receptionist wrote a note with the room number on it.

"If you do want to send your get wells in person, there's Judy Dutton coming in through the parking lot." Stacey looked out. Teetering on kitten heels was Judy Dutton, Harold's second and definitely flashier wife. She wasn't from Dawville, and she was keen on everyone knowing it. Judy hid her inevitably mascaraed and lined eyes behind glamorously large round sunglasses. The same kind of glasses that Minty Sanders wore, but Judy lacked the elegance the judge's wife exuded. Judy was always made up, even for church on Sunday, like she was auditioning for some role in the community theater productions Amy had cajoled Stacey and Addie into seeing with her.

Judy paused in the automatic doors as if walking onto a stage. Stacey waved at her, breaking the illusion. "I'm so sorry about Harold's accident, Judy. The Daw County Hams wanted me to bring some flowers by for him. We're all pulling for him to get better."

Stacey felt the scrutiny of Judy's eyes even behind the sunglasses. She must have been presentable enough that day in her pants suit with her hair and makeup done that Judy deigned to have her company. "Thank you, that's lovely." Judy turned to walk down the hallway, but paused. "Would you like a cup of coffee in the lounge?"

Judy must have needed company. For the most part, she bragged about her big city friends, girls' weekends spent with them at posh getaways, but she hadn't done much to make or keep friends in Dawville itself. Stacey had a knack for seeing someone who needed a friend, and she couldn't pass up this chance to talk to Judy when she might, for a few moments, be just a tiny bit vulnerable behind her veneer. Even if it meant getting to Gertie's in the middle of a lunch rush and the long line of cars rumbling in the drive through lane. If nothing else, Stacey was curious about Judy's long conversation with Tess Clarke, one-sided as it might have been.

"I'd be happy to," Stacey said. They made their way to the tiny coffee shop in the lobby. The coffee was unmistakably hospital coffee, bitter, slightly burnt, and with an aftertaste that reminded her of hydraulic oil.

Judy draped herself across a plastic chair. Her body was turned half toward the table, half toward the window outside. Everything outside was still so green from the recent storm, shining even through the tinted windows out to the little patch of grass and flowers just behind the hospital. Judy had ordered a latte of some sort, soy milk and two shots of espresso. Was that going to taste any better than the brewed stuff Stacey sipped at, which had been sitting in the carafe too long now? "Harold hasn't been to the ham club in a while," she said, peering over the top rims of her tortoiseshell sunglasses. "Has he paid his dues lately?"

"We don't turn anyone away for not coming regularly," Stacey said. A bit of powdered creamer that hadn't quite dissolved stuck to the roof of her mouth. "Or for not paying dues. We're more a social club than anything."

"Well, one of Harold's friends—" a word Judy squeezed out through tightened coral lips, "should have told him not to build that tower where he did. Or at all. Do you know how much that thing cost?"

The graying woman at the counter called out Judy's name. "Soy milk latte double shot for Judy."

Judy turned and waved at the woman. "Over here."

"Okay, ma'am," she said. "You can come get your coffee now."

"Or," Judy said, turning back to the table, "you can do your job and bring it to me. As I told you yesterday. Or whoever it was working here yesterday. What do they pay you for?"

No one was in line. The cashier shook her head and brought the coffee over to Judy, who muttered something about service in this place.

"Harold," Stacey said as Judy took a sip of the coffee. She grimaced. Maybe the coffee that cost three times as much as a cup of brewed was no better after all.

"How's he doing?"

"Hmm," Judy said. "He'll recover."

"That must have been quite a fall," Stacey said. "Have you been able to talk to him?"

"I come and see him," Judy said, leaning toward Stacey. "But the doctors don't think he's up for conversation yet."

"Well, when he is, we'll come and visit," Stacey said. "One of us from the ham club." Which, she feared, would be her. It was just as well, wasn't it? She could get the news first-hand on what had happened. What Jenna had told her had made her curious, even if it was like curiosity about an electric fence. Some things were better left alone. "I don't want to keep you. I'm sure you want to go see your husband, and I can't imagine the hassle you're going to have with insurance and the tower falling on the fence with his momma's old place."

"It's Tess Clarke's now," Judy reminded her. "She's wonderful, isn't she? A real sense of style. If only Harold and I weren't planning to move to the city to be closer to friends, I'd snag her for my own circle in an instant. She'd be thrilled." She sipped at her latte again. "Do stay another moment. Have you been working with those lovely wine people again?"

"Yes," Stacey said. She updated Judy on the already publicly available details of the festival.

"Tess will be there, I'm sure," Judy said. "With some of her circle."

"Can I ask a question about her place?"

"Ask away," Judy said. She slid her sunglasses up into her blonde hair with coral-manicured fingertips. Her rings weakly caught the light from the buzzing fluorescent bulbs above them.

Stacey wondered if she should ask, but Judy seemed to want to talk. And even if they weren't talking about Harold's condition, wasn't it polite to ask about his family? "How did Harold manage to part with that land? His momma lived in that cottage since she was born. It was in a state when she went into the nursing home, but it wouldn't have taken much to fix it up. And the gardens."

Judy shrugged. "Sometimes, you have to let go of the past. Tess Clarke came around looking for several acres, and we acted fast." She smiled. "We're selling the whole thing soon, anyway. Moving away from Dawville for good."

"I'm sorry to hear that," Stacey said, and she half-meant it.

"People get what they deserve in the end, don't they." Judy phrased that as a statement, not as a question. "Tess Clarke will do this community a world of good. You watch. And that antenna was an eyesore for her and the rest of us."

"Was Harold taking it down then?" Stacey asked. As soon as she did, she felt a sinking horror, him trying to do something like that by himself. He wasn't a young man, nor an agile one. Had he put it up by himself too?

"Yes." Judy lit up. "He realized the error of his ways, putting it up in the first place. Especially after I passed along Jenna's concerns. Harold refused input on putting it up, so why would he ask anyone about taking it down? You know Harold. He won't listen to reason from anyone." She smiled. "Except me, of course."

"Of course."

"I just hope Tess knows I told him so," Judy said, raising her soy latte.

Stacey looked out the window for a moment and cleaned the top of her mouth with the tip of her tongue. Clots of creamer stuck between her teeth. Gertie's would be heaven after this. "So you talked about having the tower taken down. Safely. But, Judy, if you don't mind me asking, did you warn him about putting up the tower?"

Judy stood up on her leopard print kitten heels. Dressed in black, like a widow already. But Judy was no stranger to wearing black, even to church in the middle of spring. "One day, it just sprung up. How can I give advice on something that I don't know is happening in the first place?"

****

Stacey was relieved to be back in the SUV. Judy couldn't have been right about the antenna just springing up. Putting up a tower involved a lot of work. Stacey knew firsthand from the towers she and Rick had put in. Or really, had hired out help to put in. Stacey dismissed that as one more thing that folks could be oblivious about in a marriage. She turned the new station on, but only heard static. Must have been something she'd caught from too far away to keep a decent signal. These things happened. She was hungry for Gertie's herself. She'd spent so long chatting with Judy anyway that there wasn't much of a line in the drive through lane. At least there was that.

****

Addie was up and looking much more herself. She had made a pitcher of iced tea, the peach kind they both loved, and smiled at her mother as she answered the door. Rick was at the table, grimy and looking grimly at the screen of his open laptop between the plates Addie must have set out.

"Oh, Mom," Addie said grabbing the slightly grease soaked bag from Stacey. "Gertie's, you're the best."

"There's one thing you'd miss if you left Dawville," Stacey said. "Who else makes smoked kielbasa better than Gertie?"

"Mom, it's sausage. They do have sausage in other parts of the world."

"Yes, but this is the only Gertie's in the world," Stacey said. She unwrapped a kielbasa on a long roll and put it on Rick's plate, followed by a dollop of potato salad. Addie was already a good quarter of the way through hers. "Did you eat anything this morning?"

"No," Addie said with a full mouth. "Waiting for you. What took you so long?"

Stacey told them about meeting Judy Dutton in the lobby of the hospital. Rick looked up at her over the laptop screen. "That must have been interesting."

"Not really," she said. "Addie, what kept you up last night?" In the brighter light of day, Stacey could see the remnant puffiness of Addie's eyelids, the redness in her eyes. Her nose was rough from wiping it. Something had gotten to her daughter. If she was going to be this upset at her parents telling her no to her plans to up and leave Dawville before she was ready to fly, then Stacey knew she needed to watch her daughter more carefully. Better to be gently guided out into the wider world than fall out of the nest into a world she wasn't prepared for.

Addie shrugged. "Stuff."

"Stuff?"

"Can I go back to school this afternoon?" Addie scooped a second helping of potato salad onto her plate. "How sick did you tell them I am?"

"I was vague." Stacey took the potato salad spoon from her daughter. "What do you want to go back for?"

Again, Addie shrugged. "You didn't wake me up in fifteen minutes." She popped the potatoes from her salad into her mouth with her fingers.

"I said you weren't feeling well," Stacey said. "Not *sick* sick."

Rick looked up from the laptop. "How was Harold?"

"Good question," Stacey said. "Pretty banged up but breathing."

He made a noise then went back to the laptop.

"Mom, I'm going to take the SUV," Addie said. She had covered her last bite of sausage roll with the rest of the potato salad dressing and was heading toward her room. "I'm going to school."

"No, let me take you," Stacey said. She finished her late lunch.

"I can drive, Mom. I'm fine." Addie's backpack half slid off her shoulder.

"I want to get out of the house, too," Stacey said. "You're welcome, Rick."

"What?"

"Lunch," Stacey said. "And the flowers."

Rick looked up from the laptop again. He could be a bit oblivious at times, but at least he did give her credit. When she asked for it. Stacey would have hated being in a marriage like Harold and Judy's. What was that based on, really? Rumor had it that Judy married him ten years ago after his first wife left because she thought he had more money than he did. And he must have thought she was more adventure than she was. Mostly, if what they could get out of Harold at the meetings of the ham club he did show up to was that she took off most weekends to be with her friends in Houston while he stayed home. If there was discord, it was pretty public. Rick gave her that wide grin of wonder he did when he did see her. "Oh, yeah, thanks. Thanks so much, babe. You're the best."

****

"Where are you going?" Addie fiddled with the radio in the SUV and managed to pick up the signal for the 90s station again.

"Out," Stacey said. "How'd you find that? Where's it out of?"

"What, this station?" Addie turned it up. It was FM, which she should have thought about earlier, a bit of static. Not some long-distance station coming in clear due to a fluke high up in the atmosphere. Not this time of year, anyway. "I don't know. No ID that I've heard."

"Doesn't matter," Stacey said. The high school was a good twenty minutes from their house, which meant Addie would have at most about an hour left at school, plus a few minutes after talking to the few friends she had there. It wasn't that Addie wasn't capable of making friends. She was, and she'd even held on to those she'd made who'd moved out of Daw County. Maybe that was part of the appeal of getting out. Addie was just, if Stacey was honest, particular.

"Dad told me about what happened to Mr. Dutton," Addie said over some song Stacey hadn't heard since college. "That was stupid of him, wasn't it?"

"People climb towers all the time by themselves," Stacey said. "Take unnecessary risks just because they've done so hundreds of times before and it turned out okay."

"He could have asked someone to go out with him."

"Mrs. Dutton?"

Addie laughed. "A friend from Dad's club, then."

Dad's club. Stacey took a deep breath. "Harold Dutton doesn't have that much in the way of friends. Especially friends who'd trust his work on his towers."

"Have any of his towers fallen down before?"

"Not that I know of," Stacey said. "I've only heard of one tower in the county coming down unexpectedly before, and that was an unfinished one that came down in a straight line squall." Red light. Stacey looked over at her daughter. "What did you want to go back to school for today? You have the rest of the day off. To rest." What she didn't tell her daughter was that she wouldn't have passed up the chance to stay home on any given school day, at least if she could see her friends later. It was Friday. The football team was at an away game this evening, but still the town would be buzzing with young people in what there was to do around town. Which was a lot more than had been there when Stacey was young.

"I do like school," Addie admitted. "Learning and all that."

"So why are you so eager to leave?"

Addie stayed quiet the rest of the trip to school. Stacey thought it best to leave her daughter to whatever thoughts she was having about her life. One thing she did know was that everyone had to figure it out for themselves in the end.

****

After she'd watched her daughter slip through the doors of the high school, Stacey drove over to the Bluet Café. Midafternoon on a Friday, so there would be the chance that it would be full of tourists having tea and pastries, but she'd risk it. She needed to talk to Stephanie. Stacey pulled her SUV into the café's parking lot, slowly to weave around the van and the bucket truck that were camped out not too far from its entrance.

Turned out that she didn't need to worry about the café. Maybe it was a bit too early to worry about newcomers and their quaint rituals. A few long-time residents sat at tables, and what must have been the crew from the work fleet out front drank iced tea. Mornings were a bit cooler now, but October afternoons, particularly humid ones, could warm up fast. Stephanie waved Stacey over to the counter.

"Lease is signed, and we're getting a 5G tower out back of the café," Stephanie said. Though the café did well, some months things slumped, and she'd sought out the telecom company to lease a spot for them for a new 5G cell antenna. She'd bought the land behind the shopping center a couple years ago, figuring she could find a way to make it profitable too. Stable, anyway. And that's where 5G came in, she'd explained to Stacey. Line of sight cell phone reception made it necessary to put up more antennas, and with tourism bringing in as much as it did to Daw County, Stephanie figured boasting good cell coverage—particularly fast data connections— would be even more of a draw. She set a cup of pecan coffee and a tiny pitcher of cream in front of Stacey. "The crew started putting up the small tower that we're going to need out back. Let's celebrate."

After the large lunch, Stacey needed the kick of caffeine. "Good that someone is having luck with a tower."

"It's a small one." Stephanie shrugged. "Trick is to get people to notice the amenities but not the way you get the amenities to them."

"Good plan," Stacey said. She filled Stephanie in on

her morning meeting with Judy Dutton.

"You know, I don't know why those two didn't break it off years ago," Stephanie said. A group of women came through the door, and they were swiftly guided to a table by a waitress. "Much less why they went down the aisle in the first place."

"Loneliness does that to people," Stacey said. The coffee was rich and warm, and it was waking her out of her post-lunch lull. "I don't understand how Harold could have been born and raised here and still seem like he had nothing to do with the place."

"He's not the only one, is he?"

The door chimed again. One of the phone company crew jumped up to open the door. Vanessa slipped through carrying an armload of papers to grade. The waitress went over to her, but Vanessa nodded toward the bar where Stacey and Stephanie were talking. "Glad I caught you again, Stacey," she said, pressing the papers to the floral-covered bodice of her ankle-length velvet dress. Stacey sometimes wondered whether Vanessa really liked wearing the flowing dresses and boots with the shawls and hats that made her look like something between a costume drama and a garden catalog. She was a bit younger than Stacey and Stephanie, never, as far as they knew, married. She'd come to Daw County for the full-time job at the community college after too many years tying together teaching gigs at the universities and colleges in Dallas. She'd cultivated a following here among the students and faculty. She'd also cultivated a bit of a mystery about herself. She and Stacey had always been friendly—Vanessa was a friend of Amy's after all, and they'd been to the barbecues and parties Amy and her now ex-husband had given over the years when they had lived here. "I wanted to talk to you."

Chapter Five

"What do you want to talk to me about, Vanessa?" Stacey tried to keep her voice down, but it echoed up from the pastry case.

"Obviously to apologize about bringing Addie off campus," Vanessa said. She shifted the papers, which were beginning to slip. "I'm sorry about that. I've just watched your daughter blossom from a bright girl to a young woman so full of possibilities. I know how it feels to think you're stuck somewhere."

"Stuck?"

Vanessa's face glowed. Whether from excitement or embarrassment, Stacey couldn't guess. Maybe both. "Maybe stuck isn't the right word. In Daw County, anyway. I mean, to feel like the world is just out of reach. I told her to be patient, and to do what she can right now to make small steps toward her dreams."

"What are these dreams?" Stacey said. She looked down at the sleeve of her jacket, which now sported a few spots of sausage grease along with the coffee from this morning. "And why are you giving her advice?"

"I miss your sister." Vanessa took a deep breath. "She's a dear friend to me. I can't imagine how hard her leaving must be for Addie, though. Her cool librarian aunt who indulged her travel dreams and brought her back the best treats from England has gone off on an adventure of her own. And then two of her best friends,

Ethan and Angus, go off to college. She's the last one in the nest. She's the one left behind in a less than exciting place. Don't you think that's a lot for Addie to deal with?"

"Addie's scrappy," Stacey said. "She's the one who gets through tough times the best."

"Or maybe it just looks that way," Vanessa said. "If she complained about working on the farm or having to spend yet another summer in Daw County while her friends got to go somewhere fun and exciting on vacation, what would you have said?" She shifted toward the bar and spoke in a low voice. "Do you think she wasn't devastated every summer when Amy offered to take her to England with her and Neil and Angus, and you said no?"

"I didn't want to have to worry about that while we were in the middle of our busy season," Stacey said. "Addie understands that."

"It was two weeks," Vanessa said.

"That's a long time for a kid to be away from her family," Stacey said. "And what do you know about raising kids? You don't have kids." Stacey felt a sudden pang of regret as she watched Vanessa's eyes drop. But that didn't cover over her anger at this woman who thought she knew more about her own daughter than she did.

"You're right," Vanessa said. "But I have worked with a lot of young adults." She tapped the pile of papers cradled against her. "They tell me about their lives and their dreams, and I don't pretend to be a counselor, but they open up to me about that, both in person and in writing."

"So you don't pretend to be a counselor, but you do

pretend to be their friend?"

"No," Vanessa said. "I'm their teacher. And it's my job to listen and help them express themselves better, more clearly." She shifted the papers to one arm and picked up her bag with the other. "Now, if you'll excuse me, I have a lot of feedback to give."

Stacey turned back to Stephanie. "Everyone just wants to control the world, don't they."

Stephanie wiped the counter where Stacey's coffee had dripped. "It's hard," she said. "Vanessa means well. At least Addie adores Amy and Vanessa, and not the likes of Judy Dutton."

"Or Tess Clarke. I hope." Stacey felt herself relax a bit. The cell phone tower crew shifted up from their table. "Tess and Judy. There are two women intent on controlling things."

"Controlling Harold Dutton, anyway," Stephanie added.

Maybe it was because she was feeling a little suspicious of everyone, but the sudden realization hit her hard. She didn't want to say it, because it didn't sound plausible. Stacey waited until the tower crew had left, feeling some sort of superstition for a moment. "Stephanie, tell me I'm wrong."

"About Addie?" Stephanie stepped back. "I think you're being a little overprotective, but I don't think that's a bad thing."

"Not about Addie," Stacey said. "About this. What if Harold's tower falling down wasn't an accident?"

"What do you mean?" Stephanie leaned back toward her. "Like someone wanted to hurt him?"

"Hurt him," Stacey said. "Or worse. He's been giving Tess Clarke a hard time since she bought his momma's old place, right? So she messes with the guy wires on his tower."

Stephanie shook her head. "Tess? Would she even know how to do that?"

"Or Tess hired one of her work crew from out of town to do it." That sounded a bit implausible, but worse things had happened. Easy enough to tell them that she had bought the land just over the fence line, and the tower needed to come down too. Even if the crew had no idea someone would be on the tower after they'd started to dismantle it. Stacey pressed forward, afraid if she stopped now, she wouldn't say everything. "Tess Clarke gets rid of Harold Dutton, and her problems are solved."

"But you said Judy, too," Stephanie said.

Stacey squinted her eyes at the thought of the woman in the hospital coffee shop. "She didn't look all that upset at the fact that her husband was fighting for his life down the hall." As soon as Stacey said it, she regretted it. Stephanie's wound—her own husband's death twenty years prior—was one that got reopened from time to time. But if she felt any sadness, she kept it to herself.

"Some people process things differently," Stephanie said. "If something happened to Rick, I could see you distraught, but pulling yourself together for your kids. People like Judy though? I don't know. I don't know what she'd do."

"People like Judy," Stacey started. She shuddered. "People like Judy might be more interested in the money than the man."

"So, what do we do?" Stephanie asked. "You're not going to Sheriff Williams about this, are you?"

Stacey shot Stephanie a "you're kidding" look that

had passed between them for decades, even before they'd met their husbands. "No, none of this makes sense yet," she said. "And he's so focused on his re-election campaign. I think we need to look into this ourselves for a bit first. No one can ask Harold about what happened yet, anyway." An idea struck her. "You know, Judy Dutton is just the person I could use to help me with a few last-minute things for the Pecan and Wine Festival."

"Oh, she'd love all the glitz and glamour," Stephanie agreed.

"Which is one of them. We need someone more subtle, more artsy to get to Tess Clarke, though."

"Not me," Stephanie said.

"Not me, either," Stacey said. "Besides, her place kind of gave me the creeps."

"Who then?"

As soon as Stephanie asked, Stacey knew the answer. Stacey looked over, and there she was, Vanessa, her green pen in hand, writing feedback on student papers.

****

For the rest of the hour before she picked Addie up at school, Stacey ran a few errands and picked up a few groceries for the weekend, all the time wondering how she would get Vanessa to spy on—though that wasn't quite the right phrase—Tess. Daw County was a few weeks out from the Wine and Pecan Festival, which was too late to use that as an excuse to get something artsy or literary on the schedule. Or both. Stacey turned on the radio to static again. She would figure this out. She always figured things out, at least when it came to the people in her life. And, like it or not, Vanessa remained a part of her life, so long as she was a part of Addie's life.

Stacey fiddled with the radio, finding the big AM station booming out of Austin she sometimes listened to. Nothing relevant to Daw County, but something to shut her mind off while she worked her way over to the school. She couldn't see too far in front of her, since a couple semis blocked her view, but when the light changed, the cars and trucks in front of her didn't move. Someone honked. She hated when someone honked in situations like this. Who got it the loudest? Not the folks responsible for holding up traffic, but the other frustrated drivers around them. There had been a bottleneck just ahead, a work zone where the crews were just finishing up adding in a left turn lane, which was much needed now that a neighborhood of small, quaint cottages had sprouted up, each on an acre broken off from yet another old place the now out-of-town kids were selling off. Lots of people moving in there, each with their own vehicles. The light would help traffic soon, if not now. The Austin station mentioned a wreck on I35 south downtown backing up traffic for miles. Pretty soon they'd need a traffic report for Daw County if all this growth kept up.

Lights in her mirror caught Stacey's eye. Blue and red as a county sheriff's department SUV worked its way over the shoulder to whatever was happening up ahead. She turned around to see lights coming up the other side too. Something in her neck pinged as she craned around to see cars and trucks backing up to U-turn and get off this stretch of the highway. Doubtful that the delivery truck behind her would be able to do a three-point reverse maneuver, but maybe it could back out of her way once everything behind them cleared.

She kicked herself for a moment remembering

Rick's offer to put in a scanner or at least a mobile ham rig into the SUV. She hated being stuck, but usually she had a kid in the car to pass the time with or Rick. And he carried around his handheld radios. No matter. Dwell in the mystery sometimes, Pastor Muller reminded them some Sundays. Well, it was Friday afternoon now. She wouldn't be stuck here until Sunday.

Stacey opened her window and peeked out the driver's side. Deputy Valdez, a stern young woman whose father and grandfather had been in the sheriff's department, strolled up to the delivery truck behind Stacey. She spoke with the truck driver briefly, then moved away from the truck, which began to back up slowly. Stacey waved at Deputy Valdez, who arced her way away from the truck. Hard to believe this was the girl who'd graduated just ahead of her oldest four years ago.

"Mrs. Hengesbach," she said. Her grim demeanor softened a bit. "How's Tyler?"

"Finishing up at A&M this year," Stacey said. "Time flies, doesn't it?"

"Sure does," Deputy Valdez said. She leaned closer to Stacey's window and grinned. "You remember Jeff Schneider?"

"Sure do," Stacey said. "In the class ahead of you?" The oldest son of a longtime family of farmers in the area.

Deputy Valdez nodded. "I'd show off my ring if I wore it to work."

"Congratulations!"

"Okay, enough chit chat," she said. Her stern expression returned. "As soon as the truck behind you gets clear, we need you to U-turn and detour off to the county road."

"Yes, ma'am," Stacey said. "You couldn't give us a clue what's happening up there?"

Deputy Valdez squinted at the intersection ahead of them. "Protesters. Heard there was a 5G tower going up in the new neighborhood a quarter mile in or so. They're lying down in the middle of the road, and one of them said he has an incendiary device."

"A bomb?"

"Looks like it," the deputy said. "That's why we need y'all to clear as soon as possible."

"Why is it they're so opposed to the towers?"

"Lots of reasons," she said. "Lots of people think the government is poisoning our minds with the radiation from the 5G transmitters."

Stacey sighed. A basic course on electromagnetic waves would point out the fact that unless you were right on top of the antenna when it was transmitting, you were just about as safe using your cell phone as you were driving down this highway. Much safer than lying down in the middle of it with a bomb, anyway.

"I got to go talk to the folks in front of you," Deputy Valdez said. She waved. "He's out behind you. Your turn. Good seeing you, Mrs. Hengesbach."

"You too, Deputy. And best wishes."

****

Usually taking the county road added a good twenty minutes to the trip to the high school, but with a highway's worth of traffic picking along a two-lane road with not much shoulder to speak of, much less drive on when something in front overheated, Stacey figured the trip was closer to forty-five minutes. At least this one was paved, not some washboard dirt road they'd never seem to find their way off of. She'd texted Addie, who said she was waiting in the school library with a friend. Which was just as well. If traffic wasn't going to move her way very fast, it wasn't going to move very fast in the other way either. She'd put ice in the cooler, so at least the groceries wouldn't be ruined. Good to be prepared, but not so good to have to face what she'd prepared for. There was a turn off soon that wasn't paved. Stacey made up her mind to take that, since the semis and delivery trucks in front of her weren't likely to take that. Nor, she thought with a smirk, were the newcomers in their hybrids and all-electrics.

Stacey tried not to think about Harold Dutton's accident, but there it was, plain as day. Though no one in Daw County could accuse him of being overly cautious, he was usually pretty careful even if he was stingy. Rode the fence line himself in his second-hand ATV, and then he fixed it himself. He grazed cattle on what land he couldn't use for beans. Like all good farmers out here, he knew how to put things together and when they broke, put them back together. Stacey had a hard time reasoning that he'd done something as slapdash as messing up his lines on his tower, but everyone messes up some things sometimes. He was fit for his mid-sixties, sharp too, even if he wasn't the most agile. He wasn't the most friendly of folks in the county, but if he said he was going to do something for you, he kept his word. Grudgingly, anyway. He'd made his enemies, all right. But anyone living here long enough would, especially if they weren't as interested in community as Stacey was. So there was that.

Since she wasn't going all that fast, Stacey edged her way onto the dirt road when she got to it. A few cars had turned off ahead of her, but not so many that traffic would build up here. The storm the other day must have played havoc with the surface. Good thing she hadn't let Addie drive herself to school this afternoon.

She finally arrived at the high school an hour later than she'd hoped. She'd texted Addie, who said she'd be waiting out front. Addie must have been in the library still, since she was no where to be seen out front. The high school had changed so much since Stacey and Rick had gone there thirty or more years earlier. A couple new wings flanked the original building, and a new athletic complex stuck off the back like a beacon. The stadium had been rebuilt twice, which no one minded much given how much Friday night games brought in to the local economy. Amy and the school librarians had brought Stacey and Rick on board a campaign for a new school library shared between the high school and the junior high about a decade back. It was a beautiful annex, not nearly as grand as the athletic complex, but a pretty set of windows with reading benches looked out over the schools' gardens. Stacey wanted to get out and go in, but she also wanted to get home as soon as they could, which meant ringing around another way a half hour.

She texted Addie again. She'd wait. After all, Stacey didn't want to be the police when it came to her kids. She'd actually given them a lot of freedom. Which was easy with her older two boys, Tyler and Caleb. They'd taken to driving around the farm, doing odd jobs as they could when they were younger, then later on, when she and Rick looped them in on the business side of things, showing them the financial workings, she'd watched them bloom. Both of them had gone from graduating high school straight to Texas A&M. Caleb had always had a head for math, and he was halfway through a degree in accounting, and Tyler was working on an MBA after finishing his business degree the year before. Stacey felt bad about Tyler's college graduation somewhat overshadowing her third son's high school graduation, but Ethan hadn't wanted to make much of a fuss anyway. He and his cousin Angus had graduated together, and they wanted to hold a joint party. So Amy and Neil hosted, or Amy did while Neil avoided the questions that were inevitable about the divorce. Stacey watched as Angus and Ethan disappeared into their circle of friends, surfacing only to thank relatives for coming over to celebrate. Something had been shifting in Ethan for a while now, and Stacey couldn't quite put her finger on it. Angus had followed Caleb and Tyler to Texas A&M, but Ethan, her deep thinker, was quite adamant about going to the University of Texas at Austin. He'd received good deal of grief from his brothers about his choice, but it was his after all, and Stacey stepped in when she felt she could. And he'd received a good scholarship too. Addie, meanwhile, watched wide-eyed. She wasn't the most patient kid, and she wanted to fly too.

Stacey's phone dinged.

—*On way*—

That was that, then. In the damp October heat, Stacey wilted more in her pants suit. She'd have to get it cleaned anyway. Not something she felt entirely comfortable in. Give her a pair of jeans, a t-shirt, and work boots any day over this.

Addie ran out, her backpack bouncing on her shoulder. "Let's go," she said, halfway into the passenger seat.

"Did you have a good day?"

"Mom, come on," Addie said. She slammed the door. Her bag slid to the floor. The zipper caught on her boot lace and opened just enough to let a notebook and pens fall out. "Let's go." Addie slid the seat belt over her body and jammed the latch in. She squeaked in pain.

"Did you pinch your finger?" Stacey reached over for her daughter's hand. "Let me see."

"No." She shook her hand. "Come on, let's get out of here before traffic gets bad."

"Traffic should be cleared out by now," Stacey said. "At least the long way around, where we're going." She turned the key and looked up. Coming out the door was Vanessa, bag in hand. Addie slumped against the door. "What's going on, Addie?"

"I pinched my finger," she said. "I'm impatient, I know."

"No," Stacey started. Vanessa crossed to the nearly empty faculty lot, and she was looking around. "What were you doing in the library?"

"Reading."

"With a friend."

"Like I said."

"You were reading with a friend?"

Addie made a noncommittal noise. No use going into this now. If she was going to run to Vanessa every time she had a complaint about being in Daw County, then Stacey worried about Vanessa pushing Addie too hard to leave the nest.

They pulled out onto the road that would ring around Dawville and over to their place. The rain had made what green was there pop out, and the mesquites and scrub popped out against the graying skies. "Might rain again,"

Stacey said to no one.

Addie turned from Stacey. She tapped her fingers against the window, her nails the color somewhere opposite from her hair. Stacey hadn't bothered to take art classes in high school or college. She had all the color she needed tucked away in her slice of central Texas landscape. Where the color fell on the color wheel was a better question for Amy. If her sister didn't know the answer to a question, she knew just where to look it up.

Stacey's phone buzzed. At the red light, she grabbed it and looked at the screen. "Ethan's coming after all. For homecoming next week."

Addie made her noncommittal noise toward the window.

"You're not excited? Sugar, you were so sad when he left," Stacey said. "Even if you're jealous that he's out of the house now, you should be glad to see him."

"Don't tell me how to feel," Addie said.

"I'm not," Stacey said. "I'm asking you not to feel something. That's different."

Addie turned toward her mother. "Different?" The light turned green, and Stacey pulled out into the intersection. She hadn't been by this way in a while, and she could just make out the first shifting toward fall. That was all the color wheel she needed, wasn't it?

"Different in that jealousy doesn't get you what you want, does it?"

"You've been reading too much self-help, Mom."

Stacey felt a tightening in her stomach. She had been reading some self-help books, mostly at night, and she'd hidden them away under the edge of her bed. "I'm trying to improve myself, thank you. And I'm worried about your Aunt Amy."

"You're finding yourself? By reading books?" Addie made a little smug noise. "Little late for that."

"What do you mean by that?"

Stacey felt the sudden urge to do what Rick had done to each of their three boys at least once: pull over to the side of the road and told them to get out of the car if they were going to give him or their mother lip. And he'd made them get out and walk home. Never too far, less than a half mile from the house, and only when they were old enough to make the walk home. But Addie? Neither of them would have ever considered it. "That's enough out of you, young lady." Their usual response.

"Is it?" Addie looked back out the window.

Breathing in deeply, like one of the books suggested, Stacey redirected. "So, are you going to homecoming this year? It's next Friday."

"Who would I go with?" Addie made her smug noise again. "My so-called friends all have dates, and I don't actually like football, remember?"

"But you're going to the dance, right? We can go to Madisonville and get you a dress tomorrow."

"Dance?"

"With your so-called friends?"

Addie's turn to breathe deeply. "My real friends are in college. Or they're not in in Daw County High School anymore, okay?"

Stacey pulled into their driveway and stopped the SUV. She looked at the girl who'd always fallen in so easily with the older kids, never shy about making herself heard. Her brothers' friends were her friends, boys and girls who must not have thought she was too young to join in whatever it was they were doing. If anything, Addie was less her baby and more something sophisticated that she couldn't quite put her finger on. Stacey saw that more and more now that Amy was overseas and Addie's older brothers and cousin and friends were starting a part of their lives she couldn't just yet.

"Mom, does Ethan have to come back? So soon?"

"Why, sugar? I thought you'd be happy to see him."

"I will be," Addie said. She opened the door. "They're just happier away, I guess. I mean, they're all just happier away."

Stacey looked at the house. Their metal roof would need an update soon. A couple beams on the porch needed to be repainted. And there was a suspicious looking spot between the roof and the wall that looked like a hole going into the attic. "Your brothers and Angus can be happy anywhere. Aunt Amy too. Happiness isn't tied to a place, Addie."

Except, in her heart, Stacey knew that it absolutely and inextricably was.

Chapter Six

Ever since anyone in the group could remember, the
Daw County Amateur Radio Club had met Friday nights
in fall when Dawville High's football team was at an
away game. Which meant tonight. Just about the whole
community turned out for the home games, or at least the
families who'd been in the area for a while had. Some
would tailgate, and others would push into the stands
early hoping to buy the sausage on a stick Gertie's
smoked and sold at cost to the school for fundraising. In
all that bustle, more than a few of the hams would help
out with whatever was needed with their handheld
radios, ready to report to Sheriff Williams and his team
if anything went amiss. Tonight, Dawville played a team
a good hour and a half away, and most folks didn't bother
to make that trek.

Stacey had scrambled to bake a pan of her pecan
blondies and slice up a peach cake that had been in the
chest freezer for far shorter time than whatever she'd
served Sheriff Williams had been. At least she'd
remembered to put it on the counter to thaw last night.
She'd served a quick dinner and seen Addie to her room,
where the girl closed herself in with her laptop and a slice
of cake. Then she and Rick loaded up the SUV with the
sweets and their coffee urn and headed out to Dawville
Lutheran Church, where the meeting was held in the
community room.

Even though Stacey was a licensed ham, and secretary of the club at that, she trod the line between member and the wife of a member as long as she and Rick had belonged to the group. Several of the men had grabbed slices of cake or cookies she and the other wives had baked and brought, and they were looking at the new rigs members had brought in to show. Few of the wives of hams her age or younger bothered showing up. Nights to themselves, Stacey imagined. Maybe she should have stayed home with Addie. Her job in the group was to take minutes, and community was important, after all. Besides, she wasn't sure crowding Addie wouldn't just push her farther away anyway. Stacy had become a ham to serve her community, to be there in times of crises like fires and tornadoes. Addie would be fine for the night. Wouldn't she? Stacey filled coffee cups for some of the elderly members and for their wives, who sat in a group of chairs near the window, watching the sun set.

"Stacey, could you bring over another plate of those blondies?" One of the elderly wives pointed to the coffee table in the middle of the chairs. "Best thing I've eaten this week."

"Thank you, ma'am." Stacey turned from the conversation among the hams back to the refreshments table.

Settling herself among the hams, she realized that once again, she'd have to get Rick to fill her in on details about the local news. "You remember what he did to that pirate about ten years ago, don't you?" one of the hams said.

Another one nodded. "Went out with a direction finding antenna himself. Found the guy almost on the county line."

Stacey made Addie's smug noise. She wondered for a moment whether Addie had picked it up from her, or the other way around. "Funny him going after the pirate for doing something illegal," Stacey said. "You've all heard about his tower lights."

Who hadn't? It was the talk of the meeting two weeks before. Harold himself, though nominally a member so he could use the local repeater, hadn't been to a club meeting in ages. "It's not about whether it's legal or not," one of the long-standing members said. "Harold Dutton got mad at the guy for causing interference in his own operations."

"Then you'd think he'd understand how upset the pilots are around here," Stacey said. "That's not just interrupting ops. That's dangerous."

One of the wives stood up. "Stacey?"

"Excuse me," she said. Rick could start the meeting so she could sit down and do her job, but honestly, she wanted to know more about Harold Dutton and all the hams here. Any of them—or at least any of the hams who'd been at it a while—knew enough about putting up towers and maintaining them that accidents did happen, but there was a lot a person could do to prevent them. Like not climbing up a tower without someone else on scene. Worse was the sudden realization that most of the people in this room who were licensed could pretty easily figure out how to bring a tower down and make it look like an accident, particularly when the victim of that accident wasn't prone to careful work. Stacey grabbed a pretty tray of thumbprint cookies and brought it to the women by the window. She scuttled back to her place among the hams, but her chair had been filled by the time she got there. Stacey shifted down a ways. "I imagine

Sheriff Williams has a team on this."

The club treasurer shook his head. "Naw, he thinks it was an accident. Most of us here think so too."

"Most?"

He shrugged. "Just because we didn't take a shine to the man doesn't mean we wanted him to fall off his tower."

Stacey opened her mouth to argue, but Rick smiled at her. "You ready to take notes, honey?" Stacey nodded and held up the pen and notepad she'd pulled from beneath the chair she'd previously occupied. When wasn't she ready?

****

The meeting went as they usually did, wandering from one topic to another. They didn't have a guest speaker that night, so things were looser than usual. Stacey wanted to bring the conversation back around to the question of the pirate, who they thought it could be. The station was FM, which meant it had to be someone nearby given that FM needed the listener to be within the line-of-sight of the transmitter. That narrowed things down a bit. If the pirate were on AM, then tracking him—and she'd assumed it had been a him, which maybe she shouldn't have done—down would be a harder task. Plus, FM transmitters were easier to come by. Stacey shook herself back to the club's former president rambling tale of a conversation he'd had sometime in the 1960s with someone overseas. Then someone briefly mentioned something about a drone show. Stacey wrote down "drone show" while thinking about the pirate again before she caught herself. She had to focus on taking notes. That was what she was here for, wasn't it?

After the meeting had wrapped up, Stacey sent home the rest of the cake and blondies with the wives and packed up her trays and coffee urn. She was exhausted and wanted to leave everything here until they came back for church on Sunday morning, but she pushed herself to get the job done. Rick was talking to a couple new members, so she did the job herself.

"I can't believe Sheriff Williams is not looking into the accident," Stacey said. She yawned and turned on the radio, tuning it to the lower part of the FM band, not sure what she was looking for. "Even if Harold wasn't adept at maintaining his antenna."

"You know he's got other things on his mind, Stacey." Rick stopped at a red light. Stacey remembered the years when he'd barely pause at stop signs before scooting on through, grumbling about having to stop when no one was coming. The stop signs had been replaced on a lot of the major roads by traffic lights, and Rick had been pulled over enough times to break him of the habit. After their first baby came along, Rick seemed to wise up, for which Stacey had been grateful. Had they been together that long? "The department is stretched thin as it is."

"Stretched thin with campaigning," Stacey said. The light turned, and she watched her husband's quick glances out the passenger and driver side windows before pulling the SUV into the intersection. "And pandering to whoever has the most money to donate to the effort."

"Come on, babe." Rick took his hand off the wheel to pat her on her leg. "Sheriff's not the smoothest, but he gets the job done. Besides, with Bo Sanders tied up in all those 5G protests, he's got a careful line to walk."

The Sanders family was one of the oldest and most prominent in Daw County. Bo's grandfather had been County Judge when she and Rick were in high school. Bo's father was partner in the firm that represented most of the wineries around here in their various business deals. When the elder county judge retired, Bo's father was elected in his place in an election that was never much of a contest. Stacey wondered how much Minty was involved with his election, since it was her money that financed his campaign. Stacey had been raising four small kids and helping out on the farm during the transition of power, so she hadn't paid much attention then. How much attention would she pay now? Judge Sanders was up for re-election, as was Sheriff Williams, but no one wanted to challenge the judge. Or, really, no one wanted to challenge Minty.

Bo Sanders still lived in Dawville, the youngest child who hadn't done much to speak of. His brothers and sister had both gone off to prestigious starts at Ivy league schools while Bo, a good decade younger than the last of them, had barely scraped together a degree at Daw County Community College. It wasn't as if he lacked the brains. He had smarts to spare, which he showed easily enough at the few ham radio meetings he'd attended. Knew electronics inside and out, and even corrected a few of the old-timers no one else bothered to correct. Bo never got a license that Stacey knew of. Maybe radio was just a passing phase in a life made up of passing phases. He'd tried his hand as a repair tech at Stacey's dad's machinery repair shop, and he made a go of it before deciding he was too good for all that. Whatever that meant. Bo might have had a good career as a mechanic. Probably an unkind word from his mother or grandfather put an end to all that.

Bo's father, Judge Beauregard Sanders, was a piece of work, and Stacey suddenly felt a bit of gratitude that they were in the dark and Rick couldn't see the blood rising to her face. According to Daw County lore, Judge Sanders had come home to surprise his wife only to find Dale Hillegeist, nineteen and lanky, in his underpants and digging through the refrigerator. Dale stomped the heels of his work boots against the white tile floor of the kitchen, leaving a trail of dirt as he went. The judge ran to his study to grab his rifle, when Dale must have caught on to what was happening. Dale streaked to his car in his underpants and boots, his shirt and jeans floating behind him like a trail of smoke. The Judge tore after him. In their cars—Dale in his Mustang and the Judge in his Cadillac—raced through the streets of Dawville until the patrol officer, Les Williams, pulled Dale over for excessive speeding. Word got out that Dale had intended to besmirch the honor of Judge Sanders' daughter. Except everybody knew Miss Sanders was in Boston and hadn't been back to Dawville in years. After a few beers during a summer barbecue at the pecan farm, Dale later confirmed what everyone suspected. He told Stacey, in some weird moment of secrecy between them, that he'd spent the summer sneaking into the Sanders' stately home weekdays when the Judge wasn't expected.

Dale Hillegeist had nothing to do with the Judge's daughter.

No, instead, Dale Hillegeist had been entertained for one glorious summer by Judge Sanders' wife.

Minty Sanders.

Bo, who must have been seven or eight and far younger than his siblings, had been packed off to a series of summer camps populated by other wealthy kids that summer, like he'd been every summer. Still, word must have gotten around to him. How could it not?

"You're quiet," Rick said as he pulled into their driveway.

Stacey yawned again. Or she made like she did. "Just tired."

"Thinking about Harold? Accidents happen, babe."

"They do," she agreed. But her mind went back to Judge Sanders chasing after Dale, giving Dale a bad name for the longest time. He'd gone off for a good ten years, then came back to take care of his dad when the old man had taken a bad fall down the stairs not long after he'd lost his wife to cancer. This time, though, Dale had brought an air of respectability with him in the form of his new wife, Melissa, a nurse he'd met after crashing his motorcycle into some fence post somewhere. The bike had been his last farewell to some old thrill-ride way of living he'd held on to for too long. Now he worked as an electrician, staying home with his daughters when Melissa worked shifts at the Daw County hospital.

The hospital where Harold Dutton was recuperating from his own fall.

****

On Saturday, Addie barely came out of her room. Stacey wasn't too worried. Addie slept in most weekend mornings, and unless they needed her on some farm chore, Stacey didn't bother waking her. Something in Stacey didn't quite believe the idea that you couldn't make up for a lack of sleep by sleeping in on weekends. Or maybe she did, but she liked the idea that you could control your time like that. Addie needed to feel in control—at least Stacey remembered feeling that need when she was sixteen. She shuffled out just after one pm, and Stacey warmed up leftovers from lunch and set them in front of her. Addie took the plate and walked back into her room. No use pushing—she'd just push her daughter straight out of Daw County, wouldn't she? Addie wandered out briefly for dinner, ate quietly, and then scuttled back into her room with a plate of warm peach cobbler. Stacey knocked on her door later to tell her daughter good night, and received a smug noise in return.

So it surprised Stacey to see her daughter at breakfast the next morning, wakeful and smiling. She had done her hair already, her long straight purple locks back in a tidy chignon. Addie was waiting for Stacey and Rick at the door when they'd gotten themselves dressed and ready for church. Usually, they were a few minutes late, calling for Addie who inevitably finished her hair and makeup in the SUV on the way. This morning, Addie looked pretty, in the way of the little girl she once was had been. She wore a simple blue sundress with sandals and a cardigan, so different from the black t-shirts and jeans she usually wore. Addie was pretty now in that teenaged way girls were, fresh and eager, but that was usually tinged with something frustrated and tense. Addie was sweet this morning, for lack of a better word. "Need a hand with the coffee cakes, Mom?"

Addie grabbed one of the cakes Stacey was trying to balance on her forearms and followed her parents out the door. The morning was humid, and her skirt clung to her hose. Her heel wobbled on a rock in the driveway, but she was able to catch herself on the side of the SUV thanks to her free hand.

"Think we'll need to avoid the highway this morning?" Rick started up the SUV as soon as Stacey and Addie were in.

Stacey almost turned on the radio to hear the pirate but stopped herself. "Hope not," she said. "Hope they finally shut down whoever's coordinating these protests before the Wine and Pecan Festival. But I don't know."

"You don't sound so sure," Rick said. His rough hands guided the steering wheel, and they bumped over a washed-out section of their driveway. Just getting off their land took effort some days, it seemed.

"Depends on who's behind them." Stacey looked down at the cake in her lap, which had survived the trip out to the road that would take them to the highway and on to Dawville Lutheran Church. "Oh," she said suddenly when she realized she'd left her bible on the table. No matter. It wasn't as if there weren't copies in the pews that she could use, and Rick had his. At least the parishioners didn't split up into men's and women's groups as some churches did.

As soon as they got to the church, Addie handed her father the cake she'd held and wandered off toward the direction of the room in which the teen group met. They were all kids Addie knew from school anyway, so it gave Stacey a sense of peace that she was going to be with friends instead of giving Stacey a hand with the refreshments setup. Stephanie had already put out a couple urns of coffee from the café, and she stood wiping up a drip from one of them. "You talked to her yet?" Stephanie nodded toward the doorway, in which Vanessa stood chatting with a couple of the older women. She'd been angling to start a book club, which probably explained the copy of *Fried Green Tomatoes* in her hand beside her bible.

Stacey shook her head. "Not yet." The book club

was as good an excuse as any to corner Vanessa. If Amy had any influence on her big sister, it was that she'd cultivated in Stacey—along with Rick and a good number of Daw County's residents—a love of reading by introducing them to novels they'd never have read in high school English. "You have room for a couple more cakes?"

"Those look good." Stephanie set the cakes among the others on the overfull table. If anyone would be in a hurry to get out of the adult bible study portion of church it was to get to the bounty in the kitchen.

"Thank you," Stacey said. Rick had wandered over to talk to a few of the other men. "How's the tower coming?"

"We're all set," Stephanie said. She was beaming. "Tower's up, now it's up to the phone company to put up their antenna on my tower first and scout out a few more sites around here. Supposed to come out next week. 5G in Daw County, just in time for the Pecan and Wine Festival." She looked contrite for a moment. "Maybe I shouldn't crow so proudly, not in church. The rent the phone company pays for the tower helps too, but it's a community good, isn't it?"

"It is," Stacey said. "More tourism, more opportunity for folks around here. That is a community good."

****

Community good. Someone reminded them all of the time, that Pastor Muller would begin adult services in a few minutes and that they needed to get into the sanctuary. The kids had long been ushered into their classrooms. There was something Stacey loved about the old church building, though not much of the original served its purpose anymore. The kitchen was new, and the old sanctuary was now the meeting room in which the Daw County Lutheran Ladies held their monthly gatherings. Maybe it would be where Vanessa would hold her book club, if not at the library. The new sanctuary had been built not too long before she and Rick were married in it. She'd been so proud, coming up the aisle between the beautiful new pews, the sparkle of the colorful windows. Everything seemed possible. Maybe that wasn't true, but it felt like that, especially as an eighteen-year-old bride. Now? Now she wondered whether it would be possible for her to connect to Addie again.

Sitting in a pew in the middle of the sanctuary, Stacey could see Vanessa, or the back of her head, anyway. Her brown hair had a streak of maroon, something some of the younger faculty did in support of the high school around homecoming time. Not that Vanessa was all that young anymore. She had to be nearing forty if not there yet. For years, some gossip had focused on Vanessa and "Cowboy" Jenkins, the head of the history department at Daw County Community College. They'd been a couple for just about as long as they'd both been here, but no signs of wedding bells had ever come up. Something about their relationship seemed stilted, not quite right. They never arrived together to the many events Stacey had seen them at, events Amy had orchestrated at the library. And they never left together either. Cowboy—no one knew his name for sure, but they'd all presumed it must be either embarrassingly upper crust or embarrassingly plain—never exactly fit in the community anyway. Everyone supposed he was just after their stories about their grandparents and great-grandparents for one or another of his books. Vanessa might have wised up, or maybe some of the rumors were true about Cowboy Jenkins, that he was secretly laughing at the backwoods yokels he'd found himself among and wouldn't deign to marry someone who'd so embraced them as Vanessa had, even if she wasn't one herself.

Rick shook her out of her head by offering his bible for her to read along in. She couldn't focus on the words, in some part because Pastor Muller was getting along in years and tended to ramble but mostly because she knew she had to ask Vanessa to snoop, which wasn't all that, well, Christian of her, was it?

Bible study ended, and all the adults rose together to swarm the kitchen. Stephanie and Pastor Muller's wife, who'd retired as a school teacher about a decade before, had warmed up the cakes in the oven, thus filling the church with a scent that could only mean the coziness of fall. Stephanie caught her eye and nodded toward Vanessa. The other woman pushed back her maroon lock and refilled her coffee cup, a reusable one, better for the environment. She was pious in her way, wasn't she?

Stacey inhaled and walked over. The spices calmed her in their way. For all the work she did baking for others, she did enjoy it. The spices themselves helped. "Nice of you, your hair," Stacey said. Not exactly what she meant to say or how she meant it.

Vanessa laughed. "You know, every year I say I'm going to keep it, and then I don't. This year, I'm not even making that claim."

"What's different about this year?"

"This," she said. She set down her coffee cup and reached into her hair. The maroon lock came away clean in the gold clip it had been secured to her hair with. "I didn't have time to go to the salon, and this was just easy. I can wear it anytime of year now."

"At least you don't have to worry about roots," Stacey said. She felt a sudden sense of guilt after she'd said that. Maybe it was true Vanessa didn't have roots here. Or maybe she did, but no one appreciated that fact.

Vanessa clipped the lock back into place. "You're right there," she said. "Is Addie here?"

Stacey nodded. "Look, I need to talk to you about something."

"About Addie?" Vanessa picked up her coffee cup. "You know, I was hoping she'd tell you herself, but I entered an essay she wrote into a contest, just something local to the Brazos Valley counties. Third place. I'm so proud of her. First and second place were seniors, and I think she has a chance to win next year."

Though she wanted to ask what the essay was about, if she could have a copy, if she could read what was going through her elusive daughter's head, Stacey reminded herself to stay on topic. "Thank you," she said. "How about we treat you to Gertie's to celebrate?" It would get them alone at least, if she could get Rick and Addie to stand in line for them while Stacey and Vanessa found a table.

Vanessa looked uncomfortable for a moment. "I'm afraid Gertie's doesn't have many vegan options, do they? Or any at all?"

Stacey fought the urge to roll her eyes. Ah, yes. Vanessa was vegan.

"Actually," Addie popped up behind them both, "Gertie's has vegan sausages now."

"Oh?" Stacey fought the urge to roll her eyes again.

She thought about the farm families who'd been on the land for ages growing silage and renting out their land for grazing. Is this how Daw County would end? "Well, then, no excuse now."

Vanessa beamed at Addie. "How did you find that out?"

Addie blanched a little. "I was looking it up. For a friend. Don't worry Mom, I'm not a vegan."

Stacey felt the word Addie didn't say: *yet.*

Chapter Seven

The line at Gertie's was halfway down the back
wall. Stacey loved this place. She loved the smell of
sausage which smoked behind the restaurant and
beckoned her as soon as she opened her car door. She
loved the tang of the sauerkraut and the tingle at the back
of her throat from the too-sweet tea. Their potato salad
had won statewide awards for good reason. She loved the
classic country music played too loud, the sports on the
TV, the picnic tables that were uncomfortable in a way
that spoke to summers outside at her own grandparents'
house when she was younger. There was a hammock
between two trees at the edge of the parking lot around
which children ran, shrieking joyfully in the cooling fall
breeze. A vast lot of picnic tables stood under a grove of
ancient live oaks, and these were completely full of post-
church families.

Rick had offered to stand in line for food while
Stacey and Vanessa scouted out a table. The weather was
nice, so finding a table inside wasn't much trouble.
"Take Addie with you," Stacey had said. Addie
protested, saying she wanted to talk to Vanessa, but
Stacey reminded her that Rick would need help with the
trays. At least service at Gertie's was fast. Customers
stood in line until they reached a cashier. Then the
questions were simple: which sausage, how much, and
how do you want your cabbage (sauerkraut or coleslaw)

and your potato (salad or baked)? Drinks were either tea, sweet or unsweet, or lemonade for the kids. It was brilliant. There were times when having choices narrowed down to the essentials made life a whole lot easier.

Addie trudged off toward the line with her dad while Stacey led Vanessa to a wooden table in the corner, slightly away from the speaker blaring George Strait. The tables nearest them were empty. She sat across the table and gathered herself to ask before the courage left her. "Look," Stacey said, settling her purse under the table. "I need to ask you to do something."

"If it's about Addie, I understand," Vanessa started. Her maroon lock had begun to slide down the hair it was clipped to. "She keeps coming to me, and I'm trying my best to help her understand her long-term goals. About Dawville. I don't think she knows what to—"

Stacey sighed. "Much as I'd love to talk about my daughter right now," Stacey lingered a bit on the my, "it's something different."

"Oh, sure." Vanessa sat up straight. "What can I do?"

"It's about Harold Dutton."

"Harold?" Vanessa shook her head, causing the lock to slip farther. "Poor man, falling like that. I haven't met him."

"That's okay," Stacey said. She looked out the window. Maybe looping Vanessa into this—whatever it was—would make her an ally. Someone she could talk to more easily about her daughter. Someone who seemed to know her daughter's mind better right now than her own mother did. "It's this. Harold Dutton's mother lived on the land that Tess Clarke bought not long ago. I think they were feuding over the sale of the land."

"Oh?" Vanessa's eyes were wide, eager. Did she love drama this much? Is that why she was getting between Stacey and Addie?

Stacey dismissed that thought and went on. "Harold had a radio antenna tower not too far from the fence line. Really, too close to the fence line, but technically, he thought the land had still been his, so I guess it wasn't an issue when he'd put it up."

"And you think Tess Clarke had something to do with Harold falling off the antenna?"

Stacey shushed Vanessa. "Not so loud," she said. "I don't know what I think yet. But I think it would help if someone got to know her a little better. So we can ask."

"Ask? What?"

"Okay, so I don't have this fully planned out," Stacey admitted. Rick and Addie were getting close to the front of the line. "Have you met her?"

"Briefly," Vanessa said. "She came to a visiting author's talk at the college last week."

"So, you don't know her well enough to grill her about Harold Dutton and her land," Stacey said.

Vanessa looked up, as if her eyes were scanning the open ductwork about them for an answer. "Isn't this Sheriff Williams' job?"

"This stays between us," Stacey said. Vanessa looked back at her and nodded. "I don't think Sheriff Williams is paying enough mind to the possibility that someone might have tampered with the guy wires on the tower. No one much likes the man, and it's easy enough to wave it all off like it was an accident when Harold wasn't exactly the most careful craftsman anyway."

Vanessa smirked. "And investigating would take

away from his campaigning time, right?" She nodded her head out the window. On the other side of the street, Sheriff Williams smiled down on them from a campaign billboard.

"Exactly," Stacey said. "Or there's something else. I don't know." Rick and Addie were heading to the table, laden with sausage and big cups of tea. Stacey hoped Vanessa liked her tea sweet.

Vanessa sighed. "Okay, so what do you want me to do?"

"Figure out a way to meet Tess Clarke." Stacey waved at Rick, who bobbed his head. The tray pitched a bit in his strong hands, but the food stayed squarely in place. Another thing she loved about him. If he was anything, he was steady, in so many ways. Stacey turned back to Vanessa. "Figure out a way to ask her about Harold Dutton, the land deal and all. And find out what she's building back there."

"Wait," Vanessa said. "You want me to investigate?" She must have caught Stacey's glower, because just then she turned to Rick and thanked him for getting her a lunch. Addie slid the tray between herself and Vanessa and took one of the plates and tea from it.

Stacey pointed her fork at Addie's plate. "Gertie's has a new *Käsewurst*?"

Addie shook her head and smiled. "Trying the vegan sausage." She cut off a piece and then made an unconvincing approving sound as she chewed. "Delicious. My new usual. The baked potatoes they can do vegan if you get them plain, and they have a mayo-free version of their coleslaw." Addie pointed to her own plate, which usually contained potato salad with egg and mayo and coleslaw.

"Don't tell me you're going vegan, Addie. I'm not cooking two dinners at home." Stacey cut into her own usual, the smoked kielbasa, surrounded by sauerkraut and potato salad.

"Don't worry," Addie said. "I haven't decided. Yet."

They passed the rest of lunch in light conversation. Stacey wanted to get a better idea about whether Vanessa would try to at least to meet Tess Clarke. They were of the same ilk, weren't they? Vanessa in her frumpy Sunday dress and frizzed brown hair (now that the maroon bit had fallen into her lap) looked nothing like the crowd Tess Clarke in her black pantsuit and sleek angled bob would be around. But maybe she'd fit in with the leather couch and the minimal paintings in the now-bleak interior of the late Mrs. Dutton's cottage.

At least Stacey could hope.

****

"Drive safe," Stacey said in her usual routine when Addie left for school on Monday. "Have a good day. Love you!"

"I always do," Addie said. She turned to go. At least all three of her older children said "Love you too, Mom" as they'd walked out the door. But none of them seemed to have Addie's need to detach herself from her home and fly away. Maybe it was just that way with youngest children. Maybe she should ask Amy, see if she remembered her late teens like that.

Addie had grabbed the keys to the old truck, leaving Stacey with the SUV. She hadn't planned on going anywhere this morning, just making a few changes to Rick's speech that had been hers for the Pecan and Wine Festival and rescheduling the shaker trucks to come out and get the pecans off the trees before more rain came through and the whole crop was lost. They'd used the same company for decades, and the owner always came through for them, working overnight if they needed to make up for bad weather. And in October, you never could tell.

The morning was clear and bright. If they'd had their own shaker trucks, then she could have easily done the job herself, saving them the worry. But Rick had argued against it. Too much expense for something they'd only use once a year, and it wasn't like they were set up to maintain the trucks anyway. Stacey wanted to argue that her parents had the setup—they'd owned the tractor shop and supply store they'd met in while working after they'd left school. But no, that wouldn't do anymore. The shop was taken over by the manager, a good guy, who'd do business like her dad had always done. It was time for her parents to retire, after all. Stacey had thought they'd keep the attached store at least, since it required less physical labor for them. And Stacey had so many childhood memories, best of all when the chicks came in and she and Amy would spend hours cooing over the little yellow fluff balls that always sold out fast, leaving them with none to "rescue" at the end of the season. Stacey had convinced herself that her parents would hold on to the store. Maybe one of her kids could take over after college. But Sheriff Williams had talked them into selling out to a buddy of his with a national chain. And so down went her dream of one of the boys taking over. She knew even last year that Addie wouldn't even think about the idea, much less do it.

Stacey refilled her coffee cup. She leaned against the kitchen counter and looked out the window toward the patch of garden in the side yard of the house. She didn't grow as much this spring as she usually did, and even then, she ended up giving most of the tomatoes, cucumbers, and peppers away to neighbors and friends. Usually, her mother would be there to help her jar up pickles, but her parents were in their RV this summer, somewhere near the Canadian border. Just as well that they'd gone up north during the summer.

Thinking about the shop brought back the story about how her parents had met. Her mother's father owned the place, a farm equipment repair place that did the big or complicated jobs farmers couldn't handle themselves. Her grandmother ran the store they'd built on a few years later, mostly selling seed for gardens, livestock feed, odds and ends, and candy. Stacey's mom had been married at eighteen too, right out of high school. Her husband was a good fifteen years older and took good care of her. The marriage failed years later though when her husband decided that she was the reason they hadn't conceived. So, at twenty-five, with no other prospects—who'd marry her now that everyone knew she couldn't have a family herself?—her mother worked for her parents at the store. She'd given up hope, thinking she'd never have a family herself, but she could devote herself to the family business.

One hot summer morning, Stacey's dad rolled into the shop. As a favor to a friend, her grandpa hired on an unfocused nineteen year old who was good with his hands. Definitely wasn't love at first sight for Stacey's mom, but it was for her dad. He said he saw her mom reorganizing the front counter, and he knew right away that she was the one. Took him a couple months to convince her to go out with him, but something about his willingness to get to work early and stay late made her think her parents would be okay with their going out together. And so, they did. Stacey's mom only told her the rest of the story after Stacey had done the calculations twice and asked if she'd been a premature baby. Thinking she wasn't able to get pregnant in the first place, Stacey's mom and dad hadn't been exactly careful those winter evenings they'd parked together.

Turns out, Stacey's mom hadn't been the problem in her first marriage.

So, they got married not long after Stacey's mom realized what had happened. Her dad worked hard, and eventually, he took over from Stacey's Opa once he retired. The family business passed to Stacey's mom and dad. Stacey and Rick had been too overwhelmed with the farm and family to take on the shop from her parents when they retired. Maybe she should have done more to make it work. Stacey was always willing to make it work, wasn't she? Or maybe she thought others valued family and community just as much as she had.

No use thinking about it now. The chance for that was gone.

Her phone rang. Addie. She should have been at school ten minutes ago. In the background, Stacey could hear chanting and horns honking. Homecoming rally outside? Usually, they'd save that for Friday, not a Monday before the big weekend. "Hey, sweetheart, are you at school?"

"No," Addie shouted. "There's a big protest, and the truck overheated while I was waiting." The old truck. Stacey should have insisted Addie take the SUV, but too late for that now.

Rick had already gone with his pickup. "I don't

94

think I can tow you anywhere, but let me come get you."

"Mom, how are you going to get me? I'm in the middle of things." A horn sounded nearby.

"You're blocking traffic too?"

Addie told her exactly where she was and explained that two of her classmates who'd play in the homecoming game Friday were in their truck a couple cars back from her. "They went all he-man and rolled my truck off toward the ditch. Told me to wait in their truck. Like I couldn't push my truck down into a ditch in neutral." Stacey wondered whether her daughter was capable of that feat, but now wasn't the time to argue.

"Are you in their truck now?"

Addie made her smug noise. "No way," she said. In the background, a police car must have driven by, as a police siren wailed downward in pitch. "Told them I'd stay with the truck until my daddy came and got me. Much better view of what's going on from here on top of the cab. Then I called you."

"Can you walk over to the Bluet Café? I can come the back way and meet you there." The café was on the same side of the highway that the old truck had stalled. Thank goodness for some things breaking in the right place sometimes.

They agreed on the plan. When Stacey arrived at the Bluet Café from the dusty back way, she could easily see the protesters, holding their signs. This was an odd place to protest, right in front of the boutique restaurants and shops, but that would be where the newcomers would be, right? She pulled her SUV into the lot. Stacey glanced over at the mob, who were holding up signs she couldn't quite read. Mostly young, shouting, faces red with screaming or sunburn. It was getting late in the morning.

It was then she saw a few of the Daw County deputies arresting some of the protesters. Some of them ran off throwing their signs at cars as they did so. In among them, she saw the deputy she'd spoken to earlier handcuffing the unmistakably lanky blond figure of Bo Sanders, who was shouting at the sky. Stacey shook her head and went into the café.

"Took you long enough," Addie said. She was sitting at the counter near the pastry case, her bag slung over the bar stool next to her. She bit into a croissant. "Saved you a seat."

"There's a little traffic out there, sweetheart." Stacey sat down next to her daughter and looked at her. "Though I don't know why they keep coming back to this intersection."

Stephanie brought Stacey a cup of coffee and a creamer. "Best place to stop traffic."

"But why?"

Addie swallowed the last bite of her croissant. "Didn't you see the signs?"

Stacey and Stephanie shook their heads.

"5G," Addie said. "They think it's a big governmental conspiracy."

"A conspiracy? How do you know that?" Stacey stirred the cream into her coffee. Stephanie excused herself and went to tend to a couple who walked through the door.

"It's in the news, Mom." Addie ran a finger around her plate, picking up croissant crumbs. "And some of the kids at school think they're right. Like it's a mind control thing."

"Mind control?"

"It's pretty 'out there'," Addie said. She stuck her

finger in her mouth. "We'll say these aren't the kids who aced AP physics."

Stacey laughed. This was her daughter, funny, clever, willing to call out what needed to be called out. Not afraid to go against the crowds. "And this is a popular idea at Dawville High?"

Addie shrugged. "Some of the teachers think there's something to this. And a lot of the parents do too."

"But you don't?"

"Mom," Addie made her smug sound. "Daw County is like the very last place in the US to get 5G. If there were these big bad effects, wouldn't we have seen them elsewhere by now?"

"Smart," Stacey admitted. If she hadn't learned as much as she had about electromagnetic radiation, radio frequencies, and the surrounding technology as she had studying for her ham radio license exams, would she think 5G was a danger too? "What if they're saving the really weird, scary stuff for when the whole country gets 5G? So Daw County has to get 5G for the big secret conspiracy to work, but if the protesters can stop 5G from invading here, then they can stop the whole plan?"

Addie laughed. So good to hear her laugh. More people filtered into the café. Was it nearing lunchtime already? "See? You've got it all figured out. Are you going to grab a sign and stand in the intersection?"

"I don't want to be arrested. Especially not by the sheriff."

Addie shrugged. "Didn't see him out there this time. I looked at the police cars and didn't see his Camaro. Which is good, I guess."

"Why were you looking for his car?"

"Isn't it weird that no one is looking into Mr.

Dutton's fall? You think so, even if you haven't said as much." Addie finished off her coffee. "Maybe I was hoping the sheriff was actually investigating. You and dad have a couple towers too."

"Are you worried they'll come down?" Stacey felt a sudden worry at the question she maybe should have raised herself. "No one has been up the north tower in years, and we'd never climb up by ourselves anyway."

Addie shrugged again. "Can we see if I can get to school now?"

They packed up the SUV and took the long route to the high school.

****

Addie was far from the only one late to school, judging by the long drop off line and a bus straggling in well after the first bell had rung. Stacey watched her daughter walking up the steps to the front door of the school. Someone waved in her direction, and Stacey hoped it would be a friend of Addie's that she didn't know. But another girl near Addie raised her hand and went over. It wasn't as if Addie was ever shy about making friends. She wasn't. Life among three older brothers and a cousin who was like a brother to her meant she had to learn fast if she wanted her voice heard. And she did. Stacey thought back to all the years of birthday parties she'd had and gone to, watching Addie among friends her age from her years in elementary and junior high. When had the shift happened? When did Addie go from so connected to friends in Daw County to as disconnected as possible? Stacey feared that Vanessa might be Addie's only friend left in Daw County. Now that her older brothers and cousin were off at college, who did she have left? It made sense that she'd turn to someone older and wiser to figure out what she wanted to do next.

Stacey cringed. But, she reminded herself, Vanessa hadn't done anything wrong, as far as she knew. She'd supported Addie's writing, and she was a listening ear for a girl who seemed to want to be anywhere but here. And, Stacey admitted to herself, she needed Vanessa to spy on Tess Clarke so that they could get to the bottom of the mystery about Harold Dutton's tower falling down. Better to keep Vanessa close, then. Stacey didn't want to push her away. And, more importantly, Stacey didn't want to push Vanessa away, because that would, effectively, push Addie away.

She exited the school drop off, along with all the other parents dropping off their kids, and drove slowly past the Bluet Café. Seemed the traffic that had backed up at the highway intersection and then at the school had stalled out again. One of the Daw County Sheriff's Department SUV's was parked out front. Stacey made a quick lane change, waving at the driver of the pickup behind her who let her over, and turned into the lot. Fortunately, with so much traffic, no one had been going so fast as not to be able to see her.

Traffic must have done the café some good, or at least the curiosity. At the counter, Deputy Valdez and her partner, Deputy Muller, who was Pastor and Mrs. Muller's son, stood talking to Stephanie. In her delicately embroidered apron, Stephanie waved her friend over to the counter.

"Addie left this," Stephanie said, handing over a spiral notebook. "Must have fallen out of her backpack. Do kids know how to use the zipper on those things?"

Deputy Valdez laughed. "I remember doing the

same thing."

Stacey took the notebook. She could look through it—it was probably full of notes for class—but what if it contained some clue about her daughter's dreams of going elsewhere? "Thank you," she said to Stephanie. "Y'all getting a handle on these protests?" she asked the deputies.

Muller nodded. "Best as we can. Trying to get ahead so we don't have this again for Friday."

"Homecoming," Stacey said. "Of course. Wouldn't that be terrible?" Not as bad as the Wine and Pecan Festival, but she kept that thought to herself. "Addie was just telling me that the 5G conspiracy was running rampant through the high school."

Stephanie gasped. "You didn't have high schoolers out there protesting, did you?"

Muller shook his head, but Valdez said, "We're not at liberty to say whether there were minors arrested for criminal mischief this morning."

"We can hope the science department is doing a better job there teaching these kids about effects of radio waves than the internet is," Stacey said.

"If that's all that's going on the towers," Muller said. He folded his arms over his big body, but his eyes were wide and round. "You hear things."

Valdez narrowed her eyes at her partner. "Not you, too, Dwayne."

"What?" he asked.

His partner sighed. "I'll tell you what." A voice from her radio stopped Valdez from lecturing Muller. "We've got to go. Wreck over near the county line."

Stephanie grabbed two *Danishes* and slid them in a paper bag. "Thanks for looking after us," she said, handing them to the deputies. They said their goodbyes and the deputies rushed to their SUV.

"You don't think there's anything to the conspiracy theories, do you?" Stacey asked Stephanie. Her lifelong friend didn't seem the type to entertain such nonsense, but people changed.

Stephanie laughed. "I hope not. Tower's done out back, and I'm the local evangelist for the phone company."

"Should you call yourself that?" Stacey said in a mock-serious tone.

"What, evangelist?" Stephanie laughed again. "All I do for the church, I think they'll probably let this go."

"You're right," Stacey said. "I've got to get back to the farm. Got to get those pecans harvested sooner rather than later." After they said their goodbyes, she looked down at the notebook. Stacey had driven more today than she'd planned, and she did need to get on the phone with the shaker trucks. Addie would survive one day without her notebook. Not like she didn't have others.

As she walked back out to her SUV, Stacey looked up at the new tower. The 5G antenna clung to the side of it. Stephanie could probably rent out more space on the tower. It was tall enough. Stacey made a note to talk to the ham club next meeting about putting a repeater up there, something they'd gone back and forth about for months trying to find a good place for it. But like so much else, that would have to wait for later. The tower glinted in the sunlight, and Stacey backed out, hoping nothing else would go awry today.

Chapter Eight

Jenna's voice was clipped, and even over the cell phone connection, Stacey could tell the younger woman was upset but doing a valiant effort to hide it. "I'll need a new head shot of Rick," she said. "To replace yours, of course. If you have one in black and white and one in color, that would be good. And any pictures of Rick's family going back, that would help set the scene in all our publications."

"I'll see what I can find," Stacey said. "And I don't think Rick has ever had a head shot done, if you don't count our senior pictures for high school and all the terrible driver license pictures since then." She laughed to herself. "You don't want his latest one, definitely."

Jenna didn't laugh. "Well, I need you to arrange one. My assistant can give you the contact information for our photographer."

"Same one who did mine?"

"That was a waste of money," Jenna said.

That stung. The picture wasn't bad at all. Maybe she was never pretty in the traditional sense. Stacey had her mother's big bones and was solid, but Rick seemed happy with her. Which was what counted, right? "Sorry."

The silence on the line was broken by Jenna inhaling deeply, making a weird crackling noise. "No, I'm sorry. Your picture was nice. It looks like you in a good way.

It's just that the photographer wasn't cheap, and the board is coming down on me for budget problems. Well, they're taking out the fact that one of our sponsors pulled out on me. Like I could have helped that."

Stacey asked, and Jenna explained about the scandal the CEO of the sponsor's company had gotten himself embroiled in. The wife of one of the CEOs had been caught with a much younger man, and the CEO had retaliated in a less-than-legal manner. Officially, the company had taken their sponsorship money to put toward legal fees, but Stacey could hear the story beneath the story in Jenna's voice. One wife in particular on the Wine and Pecan Festival board did not want to be associated with any such rumors. "How can you help that?" Stacey asked. "That's not on you."

"I'm scrambling to find another sponsor, last minute." She sighed again. "I'm trying to figure out how to sell whatever companies I can on the merits of associating with Daw County. It's hard, though, with these protests making statewide news. And then we're getting another tower in the middle of the shopping center that took years to become chic."

"Stephanie's tower?"

"I know it's a good thing, because we need the 5G, but," Jenna stopped herself. "Couldn't she have waited for the Festival to be over before sticking that eyesore up? Towers are just, I don't know, ugly. They're just ugly. And I think if Daw County is going to become a tourist destination, particularly for its natural beauty, then we need to bring as many towers down as we can."

"And replace them with?" Stacey didn't want to argue with the fact that towers needed to be there for the good of the community, but she didn't have any ideas about replacements either.

"They're making wind turbines less intrusive on the landscape now," Jenna said. "Like floral arrangements instead of ugly metal sticks. Why didn't Stephanie think of that?"

"Because most of the time, people pay them no mind," Stacey said. "Especially after they've been there a while. Month or two from now, no one is going to notice the one over by the Bluet Café."

"I hope you're right," Jenna said. She coughed that "clear the emotion out of your throat" cough that Stacey was all too familiar with herself. "The committee doesn't see it that way, though."

"They're just taking the sponsorship problem out on you," Stacey said. "Unfairly."

Jenna thanked her. "There is a bit of good news," she said. "I'm hiring some of Tess Clarke's construction crew to help with last minute details. Some trees came down in the storm the other day and damaged the structures in the park. They'll be restoring the pavilion where Rick will give his speech, and helping out with a few new things the committee wants. There's so much construction on new homes here, that it's hard to find a good crew anywhere near Daw County who isn't booked a year out."

"That's got to be expensive," Stacey said. "Have you seen the kind of buildings they're putting up out there at the old Dutton place?"

"Construction stalled because of the Dutton incident," Jenna said. "Which was all the better for me. I mean, the festival. Besides, the extra cost is worth it. I've seen what they've done already, restoring the old cottage, and it's just beautiful."

"Just the sort of thing Daw County needs to bring in more tourists?"

"Yes," Jenna said brightly. Stacey could hear the smile in her voice. "Exactly."

****

Stacey rebooked the shaker trucks and got the rest of the pecan harvest details hammered out with the various crews she had to hammer them out with. There were at least a dozen other pecan farmers in the county, some of them big operations like hers and Rick's, and some of them much smaller. It helped that her ties to the companies she hired went back to Rick's parents' days farming the land. They'd retired just as soon as she and Rick had established themselves. Rick's mother, Sue, had been particularly helpful, watching the kids while Stacey needed to lend a hand in operations outside or to learn how to do the books. Helped too that Larry, Rick's dad, took the kids out as much as he could onto the land, just as he'd done for Rick and his brothers. Larry and Sue had a cottage built for themselves on the land not too far from the main house that Rick and Stacey had taken over. They'd put in a garden, giving the kids small trowels and watering cans so that they could claim some of the vegetables as their own work. The chicken coop stayed with Sue, if not in location then in spirit, and she taught the kids to be gentle reaching under the hens' warm feathered bodies to find eggs they'd scramble and eat alongside the tomatoes and peppers they'd grown. Hadn't it been a charmed life she'd led so far? Even if things were falling apart around her, even if it looked like none of her children were interested in coming home to farm, at least she'd done what she could to make it inviting to them.

Soon, it was time for her to pick up Addie again. She started up the SUV and turned up the radio. "Sheriff Les Williams is proud to have served Daw County for twelve years as County Sheriff," the voice on the radio intoned over a band playing some patriotic-sounding march. Stacey tried to think whose voice that might have been, but gave up and concluded that this ad must have been made in Houston somewhere by some big ad agency. Sheriff Williams had enough money in his coffers to cover such things, especially when folks like the Sanders family chipped in as much as they were rumored to do. She and Rick had voted for Sheriff Williams in the last three elections, on the advice of most of the community around them. She figured Rick would probably vote for him again. Stacey didn't know much about his woefully underfunded opponent, Josie Neuenschwander, other than that she'd gone to Sam Houston State University to study criminal justice right around the time Stacey and Rick were about to graduate. She'd gone on to law school at the University of Houston after that, then came back to Daw County to work first as a prosecutor for the county and then as a judge. The sheriff usually put on a show during his re-election campaigns, but this year, it was bigger and much, much worse. Was he worried about Josie having a chance against him? "Your vote for Sheriff Williams is a vote for your personal freedom. Protect your rights and vote Sheriff Williams." Stacey felt the groan in her throat rising, and, not looking at the radio, she pressed a button to change the station.

"5G," the voice on the new station repeated a few times. Static washed over the audio, but she heard a man's voice that was almost familiar but a little mechanical, like it was processed to hide its source.

"You'd think people would be more careful with this," he said. "Like this and other towers. I don't think I need to remind you what happens when you build a tower and you're not careful with it. Towers come down. Especially if you go climbing up towers you weren't especially good at building in the first place." Another wash of static over his voice. When the audio came back, music came up from the static. Another song from her high school days. Stacey didn't know whether to be disturbed by the music with its new connection to whoever it was talking or not. 5G, towers. If she was going to help Harold Dutton, then she needed to get to the bottom of this mystery first, it seemed. Who was this pirate and what was his connection to Harold Dutton's tower falling?

"You look like you had a good day." Stacey watched her daughter swing her backpack in the passenger seat with the same joyful force she'd done swinging hay into a trailer for the cows her older brothers had raised for 4-H. Addie's project this year was in computer programming, a web application of some sort, and Stacey didn't want to press her, whether she was working on it or not. 4-H had certainly changed since she'd been in decades ago.

"Frau Weber told me about a program where I can go to Germany for the summer." Addie leaned back and adjusted her sunglasses. "Maybe it's too late to spend this year there, but you and Dad have to let me go for the summer."

"What's this *have to*?" Stacey felt irked by the fact that her daughter's current German teacher seemed to be in the same league as her future English teacher.

"I don't have to be here this summer, do I?" Addie's

good mood collapsed. "Tyler and Caleb don't come home for the summers anymore, and Ethan's trying to get an internship already for June."

"He told you this?" Her youngest son was never as forthright with her and Rick as his older brothers, but at least he'd never pushed on leaving the way his younger sister had. "When? He didn't mention this to me."

"Maybe if you'd asked."

"Has Ethan even decided on a major yet?"

Addie shut the conversation down. Stacey felt guilty for not knowing how to navigate the waters of her daughter's late teen years. With her older brothers, it had been simpler, more straightforward. With Addie? Well, Stacey had been a teenage girl and so had Amy. Though Amy was hard to reach now, working on a cruise ship as a librarian must have kept her busy, and to be fair, neither one of them was much good at deeper conversation. There never seemed to be a reason to get better at it either.

"Addie, look, I'm sorry," Stacey began. Something blowing around in a ditch caught her eye. A white sign that must have come loose off some telephone pole—people were always sticking them up advertising suspect job prospects and garage sales. It flipped up in the wind. 5G, the sign said. There was more text, but she couldn't read it. The bottom edge was at an angle, like it had been torn in half. "Wait, Addie, I need your help." Stacey turned into a side road, a dirt road that led to the Kellers' farm so no traffic was likely to come in or out on. She parked. "Wait here."

Stacey turned off the SUV and made her way down to the ditch. Addie must have seen what her mother was doing, and she got out too, looking up. "Addie, wait,"

Stacey called, but the girl ran back toward the main road. Stacey used a stick to work the sign up to her as fast as she could and grabbed it. 5G. Most of the text had been cut off though.

"Mom, look at this," Addie said. Stacey followed her daughter's voice. She was pointing at a telephone pole, on which half a white sign had bent in the wind. Stacey ran over and held up the top part, which was in her hand.

"Think we can get it?" Stacey wondered.

Addie made her smug noise at her mother, then pulled her phone out of her pocket. "Don't need to. Besides, it's evidence, isn't it?"

"Evidence?"

"Maybe." She pulled up the picture on her phone and zoomed in on the writing on the sign. "Or definitely. Look at this."

"Um, 'is coming be prepared.' What does that mean?"

"It means we have conspiracy theorists," Addie said. She shielded her eyes from the sunlight and looked to the south. There, standing in the middle of the Kellers' field was a short tower, one probably leased to the phone company already. "And I think it means we have a problem. I'm going to climb up and see if I can get the rest of the sign down."

"Addie?" Stacey took a deep breath. Maybe it was good she and Rick hadn't let her go abroad just yet. "Think about Harold Dutton. What happened to him."

"Yeah, Mom, I don't think the 5G protesters are capable of setting up the telephone pole to fall down like they did with Mr. Dutton's tower. I think they would be sad if the electricity went out. Where would they get their weirdo ideas if they didn't have access to the internet anymore? But better safe than sorry." Addie shrugged. Stacey wanted to laugh, but she could see Addie was serious. And she was right. "I'll stay on the ground though."

Stacey had, once again, underestimated her daughter.

"Come on," Stacey said. "We need coffee." She put the half of the sign she'd rescued from the ditch into the back of the SUV. "And we need to talk."

****

As she parked the SUV, Stacey watched Minty Sanders leave one of the boutiques that flanked the Bluet Café. Stacey herself had never had much occasion to go inside, since she'd left her "dressing up" days long behind her. Minty stopped and clutched the floral-covered boutique bag to her side. She strode over to the SUV and tapped on the window.

"Mrs. Hengesbach," she said sharply.

"Good to see you, Mrs. Sanders," Stacey said. She elbowed Addie who waved and flashed a smile worthy of the worst school portrait. "Please, do call me Stacey."

"You are Mrs. Hengesbach, so I shall call you Mrs. Hengesbach." Minty peered over the top of her oversized sunglasses. "You've deferred to your husband on the matter of the festival speech, I presume."

Stacey held back what she wanted to say, which was not that she'd deferred. She'd been ordered, more like. "I'm rewriting the speech for him, yes."

"You ought to let your husband speak for himself," Minty said, pushing her glasses back up on her face. "It's not a woman's place to control her man."

"No one controls Rick, that's true."

"Good."

"How's Bo doing?"

Minty Sanders glare was strong enough to reach through her dark sunglasses. "My son is his own man." She nodded and strode off.

"What was that about?" Addie asked after Stacey rolled up the window.

"I have no idea," Stacey said. Which was probably half-true at the very least. But at least she knew now exactly who had pressured the committee into booting Stacey's speech in favor of Rick's. One that she was writing.

****

The Bluet Café was half-full, as Stephanie liked to say. She'd hired a few of the high school kids to wait tables part-time, so she could take a break. So Stacey didn't feel bad waving her over and pointing at the picture of the sign on Addie's phone. "We have a problem," she said. "Maybe."

"Maybe?" Stephanie caught the attention of one of the wait staff, who came back with three cups of pecan coffee and creamers. "What do you mean by *maybe*."

Stacey explained the sign. "Doesn't it seem weird to you, all the protests, and Harold's tower falling down?" She wrapped her hands around the mug. Didn't matter that the afternoon was nearing hot. There was something that was always good about wrapping her hands around a warm mug of coffee. "There's got to be something here that we're missing."

"Maybe?"

Addie grabbed one of the notebooks she carried in her backpack. Most of her friends had tablets, but, she'd explained to her mother, there was something about the act of writing that she liked and that made what she was learning stick. "Let's write down what we know."

Stacey nodded. Maybe this was what they needed. A project to work on together. When Stacey and Amy had fought during their high school days, their mother would often usher them into the kitchen with a basket of fruit, a big pot of water, and a whole box full of mason jars. "Don't come out until you've worked it out or canned all this fruit. Or both," their mother had said. It worked. Over washing, cutting, and cooking fruit, Stacey and Amy worked out their problems. "Okay, let's go back to the beginning."

In her looping script, Addie wrote "Mr. Dutton's Tower" in purple ink at the top of a page. "So, what do we do now?"

Stephanie tapped the side of her coffee mug with her index finger. "We can start there. Good thinking, Addie." Addie smiled. If Stacey was going to keep at least some part of her daughter in Daw County, reinforcing her ties to the people here was a good start. Stephanie narrowed her eyes. "I don't want to point out any customers, though."

Addie must have picked up on what Stephanie was thinking. "The two obvious ones are Mrs. Dutton, because she doesn't like living in Dawville."

"Hey now," Stacey said. "How do you know that? I mean, why do you think that?"

Stephanie stifled a laugh. "Judy Dutton couldn't make that clearer if she wore a sign saying so."

"So there's Mrs. Dutton," Addie said. "If Mr. Dutton couldn't work on the farm anymore, then they'd have to leave, right?"

Stacey nodded. It was a dark thought, but Addie was

right. "You said you had two obvious suspects."

"Mrs. Dutton and Tess Clarke. We don't know what she's planning on the land, and, I don't know, maybe she just didn't like the tower? Maybe she believes in 5G conspiracies. Or aliens." Addie wrote down Tess Clarke's name under Judy Dutton's.

Stephanie looked around for a moment. "There's word there was a dispute between Harold and Tess about the sale of the land."

"I saw that much when I was out there bringing by a pecan cake," Stacey said. "I hope she passed that along to the crew if she didn't think it was good enough for her."

"Mom, you have the best pecan cake in Daw County," Addie said. She looked up at Stephanie. "I mean, homemade."

"Well, those are the two obvious ones," Stacey said. "Who else?"

"Next question is who else was affected by Mr. Dutton's sale of his momma's land. Or the tower. He wasn't interfering on the radio, was he?" Stephanie looked over her coffee cup at Stacey.

"Not that I was aware of," Stacey said. "I don't get much time on air unless it's training for storm season communications. But Rick hasn't said anything. And the hams in Daw County are the worst gossips. So we'd have heard about it, I'm sure." There was one other person who'd just revealed that she'd benefited from the tower's collapse. Jenna got the idle construction crew, didn't she? Well, that wouldn't put her on the list, not if she just took advantage of an accident. Being savvy about that wouldn't make her a suspect. Besides, Stacey considered Jenna a friend of sorts, even if Jenna hadn't stood up for

Stacey as a speaker at the festival.

"What are we going to do with this list?' Addie asked. "Are we going to Sheriff Williams with it? Are we going to investigate?" Her eyes were round, though Stacey couldn't tell with excitement or fear.

"We're going to think about it," Stacey said. "We're not going to do anything with it yet."

"Yet?"

"I don't know," Stacey said. "It's none of our business, really, is it?"

Stephanie sighed. "It's community business. Which makes it our business."

"You're right, Steph. Here," Stacey said, holding out her hand to Addie. "Let me hold on to that list. You tend to leave notebooks lying around."

"What are you worried about, Mom?"

Stacey could have named a thousand things. "I don't want anyone getting the idea that we are investigating. We're not. We're just thinking about what might have happened."

Addie held her notebook to herself for a moment, then tore out the page and handed it to Stacey. Wasn't this the way they had to do things? She had to let Addie in on the investigation, whatever that meant, but also she had to protect her daughter. Community business was important.

Addie, though, was even more important than that.

Chapter Nine

"You know better than I do where all that stuff is," Rick said to Stacey from the back of their disorganized storage closet. "Have you called Mom? She can come over to look for this. She'll know where the pictures are."

"Your mom is in Houston with your brother, if you haven't forgotten that," Stacey said. She emerged from the attic with a box of what she'd hoped contained the pictures of the Hengesbachs when they'd first bought the land in Daw County not long after they'd arrived in Texas from the land they'd left behind in Germany.

"Maybe that stuff should go to a museum?" Addie, who'd been waiting for her at the bottom of the attic stairs, took the box from her mother. "Can I go up and look now?"

"For what?"

Addie shrugged. "I just want to see what's up there."

Stacey closed the attic door. If she looked hard enough, she could see the places where the farmhouse had been renovated, walls taken down and rooms added on. It wasn't the original farmhouse that Rick's ancestors had built. That one was a cabin Rick's Opa had restored and now housed some of the original farming equipment and other household necessaries. Stacey had wondered aloud more than once whether the cabin and its contents ought to go to the Daw County Historical Society along with the letters and pictures they stored in the attic at the new farmhouse, but Rick shot that down every time. Not that she didn't think he'd agree with her that the cabin and the equipment would be better cared for by the society, or that the community might enjoy seeing the pieces of their past, though most of the Hengesbach cousins had gone elsewhere over the years. The thing that kept Rick saying no, Stacey knew, was that the Daw County Historical Society was headed up by Cowboy Jenkins, and there was no way the Hengesbach family heirlooms were going to that man. Stacey had never quite gotten the full story out of Rick, what Cowboy had said that so bothered Rick. But there it was. Stacey hoped all the pictures were here. If they'd been over at the cabin, they were long gone, the victims of time, rain, and heat. Like everything else.

"How about you help me sort these instead." Stacey took the box from her daughter and sat down at the dining table.

"I've seen those before." Addie looked hopefully at the attic again.

Stacey sighed and handed Addie the flashlight she'd put in her pocket. "Be sure to scare off any rats you see."

Addie did her best farm cat impression, grabbed the flashlight, and jumped up the attic door.

Of course, they'd all be here, inside the box. The ones she knew about, anyway. All the wedding pictures, family portraits, letters to and from Germany, and then later across Texas and the wider US. They weren't her family, but they were, in a way. The later pictures, anything from Rick's grandparents and after, were stored elsewhere. Sue had massive photo albums, each picture and memento lovingly labeled in her fine, clear script. She'd made a project of that over the years, right after she'd married Larry Hengesbach. She'd included what photos she had of her own family, and she'd made a massive family tree, which Larry had dubbed "the tapestry," and she spent hours updating the embroidered branches with names and dates as the family grew. After Rick's oldest brother died, the tree came down for a while. But then Tyler was born, then Caleb, Ethan, and Addie, and eventually, Sue returned the tree to its former place, updated with new names, new dates.

Stacey made a note to ask her own mother where their family box was, now that her parents had sold their shop and bought an RV. She felt silly for worrying—they hadn't sold the house, since they still lived there between trips. So their family history was, most likely, sitting exactly where it had since Stacey and Amy were kids. But maybe it was time for their parents to hand over the task of preserving their boxes and albums to Stacey. She was the one who'd stayed, after all. She was the one who'd put down the longest, deepest roots of all.

Rick put his hands on her shoulders. "Cool," he said. "I can't tell you who's who, though."

"This," Stacey said as she took a picture out of the box, "is your great-grandmother as a baby."

"You can tell that from a baby picture?"

Stacey sighed. "I've read the back of the pictures enough times to know. Maybe you should too?"

"Wonder which one of the kids will want those?" Rick took his hands off her shoulders. She could smell the dust on him, which he'd transferred to her shirt. Or maybe she'd collected it in the attic.

"We'll ask," she said. "When the time comes."

Rick went off to the kitchen. She heard his footsteps, still heavy in his slippers, on the linoleum tiles. Her rule, trying to keep the house clean, or maybe just in the shape it had been when Sue and Larry transferred it over to them. No shoes in the house. Rick insisted on no cats or dogs in the house, either, mostly because he had a clear line in his head between people and animals, which he must have picked up from when they'd raised beef cattle for FFA in high school or from Sue and Larry, who'd run cows on the land to graze, land they couldn't farm profitably. To Stacey, the idea of raising kids without pets was sad—she'd grown up with a series of cats and rabbits roaming the tiny house of her childhood, and always, there was an old dog who'd command their porch. Even when they'd got a young dog after the old one died or when the new one needed a companion, the dogs seemed old and world-weary. She supposed if she'd napped on a porch, maybe she would be too.

Stacey heard a crash overhead and jumped up. The box upended, and a few of the pictures spilled out onto the floor. Addie screeched. Stacey stepped forward, feeling after it was too late the heel of her house shoe on the old photo beneath it. Addie wailed. Stacey picked up the picture instead, trying to smooth out the indentation her heel had put into the face of some now long dead ancestor.

"We do have rats." Addie popped out of the attic doorway. She rubbed her head with the back of the hand she held the flashlight in. In the other, she had a small box. "Turns out I'm a terrible farm cat. You could have helped, Mom."

"I'm trying." Stacey gave up on the picture. It would be wrinkled. Every time she looked at the picture, it would be creased, wouldn't it? "You going to take some traps up there for me?"

"That's Dad's job." Addie sneezed. "Speaking of Dad, if he won't let you give that stuff to the museum, then maybe they could be scanned? Vanessa told me that Cowboy was working on a project where they scanned a whole bunch of historical documents and pictures just in case the originals were destroyed."

"Vanessa? Cowboy?"

"Sorry, Dr. Dumont. Dr. Jenkins. Is that better?" It was, but the damage had been done. It was bad enough that Addie was calling the head of the Daw County Community College English department by her first name. Had she been talking to Cowboy, too? What sort of nonsense was he filling her head with?

Stacey filed away the idea of scanning the pictures for later. "What's in the box?"

Addie shrugged. "Just kid stuff, I think. I'm not sure." Kid stuff. Stuff from a simpler time, for Addie and her brothers, anyway. Maybe not for Stacey. Her daughter went down the hallway to what was the newest addition to the farmhouse. After Addie was born, Stacey and Rick decided putting three boys in one bedroom would mean too much chaos. They'd knocked down a wall and taken out an old oak that was threatening the roof anyway and put in two more bedrooms.

Rick plodded back into the dining room. It was late, and Rick sat heavily next to her. "Finding what you need for the festival?" He popped the top of his beer can. Bubbles sprayed Stacey's arm, and she feared a few would land on the pictures. Well, what if they were all destroyed? What then?

"I need to organize these," Stacey said. "By time or family, I don't know yet."

"Does it matter? You can tell them this was my

great-great-great uncle Karl, who'd been a baron back in the old country before he denounced his title and fortune to come to Texas and marry the Cherokee princess of his dreams." Rick took a swig of his beer. "And then he fought alongside Sam Houston, Stephen F. Austin, oh, and William Travis and David Bowie and Davy Crockett at the Alamo to win the freedom of the state from the Mexican dictator Santa Ana."

"One, that's your great-grandmother as a baby, so wrong timeline. Two, since when do you have Native American ancestry?" Stacey shook her head. "And three, David Bowie? I think it was James Bowie at the Alamo. Do you even remember your Texas history? We had a whole year of it in school." Stacey probably wouldn't have remembered as much as she did if she hadn't ushered four kids through the year of Texas history homework and projects as recently as she had.

"You're going to tell me that this stuff belongs in a museum just because I can't keep Davy Jones and Davy Bowie straight?"

Stacey put out the pictures in straight lines. "Don't joke right now. I'm working."

"Jenna's got you on a chain." Rick stood up. "I'm going to watch TV."

"Jenna does not have me on a chain, Rick." Stacey couldn't face her husband. "I am invested in the success of the Wine and Pecan Festival. It'll do us some good to have some publicity, and it's very good for the community. You know tourism took a hit these past few years."

"Why do we need publicity?" Rick slurped his beer. Ugly habit, but if she hadn't been able to get him to stop in well over a quarter century of marriage, then she probably couldn't now. "We sell our entire crop at a good price every year. We don't need publicity."

"The wine industry does."

"Well if we're pulling the wine industry along, then they should call it the Pecan and Wine Festival." Rick put up a fight every year about this. The half dozen other pecan farmers in the area were happy enough to have second billing. Why not Rick? "I'm giving the keynote, after all. A pecan farmer. Not some winery snob who trucks in grapes from California and smashes them here and slaps a Texas wine label on their bottle."

"I'm not having this argument right now." Because they'd had it before. Most of the grapes were grown in Texas, many of them here in Daw County. Jenna had shown her the documentation, and any that they'd trucked in were varieties that were popular German-style wine grapes that couldn't be grown in Texas. "Least you could do is sit down with me and find the pictures I mentioned in your speech."

"Which ones?"

"Have you even *read* the speech? I rewrote the whole thing when the association decided they wanted you to talk, not me." They wanted the farmer, not the mere farmer's wife. And Stacey wondered now if it was the pecan growers who'd cared about this or if something else influenced them. Someone. Someone with wealthier roots in Daw County than Stacey or Rick had. "In the speech, I mention your Hengesbach relatives, the stories your dad told us over and over? I mean, you mention. It's your speech."

"Which stories did Dad tell?" Rick asked again.

Stacey inhaled deeply. "The festival is in two weeks, Rick. Please, go read over the speech. Practice it. It's not

121

long. I'd already memorized the one I was going to give. You'll have notecards, too. And slides."

Rick took another long drink of his beer. "Got other things to do. You know that."

"I rescheduled the shaker trucks," Stacey said. That was hardly the only thing they had to think about right now, and she knew it, but she needed to feel useful. "And I need to get Ethan's room ready for this weekend. He's going to be home Friday around lunchtime, after his morning classes."

Stacey tried hard to read Rick's face. Sometimes, she wished people in this house just talked to each other more, rather than hiding everything behind a mask of okayness. Something her ancestors had done, something his had done too. "Just Ethan?"

"Caleb has an exam Friday afternoon," Stacey said. She lined up the pictures in straight rows, trying to ignore any wrinkles time or her carelessness had imposed upon them. "And Tyler has a group project to work on. They're sorry they can't come."

"But Ethan can," Rick said.

"Don't sound so disappointed your kid is coming home for the weekend, Rick."

"I'm not," he said.

"They're coming to see you the festival weekend, though." Stacey tried to sound hopeful. Tyler and Caleb were both comfortable in their new selves they'd blossomed into at Texas A&M, selves that were, really, just extensions of who they had been on the farm. Stacey wouldn't hesitate to turn over all the farm's books to either one of them now. In fact, they might make them better than she had for years now.

"So Ethan's not coming for the festival?"

"Don't make that sound like such a good thing," Stacey said. She steeled herself for a fight that she'd been preparing for years. Not that it ever happened. She knew one day, she'd have to fight for her third child, her youngest son. After the near stereotypical boyhoods of Tyler and Caleb, Stacey didn't know what to do with Ethan. He wasn't exactly boyish like his brothers, enjoying the roughness of their existence. Nor was he girlish, either. After Addie came along, Stacey hoped Ethan would fall in more with his older brothers. Not so. Addie was definitely queen bee around her brothers and Angus her cousin, but Ethan never settled into anything. He was, as Amy had once said, neither fish nor fowl. "He's Ethan," Amy said. "He's great. He's a really good kid." And he was a really good kid turning into, for all she could see, a really good young adult.

There was something neither fish nor fowl about him, though. Rick never said anything much about it, only worried when Ethan would rather read than watch football on TV with his dad and brothers. Stacey stood up for Ethan. He could drive a tractor better than his brothers, and he had no problem splitting logs all morning for their wood stove. Rick never quite said what he thought was wrong with Ethan. Stacey had convinced herself nothing was wrong, and she'd steeled herself for a fight against anyone who said otherwise. What she didn't know was who she was going to have to fight with. Would it be Rick? Or would it be a lifelong fight with herself? "Ethan's always been right at home at these things."

Rick shot her a look.

She shook her head. "Like Tyler and Caleb."

"Not like Tyler and Caleb," Rick said. He finished

his beer and wandered back to the kitchen. Stacey felt the nerves in her back jump when she heard Rick crushing the beer can and tossing it in the recycling bin.

Rick was right. Ethan wasn't like Tyler or Caleb.

Question was whether that was such a bad thing?

****

Like she had for so many years, Addie waited for Stacey the next morning at the back door, backpack slung over one shoulder, eager to get on with the day. "Wait a minute," Stacey said. She got out her phone and checked the local traffic. If there was something good about so many people moving into the county, it was that they'd brought their technology with them. She opened up her maps app and scrolled over to the major intersection they'd need to take to get to the high school. "Looks like there's another protest. The intersection is red for a good ways," she said. Good that Addie was a bit early. "We need to take the long way around."

Addie swung her backpack up on both shoulders then winced. "Ugh," she said, dropping her backpack. "Hold on." She opened her backpack and pulled out the offending object. Addie held up a piece of curved metal, one that was just like the one that had punctured her tire.

"Where did you get that?" Stacey reached for it.

"Found it as I was walking from the protest," she said. "Opa's always picking up stuff like this. Thought he might like it when he and Oma got back from their trip."

Stacey looked at the time. "You and Opa with a metal detector. That was always a fun day. Let's get going," she said. "We'll put this out in the shop." She grabbed her keys and ushered her daughter out the door. "Might be a coincidence, but I pulled one of these out of my tire near Mrs. Dutton's old place." The truck had been towed to the farm, but neither she nor Rick had time to look at it for damage yet. Probably just needed some coolant and it would be fine. In the morning light, she made out what she was looking for. Another piece of metal, slightly rusted and damaged from the drive, still sitting in the truck bed. She grabbed that one too, slid open the door to their machine shop, and placed both on the workbench. Probably just a coincidence.

"You haven't called it Tess Clarke's place," Addie said. In the passenger seat, she was digging through her backpack, losing pens and paper from it as she dug.

"Well, it takes me time to get used to Mrs. Dutton not being there anymore," Stacey admitted. "You know Mrs. Dutton taught Amy how to make lace for her 4-H projects, right? I went over there a lot too. She loved beautiful things. Shame what Tess Clarke has done to Mrs. Dutton's home."

"Vanessa says it's gorgeous," Addie said. She looked up from her backpack. "She says it's done in a style—oh, I wrote it down somewhere."

"I don't know whether I'm more worried about you losing things or calling your teacher by her first name, Addie." Stacey stopped at a red light. No one coming out this way, but the county had to do something with the increased tax revenue, and putting in more traffic lights was a safe call. Like the county judge, the county commissioner was in cahoots with Sheriff Williams, though Stacey couldn't quite figure out why. Something for later. So much for later. The county commissioner took care of the roads and bridges, which had needed taking care of for a good long while. "Do you call her Vanessa to her face?"

"Sure," Addie said. "She asked me to call her Vanessa. And she's not my teacher."

"She teaches the senior English dual credit class at the high school," Stacey said. "Which means she will be your teacher next year."

"And she's Aunt Amy's friend. She'd be your friend too if you'd let her. Come on, Mom," Addie said. "You're not even giving me the chance to skip out next year. It's not fair."

"What's not fair?"

"Dawville?"

Stacey pulled through the green light. She didn't want to get into this topic this morning. Addie would change her mind. High school had been much different for Addie than it had been for Stacey, but Stacey's senior year had probably been the best in her life. "You said Dr. Dumont has been over to Ms. Clarke's house. Did she tell you anything else? What Ms. Clarke is building back there?"

"No, she said *Ms*. Clarke was just annoyed by *Mr*. Dutton's tower falling down, so *Dr*. Dumont changed the subject." Addie drew out the titles and last names as she spoke them.

Stacey decided to ignore her daughter's insolence. "I'd be annoyed too if someone's tower took out my fence and almost crashed into whatever I was having put out there," Stacey said. "Even if it was destroying something beautiful. One of these days, we should go back into the attic and find some of the needlework she taught me how to do. I'm not as good as Amy was, not nearly as good as Oma Hengesbach is. Maybe you could pick that up?"

"I'm not going back in the attic until Dad gets the

rats out," Addie said.

"They're just rats, Addie," Stacey said. "If you'd grown up with cats and dogs in the house, maybe you wouldn't be so skittish around animals."

"I'm not skittish around animals," Addie said. "I hang around the barn cats enough. Pfeffernuss even lets me pet her. And I've gathered more than my share of eggs. Rats bite."

"Hens peck, and cats scratch," Stacey said. "But only if they feel threatened. As long as you don't go up and stick your finger in their faces, they're not going to bite you." She paused a moment. "Wait, who's Pfeffernuss?"

"The young calico," Addie said. "She's getting kind of fluffy, though. Really fluffy, actually. Pushes the other bigger cats out of the way to get her fill. She's spicy."

"Oh," Stacey said. Getting the new barn cats that had shown up over the summer fixed had been on Stacey's to do list. She made a note to put that at the very top of her list, though she'd wait until Pfeffernuss had weaned her forthcoming kittens before she'd take her to the vet. And find good homes for the kittens. At least the new well-to-do around Dawville loved rescuing animals, and Stacey had no doubt Addie would tame the kittens well enough. "Pfeffernuss is spicy, then, huh."

"I haven't seen her in a few days, though."

Stacey didn't want to explain now that spicy, fluffy Pfeffernuss has probably holed up in a nest somewhere with her new babies. Too much else to think about right now.

Addie went quiet anyway. Stacey listened to the sounds of the tires over the road. "Can I tell you about Mrs. Dutton?"

"I knew her too, Mom," Addie said. "I used to play in the backyard when you took me to visit her. What did you talk to her about? And why did you only ever take me?"

Stacey sighed. Maybe she should have taken her boys to see Mrs. Dutton. "Every time Oma Hengesbach tried to teach you how to embroider or cross stitch, quilting, anything like that, you shook your head and went out to play with the boys. I guess I wanted you to learn something from Mrs. Dutton the way your Aunt Amy and I did."

"I wasn't interested in that," Addie said. She sniffled and ran her arm across her nose. "I liked her cookies, though. I wish she would have taught me that, I guess."

"You miss her, too?"

"No." Addie sniffed again. "It's been ages."

"Addie, it's okay." Stacey felt her eyes prickle. She looked up for a moment, long enough to stop the feeling of sadness but not long enough to keep her eyes off the road dangerously. "It's been a few years, but you don't ever have to stop missing people you loved."

Out of the corner of her eye, Stacey saw her daughter nod.

"Mrs. Dutton left your Aunt Amy a box of some of her old needlework supplies, and some pieces she'd done. It's probably in the old barn, where Amy stored her stuff before going to sea," Stacey said.

Addie groaned. "Everyone gets to leave Dawville except me."

"Be patient," Stacey said. Which was hard, she knew. In the ditch in front of them, something small and rust colored moved around. Someone's lost dog? She looked closer for a moment. "We should move the box to the attic anyway. The old barn is pretty weather tight, but I don't know what the heat will do to that next summer."

"I've been patient."

Stacey nodded toward the ditch. "Is that a fox over there? See it?"

"I've been watching them, Mom," Addie said. "They're coyotes."

"Are they?" Stacey didn't look over again. "At least let me tell you about Mrs. Dutton. You won't have to listen long, since we're almost to the school."

Stacey took Addie's silence not so much as permission but as a lack of protest, which was probably all she was going to get out of the girl this morning. Mrs. Dutton was a small woman who'd raised three boys, mostly on her own. Her husband drove long haul trucks and was gone most of the time. One trip out, not long after Harold's younger brother went off to work in the oil fields, Mrs. Dutton's husband called and said he wasn't coming home again. He'd met someone younger and more exciting. Mrs. Dutton packed his bags and set them on the porch for him to pick up so she didn't have to see him.

When Harold, the oldest of the three, came back from the Army, he took over the care of the land, all except the house he'd grown up in, the cottage Mrs. Dutton wanted for herself. She'd raised a nest-full, then when it was empty, she wanted her own space. It was a beautiful little cottage, lots of windows for natural light, dollhouse sweet but with the edge of a woman who'd done a lot in her life by herself. Harold built himself a modern house where he raised his children with his first wife. Where he still lived with his second.

Stacey had only ever known Mrs. Dutton as a single woman. After Stacey's mom complimented her on a needlework cover she'd made for her bible one morning in church, they decided maybe it would be a good thing for Amy and Stacey to learn the craft, something Stacey's mom didn't do herself. So, every other Saturday morning, the girls would go over and help with a chore before learning how to make small flowers and knots and lines in thread. Stacey doubted she could remember any of it, but she'd never let go the feeling of Mrs. Dutton's warm hand on hers, guiding her finger and thumb holding the needle back up to just the right place in the fabric.

"After she had the cottage to herself, everyone said, Mrs. Dutton became a new woman," Stacey said. "She went to the drugstore for new makeup, had her hair done in the salon, always had her nails nice. She couldn't afford really nice dresses, but she knew how to tailor and embellish what she could buy so that they looked beautiful on her. She tried, and she made it work."

"What does any of this have to do with Tess Clarke, though," Addie asked.

"Tess Clarke is destroying what Mrs. Dutton worked to build. Don't you get that?" Stacey was surprised by the edge in her voice. "Tess Clarke came in, dozed over the garden, covered over the cottage with ugly new style decoration, and now's she's building a giant house for herself behind the cottage she ruined. Don't you get that?"

Addie made her smug noise. "Mom, the design is called Deconstructivism. Vanessa told me that."

"I don't care what it's called," Stacey said. "Maybe Dr. Dumont thinks this is part of your education, but maybe you need to focus more on math and science than English."

"Maybe you need to focus less on history, Mom. Past history."

Stacey pulled the SUV into the school drop off lane. Few cars were there, and even a few buses seemed to be missing. Whatever was going on over there by the protest, she needed to see. "Maybe you need to focus more on community, Addie. Just appreciate what you have here before you go. You'll miss it."

"Are you so sure of that?" Addie slid out of the passenger seat as soon as the SUV came to a stop. The drop off lane moved swiftly, almost too swiftly, for Stacey to see her daughter going through the doors of the high school. Caleb and Tyler might have been better at math and science, but Ethan and Addie held their own in both subjects. Ethan had even won a full scholarship, which had helped convince Stacey and Rick to send him to the UT in Austin. Why had she wanted Ethan to stay close, closer than Austin? Really, Austin wasn't that far away. Even if College Station, where Caleb and Tyler were now, was closer, none of her children were all that far away. Still, something about letting Ethan go bothered her. Caleb and Tyler both had a handle on life in ways Ethan didn't seem to, the way Addie seemed to think she did. Maybe it was just that Stacey didn't want her nest to empty this soon. Almost, it felt, all at once.

Maybe Addie was right. Maybe Stacey shouldn't focus so much on the past. But that's where her anchors lay. That's where her identity anchored itself. But maybe there was something to this. Maybe Stacey should focus more on math and science herself. Something dawned on her, something vague, but she knew she needed to see Stephanie, and she knew she needed to see her now.

Chapter Ten

A strong wind blew through Daw County, pushing the trees dotting the dusty landscape back and forth. Stacey had loved the pines of east Texas when she went to college there, and she and Rick never missed the chance to take their kids to Sam Houston State's homecoming weekend, as much to hike through the piney woods as to see their college friends. They were missing the event this year. The Wine and Pecan Festival took up too much of their time, and anyway, without the boys, the hike was less fun. Addie was a good sport about it, but last year, she'd begged to stay home that weekend. Reluctantly, Rick and Stacey let her. None of their fears had come true. The worst that had happened was that Addie had dyed her hair purple and burned a bag of popcorn in the microwave.

Maybe Stacey shouldn't fight so hard after all about keeping Addie home one more year.

Stacey pushed the SUV's door open against the wind. A gust caught the door of the Bluet Café and held it open for a moment, vigorously ringing the bells hanging from the pneumatic arm at the top. A paper sign on the inside of the door was lifted then torn from it, probably something advertising a choir bake sale or some event at one of the local churches.

Inside, a few tables were occupied, but not nearly as many as there would be on a normal morning. "Protests keeping people from your kolaches?" Stacey asked Stephanie as she sat down at the small bar beside the bakery case.

"Something is," Stephanie said. "It's been quiet since the 5G conspiracy nuts set up camp in the intersection this morning."

"They have a whole camp there?"

"That's what I've heard. Deputy Valdez and her partner were here briefly this morning after my alarm went off," Stephanie pointed vaguely behind her. "Didn't see anything, and with this wind, it was probably a false alarm. Or a possum."

"Possums do love kolache scraps," Stacey said. She was trying to keep her spirits up, but something dark hung over her. She thought of her daughter, so eager to get to school—but eager to get away from it. Did she know something about the 5G group at school? Was she a part of the conspiracy? For a moment, Stacey let herself think about the possibility that Addie had used the metal piece that she'd found in the ditch on her own, that she was an accessory to the protests, even distantly. But Addie was smart. She knew there was nothing to the 5G conspiracies, and she wouldn't have shown her mom the piece of metal if she had believed in stopping the new 5G installations.

Stephanie nodded. "And the raccoons and the skunks." She set a cup of coffee in front of Stacey.

Something moaned outside.

Stacey poured cream into her coffee and stirred it. "Why that intersection?"

"It's the busiest in the county," Stephanie said. "Unfortunately, it's the main way to get to the shopping center. How'd you manage to get here?"

"Back roads," Stacey said. "Dropping Addie off at school."

Something banged outside. "I need to get the lids on the garbage bins to stay down," Stephanie said. "They bang, but I've never heard them this loud. We're getting some storm."

Stacey sighed. She'd have to reschedule the pecan harvest again, try to squeeze into the narrowing window of time when the shaker trucks could come out while the pecans were at their best. The lights flickered and went out.

From the kitchen emerged the morning cook wiping her hands on her apron. Two retired women who'd worked as wait staff followed behind. The light from the windows still made the food easy to see, but with the prospect of no more coffee refills, many of the customers finished their last bites, drank up their coffee, set cash on the table, and left.

"Well, I should get going too," Stacey said. "You need anything?"

"No, thanks. I need to call the power company, though," Stephanie said. She picked up the phone by the cash register. "That's funny. The phone's out too."

"Would the wind do that?" Stacey said. She and Stephanie waved at the last of the customers to leave, a ham and his wife. After they were out the door, one of the wait staff locked up.

"This is not what we needed after having a slow morning." Stephanie found her cell phone in her apron pocket and pulled up the number for the power company. "At least this isn't the protesters."

Something moaned again, this time, louder. Something in Stacey told her to grab Stephanie by the arm and pull her away from the counter. The cook and wait staff had sat down at a far booth. Just as Stacey and Stephanie cleared the counter, something loud and large came crashing down into the ceiling. They unlocked the door and ran outside just as something grazed Stacey's forehead.

Stacey couldn't believe what she saw. Lying across the top of the Bluet Café was the newly installed antenna tower. Stephanie shouted something at the power company person she was talking to. Stacey grabbed her own phone and quickly dialed the police with one hand while pushing against her forehead with the other.

Customers and staff from the surrounding shops rushed out to see what had happened.

Another antenna tower had fallen.

****

Deputy Valdez and her partner had been the first on the scene. They'd left the protest in the hands of a couple new recruits, mostly just clearing out what was left of the traffic after the protesters had been hauled away.

Deputy Muller whistled. "Some wind this morning." He held on to his hat as it gusted again.

"You think this is an accident?" Stephanie shouted. Stacey had rarely seen her friend get upset, but then again, this was upsetting.

Stacey took Stephanie's arm. Deputy Valdez shook her head. "We can't say what happened yet, not until a full investigation has taken place." The young woman was serious, in charge. "Sheriff says he's on the way, too."

The sheriff. Stacey tried hard not to roll her eyes, but he was needed here, wasn't he? A good number of the people crowding around were voters, after all.

One of the shop owners took the café staff and Stacey into her shop's office. She brought out coffee, not as good as Stephanie's, but much needed, and a bandage for Stacey's forehead. The bleeding had slowed at least. "Can you tell me again what happened?" Deputy Muller said. Stacey repeated the noises she'd heard, the wind banging but also the moans and the creaks.

Outside, she could hear the wind banging up against the side of the shopping center. Cold front coming through. Might knock down a fair number of the pecans anyway.

Deputy Muller wrote down what she said on a tablet, his pencil making scratching sounds across the page. Once she'd finished, he nodded and stood up. "You okay, Mrs. H.?" His broad smile made him look goofy, childlike. "You sure you're okay?"

"I'm fine." Stacey took a deep breath in and squeezed her arms around herself. Despite the coffee and the warmth of the little office, she felt cold. Deputy Valdez had interviewed the waitress and was on to the cook. Stephanie hadn't spoken yet. "Mind if I sit with Stephanie while you interview her?"

Deputy Muller agreed, and Stacey shifted onto the small couch alongside Stephanie. Muller rolled the office chair he sat in over to the couch. Stacey held Stephanie's hand in hers. She'd expected it to be cold like hers or cool at least, but her hand was almost hot to the touch. If there was one thing Stephanie had become better at over the years than running her café, it was holding in her feelings. Not unusual around here. People were pragmatic, for the most part. Stephanie had held it together after her husband died. She'd held it together after the café had once nearly gone under with the recession in 2008 and again a few years later when a fire wrecked much of the shopping center. Stephanie held herself together. But now? Something was cracking.

Deputy Muller repeated his question. Stephanie took a ragged breath in and tried to answer, but not much came out. Deputy Valdez turned from the cook and put her hand on Stephanie's shoulder. "Mrs. Duran, do you need some water?"

Stephanie looked up. "This is my fault, isn't it?"

"What?" Stacey squeezed her hand.

"Putting the tower up there in the first place," Stephanie said. "Greedy. I've had half a dozen people come by and tell me that the tower was a bad idea. Jenna Bailey's assistant, she came down to pick up kolaches for a meeting and dropped a hint that the festival committee wasn't pleased. And, I've had a few fliers left at tables making noise about the dangers of 5G. I thought they were just things brought in by people who'd been given a flier and they'd just left it. But I don't know."

Deputy Valdez pulled her chair over to the couch. The cook and the waitress were nodding along. "Can you remember who left those fliers? And when?"

The waitress shook her head. "They were never at tables I'd just served. More like they were on chairs or on the floor for whoever to find and read."

"Did you save them?"

The waitress shook her head again, but Stephanie nodded. "I left one under the cash register. it's probably still there. They were all the same, though there were more of them after I had the tower put in. I thought the protesters had gotten to the customers or something." She leaned forward. "I run a business where all are welcome, but," she said with a sigh, "we don't invite in the types who are protesting, you know?"

Stacey did know. Some of the protesters looked as if they hadn't showered in a while. But these were all middle class kids, or in the case of Bo Sanders, upper middle class. All had solid, stable homes to go back to. "I don't think they're the brunch crowd," she said. "Or the afternoon tea types."

The deputies thanked them and assured them that the county sheriff's office would do a thorough investigation. Deputy Valdez also made Stacey promise to go to the emergency room to get the cut on her forehead looked at. Outside, the wind howled. Stacey bristled against the weather, these winds that teased a rainstorm but never brought one. Not that they needed a rain, not so close to harvest time. They didn't need downdrafts strong enough to push over a tower, either.

"Can I drive you home?" Stacey offered Stephanie as they walked out of the shop.

She shook her head and took her keys out of her apron pocket. "I'm going to call my lawyer, and my insurance company, and my daughter in that order." Briefly, she glanced back at the café then down to the keys in her hand.

"Why don't you call your daughter first?" Stacey asked. "I'm sure the others can wait."

"No," Stephanie said. "If I call her first, then I'll start to cry, and I won't stop for a while." She looked up and smiled. "I know how to do this. I'm good at losing things." Which was true. With a pang, Stacey suddenly thought of Mrs. Dutton's funeral, how she and Amy had sat together, bleary-eyed and wistful for their childhoods. Stephanie had been there too, of course. Mrs. Dutton had been like another grandmother to Stephanie's daughter, watching her after school so many afternoons, trying to teach her how to make beautiful things. She'd been one of the first over to visit with Stephanie, pregnant and widowed. Stephanie had her arm around her daughter the whole time, as if by holding her, she could hold on to the old woman and everything she'd done for them both. Everything she'd done for Daw County.

"Will you text me when you get home? Let me know you're safe?"

Stephanie nodded. She inhaled as if she were going to say something, but the words must have stopped in her throat. The tower did some damage, but the café could be fixed. The café could be made better even. Stacey knew that when things changed, even for the better, a person still had to mourn the old way things had been.

For now, though, things looked bad. Stacey watched Stephanie get into her van that doubled as the café's catering truck and pull onto the highway. She didn't live far. The cook and waitress had left too.

Stacey touched the cut on her head. She thought for a moment about the Wine and Pecan Festival coming up in a couple weeks. Would her cut heal by then? Suddenly, the pain came. Nothing she couldn't drive with—she'd driven herself to the hospital with a fractured wrist when Rick was away and fortunately the kids were in school. Stacey didn't want to take off the bandage just yet, though. She'd heard about injuries that don't seem bad in the moment, but then they show their real severity later on, once the shock wore off. She sighed, got into the SUV, and pulled onto the highway and headed for the hospital.

In the rearview mirror, she saw herself briefly. The

cut was covered up, but a trickle of blood had run down the side of her nose. First, she'd get the cut taken care of. Then, she'd go home, wash her face, and figure out why someone wanted to knock down two towers in Daw County.

Someone wanted them down. Stacey just had to figure out what the connection between the two towers was. Harold Dutton's was too far from anything to be a good candidate for a 5G antenna. No, something connected the two towers.

Or someone.

Stacey thought briefly of Mrs. Dutton and all the good she'd done for Daw County. Then she wondered who would want all that good undone.

****

The wait in the ER had been thankfully short. Turned out all Stacey needed was a couple stitches and a prescription for antibiotics, which, she figured, she might as well get filled in the pharmacy in the hospital lobby. She could easily spend the half-hour expected wait time for the pills in the coffee shop. She felt a twinge of guilt—shouldn't she be working on the pictures for Rick's talk? Quickly, she dialed the number for the photographer and settled on a time for Rick's head shots.

As she hung up from the photographer's, she heard a sob behind her. Judy Dutton clutched a water bottle, her long nails tapping the sides of the plastic. If Stephanie was the picture of emotional strength, Judy was her opposite, showing every flit of emotion. Still, her husband was in the hospital, and Stacey figured that repairing whatever damage had been done at Tess Clarke's wouldn't be cheap.

She picked up her coffee and bag, still feeling a bit

woozy not from blood loss or the stitches, but from the whirl of activity of the day, and made her way over to Judy's table. "May I sit here?"

Judy nodded.

"How's Harold?"

"Oh." Judy straightened up a bit. "His doctors are hopeful. He's making progress. They don't want him talking just yet, but I talk to him—he's used to that—and hold his hand. He squeezes mine back. Oh." She sniffled. "I was afraid I was going to lose him."

"That's hard to think about," Stacey said.

Judy shook her head. "I'm hopeful."

"Hopeful is good."

Judy lifted her sunglasses. "Oh, dear. What happened to you?"

Stacey recounted the morning's events at the Bluet Café. "Everyone else is fine."

"But the Bluet Café?" Judy said. "And I was going to bring that nice Tess Clarke another cake. She's classy, you know."

"Have you talked to her lately? After the tower falling?"

"She's been a peach," Judy said. "Not pressing charges, and she's waiting for the official report from the sheriff's office before her lawyer talks to our insurance company." Judy took a ragged breath in and whipped her sunglasses back over her eyes.

"What's wrong? You have insurance, don't you?" That was the one thing Stacey insisted on after Rick showed her his initial plans for the tower. Not so much for what the tower might fall down on—it was in the middle of pastureland and at most, might take out a cow or two. The insurance was for just what had happened to

Harold. She imagined Rick and his ham buddies scaling the tower to make adjustments or additions, and she feared the worst. "They'll cover this?"

"We do," Judy said. She leaned toward Stacey. "It's just that Sheriff Williams thinks this was just Harold doing something bullheaded. An accident."

"You don't think it was?"

"Harold might be bullheaded," Judy said. "But he wouldn't do something that stupid. The last couple years, the farm hasn't done as well as before, and we haven't been the best at saving. Don't tell anyone. I had just about convinced Harold to sell his radio equipment since he's never on it anymore anyway. And when Sheriff Williams told us he was just about to wrap up his investigation, because obviously, this was Harold's fault, oh." A high-pitched whine came from between Judy's pinched coral lips.

"Have you told Harold?"

Judy breathed in again. "If I told Harold, I'm afraid it might kill him. Tess Clarke is nice now, but how will she be when the sheriff tells her that this was Harold's fault?"

Stacey nodded.

"Judy?"

Her bleached hairdo bobbed as she looked up. "Is he awake again?"

Melinda nodded. Melinda Hillegeist, Dale's wife and mother to their two daughters. She was not the woman Stacey had figured Dale would have gone in for, but they'd been together fifteen years now, quite happily.

"He is," Melinda said softly. "He's asking for you."

Stacey couldn't quite read Judy's face. She pushed the sunglasses up to her eyes, ran her hand through her hair, and stood up, wobbling on her kitten heels. "Well, then. I suppose I have to go, Stacey. Thanks for the chat." She picked up her water bottle, coral lipstick around the opening.

After the clicking of Judy's heels against the tile floor was gone, Melinda sat down. "Stacey, it's good to see you." Stacey and Melinda hadn't exactly been friends, though they'd worked together on projects for the Daw County Lutheran Ladies' Society. Melinda was a good decade younger than Dale, a steady woman who had worked her way up the ranks at the hospital not long after she'd arrived as Dale's new bride. She had a good head on her shoulders and was practical as anyone could be around here, but she must have had some dreamy side to have fallen for Dale and married him. "Mind if I join you? I'm on break for a bit and could use some non-patient-related conversation."

"Good to see you, too, Melinda." Stacey picked at a sliver of cardboard coming off the holder around her cup. "Suppose I can't ask you about Harold Dutton."

Melinda shook her head. "Patient privacy. Sorry. I can ask you what you're here for. Look at that bandage on your head."

Stacey told the events of the morning again. Each time she told the story, the café as it was receded from her memory. Would she ever see it without the metal sticking through the ceiling? "I'm fine," she said. "I'm not sure Judy is, though."

"She's got a lot to deal with," Melinda said. "You've heard the gossip even before the tower accident."

"You're never one to gossip," Stacey said. Which was true.

Melinda nodded. "I'm dealing with my own gossip.

Look, I'm glad I saw you here. You know, I don't know the first thing about radios, other than the presets in my car. Can I ask you about radio things?"

"Anytime."

"It's Dale." Melinda sighed. "I don't know what he's got going on, but it's something to do with radio. He's bought a few pieces of equipment. I know he has a license like you and Rick have, but this doesn't seem like any of his other amateur gear. And it's not like he's ever on the radio, anyway."

"What did he tell you it was?"

"You're going to laugh," Melinda said. "A very important project. Something about preserving part of Daw County. Something about fixing up something old and important to him and to all of us. I have no idea what that would be, though."

"I don't know," Stacey said. Which is what she said to everyone most days now. "Does he have the equipment with his other ham stuff?"

Melinda sighed. "I wouldn't have found out about it, but Michelle has to do everything her dad does, which is great because she's a teenager now, and I'm glad they're still close. But when she found the equipment with his ham station, Dale was cagy about it. Like he didn't want her to know about it. Usually, he's fine with Michelle and Mae poking around his radio gear. But, I don't know about this." She lowered her voice. "Is he trying to do something his license won't permit him to do?"

"I wouldn't worry about it," Stacey said. "Dale's got the highest level license you can get as an amateur. So he knows what he's doing. And he knows what he shouldn't be doing, too."

"Knowing Dale, it's probably something for one of the girls," Melinda said. "Probably doesn't want to ruin the surprise. Last year, I don't know if you heard about this, he set up a ham radio conversation between the middle school students and the International Space Station. The kids got to ask questions about space and experiments and life up there and hear the astronaut's answer." She sat back and smiled. "Mae was just over the moon for weeks after that, talking about how amazing it was to talk to someone in space like that. Michelle wrote her first story for the Daw County Newspaper's student voices column after that. He's a good dad."

"Sounds like he's a wonderful dad," Stacey said. Something in her heart turned over a bit whenever she thought of Melinda and Dale and the family they'd made. Melinda hadn't exactly had an easy time of it when she first arrived here, rather unexpectedly. Dale's family refused to come to the small wedding they'd had in Houston, where Melinda's family lived. Stephanie insisted on hosting a reception at the café, complete with a beautiful cake after word got out about that. Much as Stacey wanted Daw County to be open-minded with regard to things that seemed to be settled everywhere else in the world like interracial marriage, she knew that wasn't the case. Even Mrs. Dutton, who welcomed everyone into her cottage, seemed a little shy of Melinda at first. Stacey wanted to think that the coldness was due to Melinda's being an outsider, though she knew better than that. But fifteen years and a lot of work on Melinda and Dale's part, and the community was a little better. "Y'all coming to the Wine and Pecan Festival?"

"Wouldn't miss it," Melinda said. "The girls have

been talking about it non-stop."

"Dale's coming then, too?"

Melinda nodded. Why was it that she was suddenly stuck on Dale Hillegeist? "I'll be working that weekend, so he's on festival dad duty."

Rick generally left the kids to their own devices—in Addie's case, literally—during events like this. Oktoberfest, the Wine and Pecan Festival, the Halloween carnival in the school parking lot, it was all the same. The kids were Stacey's to deal with while Rick went off to talk shop or who knows what else with his buddies, all of whom had probably left their kids to wander alone or with their mothers through the crowd. Not that danger lurked much around them. The community knew who was who, and when newcomers came, they were filled in pretty quickly. Still, it would have been nice, wouldn't it, for Rick to do something more in public with his own kids? "We'll keep an eye out for them."

"Actually, my parents are coming out for the event too," Melinda said. "They're always coming up here, but they say they can't ever get enough time with their granddaughters." She smiled. "You must know how that goes."

"I don't know how I would have coped without so much family nearby," Stacey admitted. "Not with four, anyway."

"Four, that's always impressed me," Melinda said. "The thought kind of scares me, though."

"You wanted more?"

Melinda shook her head. "It was me and my younger brother growing up, and two seemed like a good number to me. Dale wanted more, but he understood that wasn't going to happen. Not easily. Maybe growing up as an only child made him have fantasies about a big family, lots of siblings."

Stacey started to say, well, there's Dale's mother, but, truthfully, there wasn't. Dale's parents split up before he was born, and Dale was shuttled back and forth between a kind but benignly neglectful elderly great aunt and a stern, overly managing uncle and aunt. Dale got the wrong end of a hard situation. He turned out pretty well, though. Stacey smiled. "Well, you know what they say about farm families. Free labor and all that."

"Must have been somewhat expensive, though," Melinda said. "All those tiny work boots they must have grown out of so fast."

Stacey laughed. Melinda was kind, funny, and the sort of friend she'd eagerly add to her circle if she'd allowed herself to get close. Something about Dale Hillegeist still ate at her though. "You know it." Kind, funny, and Stacey hated to admit it, younger and prettier than she was. Probably smarter too, a respected nurse with a career.

"I have to get back to my patients," Melinda said. "You take care of that head, okay? Good talking to you though."

"Good talking to you, too," Stacey said. Good talking to Dale Hillegeist's wife. And she meant it.

The pharmacy tech called her name, and Stacey picked up her antibiotics. Her forehead would heal soon enough, and the cut was close enough to her hairline that she could sweep her hair down over it to cover the wound.

Back in her SUV, Stacey's phone buzzed. She looked down at her phone and saw the text from Stephanie. She put the keys into the ignition but didn't start the car yet.

—*Can you come down to the café?*—

Stacey texted her friend back, started the car, and left.

Chapter Eleven

Stacey pulled into the café lot. A crowd stood around, looking at the collapsed tower still sticking out of the café's roof. Police tape surrounded the building. Almost lunch time. Word must have started to spread, on social media as well as in person. The folks crowding around could always go to Gertie's or any number of sit-down places nearby, but they were hungry for details, weren't they.

Stacey was too.

Stephanie leaned against her catering van, between the words Bluet and Café, a wreath of the small four-point star flowers just above her head. She was glowering, though Stacey didn't know if she was glowering at the tower, the crowd, or both. "Where are they?"

"Who?" Stacey asked.

Stephanie sighed. "The police. They're supposed to be investigating the tower so I can get the tower off my café and start the repairs. It's not like they don't know how hard it is to find contractors around here who aren't booked months out. And I'm not going to use some outsider company. Who knows what they'd say if I did."

"If you had to, I'm sure they'd understand." Stacey tried to put her hand on Stephanie's arm, but she shrugged it away.

"I need the insurance people to come out, too,"

Stephanie said. "But they can't inspect until after the sheriff's office gives them the go ahead. The construction company who put up the tower needs to come out and tell me what they think happened. It's not like the wind was that strong, not as strong as wind gets out here. Maybe the wind doesn't blow so hard in the big city. And the phone company, they'll need to come out too. I hope they're not going to charge me for their broken equipment." Stephanie's voice was at the edge of breaking. Stacey knew, though, that her friend would do all that she could not to let it.

"What is it?"

Stephanie put her face in her hands, then drew them away. "The damage, Stacey. The damage is too much for just the tower falling down off the back of the building. It was bolted on, and I can see it ripping up part of the roofing, but to take out my entire kitchen?"

They'd all been so shaken up. Stacey looked over at the building. A good chunk had been blown out the back. Stephanie was right. "So someone planted an explosive to take out the tower?"

Stephanie nodded. "I don't see how this could be just wind."

"What can I do to help?" Stacey asked. "Anything."

Stephanie turned to her. "You have the harvest to take care of," she said. "And the festival."

"How can I help?" Stacey asked again. "Usually, I'm good at asking if I can do something specific, like bring over dinner or feed the cats and dogs. But I don't know what you need right now."

Stephanie sniffled, then she burst out laughing. "I need someone to gripe at."

"I'm your woman, then," Stacey said. She put her

arm around her friend, who leaned against her.

"I have insurance," Stephanie said. "I'm not worried about the money. But I am worried about all the people who come here for a conversation and coffee and just to be around each other."

"You know what?" Stacey said. "They're here for you too."

"What if they find someplace else?" Stephanie nodded her head toward an excavator sitting in a lot nearby. "They're putting in a tea room over there, can you believe it?"

"I cannot believe it," Stacey said, though she did. "Look, they'll be back. They'll be back for you and for your food. People love the Bluet Café. It's an institution around here. You're in magazines all around the state. You'll be back, and they'll be back."

A car door slammed nearby. Vanessa Dumont emerged, looking slightly harried, her maroon hairpiece slipping out of her brown waves. "Oh, goodness, Stephanie, I'm so sorry. I didn't believe it. I had to come down here on my lunch break to see it for myself."

"You and the rest of Daw County," Stephanie said, pointing to the crowd.

Vanessa gasped. "They're all taking pictures. That's horrible."

"Hmm," Stacey said. "Reporter from the paper was already down here asking me questions. No comment, of course, but she wanted to get my permission to take a picture of the building. I told her she had to wait for me. That's why I'm back here, instead of on the phone with, oh, I don't know who else I can be on the phone with. I've already called everybody who needs to be called." Stephanie's voice edged toward breaking again.

"Speaking of calling, you'll never guess who I talked to," Vanessa said. Stacey glared at Vanessa for a moment, changing the subject when Stephanie needed them. But then she saw how Stephanie's urgent sadness passed from her face. "Tess Clarke."

"Do tell," Stephanie said.

"Well," Vanessa began. "I wasn't sure I'd be able to get her to see me. But I did some online snooping—I hope that's okay, since you asked me to, Stacey—and found out that she's on the board of a small literary grants organization that one of my classmates from forever ago won a couple years back. I contacted him out of the blue, asked what's going on, and turned the conversation toward the prize. Turns out, that they'd met for dinner and had a nice conversation. I said, oh, what a coincidence, she just moved here. I have no idea if he believed it was just a coincidence because I am terrible at lying." While the wind blew through the police tape, Vanessa chattered away, taking Stephanie's attention away from the café and Stacey's away from Stephanie.

Tess Clarke, as it turns out, was more than happy to see the chatty head of the Daw County Community College English department who was friends—if distant friends—with one of her recent prize winners. She invited Vanessa over for coffee, and the two sat for hours talking about literature.

"So, you asked her about Harold's tower?" Stacey asked once Vanessa's winding description of the interior of the late Mrs. Dutton's cottage and all the books now housed therein. She had a far-away dreamy look Stacey recognized. It was Amy's look when she talked about books or going to England with her ex-husband and son or, worse, the job she'd gotten on the luxury cruise liner.

Vanessa eyes widened. "Um, no."

"You asked her about the tower and about the repairs, at least, right?" Stephanie leaned away from the van as if she were waiting for Vanessa to reveal all.

"No, not really."

"Not really?" Stacey shook her head. "You'll talk to her again."

"Oh, I will," Vanessa said eagerly. Amy's dreaminess. This better not mess up their chances to get something useful out of Tess Clarke. "We're having dinner tomorrow night. Her place. She said she wanted my opinion about some local poets."

"Do we have local poets?" Stephanie asked.

"Vanessa," Stacey said in a voice too close to the one she used on Addie when the girl had done something wrong. "This is good, but you need to ask Tess Clarke about Harold and his tower, got it?"

Though she still seemed to be off in a dream, Vanessa nodded. "I will."

A sheriff's office SUV pulled up behind the catering van. Deputy Valdez and Deputy Muller got out of the car and waved Stephanie over. "Thank goodness, y'all are back," she said. "Excuse me. I have to get these people moving."

"I'm glad I caught you here, Stacey," Vanessa said. "I need to talk to you."

"About Tess Clarke?"

Vanessa shifted her large bag back onto her shoulder. Was she ever put together well? "About Addie, actually."

"What about Addie?" Stacey looked at her phone. She had a thousand things she had to do at the farm and a thousand more she had to take care of for the festival.

Plus, apparently, she had rat traps to buy and set, because Rick couldn't find any out in the shop.

"There's a program I think she would benefit from," Vanessa said. "You know I'm friends with Frau Weber, who teaches German at the middle school, high school, and the college, right? She told me about this program where high school students can travel to Germany and live with a host family for six weeks over the summer."

"Addie has farm chores to do over the summer," Stacey said. Which was somewhat true, though much of the summer work was either hired out or automated, so Addie wasn't needed there, strictly speaking. "And I would appreciate it if you didn't go around putting ideas in my daughter's head about leaving Dawville. Do you know that she wants to drop out of high school?"

"I haven't spoken with her about the summer program yet," Vanessa said. For the first time, Stacey saw some fierceness behind her eyes, not just the gauzy wisp she seemed to be. "I only mention it because the German teacher thought it might be a good opportunity for her. For all the students in her class. Not just Addie."

"Are you sure it's not just Addie?" Stacey grabbed her keys, which dug into her palm.

"Absolutely, it's not just Addie," Vanessa said. "I look out for opportunities for all the students."

"Because you seem to know an awful lot about my daughter," Stacey said. "I don't see you hanging around other families, butting into their business."

"I do, thank you, because it's my job," Vanessa said. Her bag slipped from her shoulder, and a few things tumbled out onto the asphalt. She bent down to pick them up.

"Really? Who else are you pestering to send their

kid thousands of miles away?"

Vanessa stood up, shoving the notebook back into her bag, which hung off her at an awkward angle. "Okay, look," she said, shaking her head. "I promised Amy I'd look out for her. You know Addie and Amy have always been close. Addie's just as much of a dreamer as Amy, and she just wants her to see the world, have the chance to spread her wings."

Stacey felt a sudden pang. "Oh, the same Amy who broke up her marriage, left town right before her only kid went off to college, and is now gallivanting around on a cruise ship giving books to rich people?"

"Amy's marriage was bad from the start, and you know it," Vanessa said. "Not everyone gets to marry their perfect high school sweetheart, okay?" She looked down at the asphalt. "Not everyone gets to get married in the first place." She inhaled sharply and looked up again. "And besides, Angus can hold his own. You know this. He went off to school with Tyler and Caleb, and from what Amy tells me, he's adjusted fine and is thriving there."

"I know that," Stacey said. Tyler rarely reported in, busy as he was, but Caleb sent her occasional texts. One or two had mentioned Angus, but otherwise they must have gone their separate ways. Angus himself had reported in weekly at first, then contact dwindled. Maybe as it should have—he was, he reported, busy with classes and his new friends. Amy had sent a couple glowing reports about him as well. "You talk to Amy?"

"Email," Vanessa said. "She keeps me updated. Group email with Tiffany at the library, a few of her library school friends, and me."

Stacey stung. She wasn't included? "That's nice.

156

But being friends with Amy doesn't entitle you to intrude on Addie's life."

"I'm not."

Across the parking lot, Stephanie was gesturing wildly at the deputies. Stacey wanted to end this conversation, go over to her and stand by her friend. Be her friend, unlike whatever Vanessa was doing. But she had to stay here. "Well, please continue to not intrude, thank you very much. Excuse me. I have a friend who needs me."

"I'll give you a call about Tess, after I go see her," Vanessa said. She walked off to her car, bag swinging awkwardly behind her in the gauze of her long filmy skirt.

Stacey shook her head. Stephanie was smiling. The deputies were heading toward their SUV. "What did I miss?"

"If I don't start laughing, I'm going to cry," Stephanie said. "Sheriff thinks it's an accident. They're not going to do an investigation beyond just taking our statements." She sighed. "At least I can get the construction people in now. Insurance. Those balls rolling."

"It was pretty windy today," Stacey said. "The tower company would be responsible for not securing it, right?"

Stephanie shook her head. "Don't you think it's weird that in less than a week, two towers have come down in Daw County?"

"Two towers that have nothing to do with each other," Stacey said. "A ham radio antenna tower and a cell tower. Unless someone totally has no idea about what they're for, I don't think there's a reason for someone to bring down both. Besides, Harold Dutton's beef with Tess Clarke has nothing to do with the Bluet Café."

"I can't think of a link, either." Stephanie shrugged. "Got to get back on the phone now."

****

Stacey promised she'd check in with Stephanie later. Stacey made her way back to the farm, going the long way around the protesters. Soon enough, going the long way around would become automatic, if the protesters kept this up. Sheriff's office didn't seem up to keeping the protesters away, so why would they look into what happened to the towers at Harold Dutton's place or the Bluet Café.

Coming up the road to the farm, something caught Stacey's eye on the side of the road. Something the wind must have blown in, cardboard boxes or something. As she looked closer, though, she could see that the large flat boxes were tethered to the ground, one facing her and the other facing the road. She stepped on the gas, and the SUV's tires spun on the gravel road.

No, not that, she thought.

But it was that.

Just at the entry way to the Hengesbach farm, with its lovely wrought iron archway with the pecans, waved not two but a half dozen signs facing the road, all of them shouting "Re-elect Les Williams for Daw County Sheriff."

"Rick!" Stacey shouted as soon as she opened the door to the house. Her voice echoed through. "Rick, what on Earth did you put out on the entry way?"

Rick stood in the kitchen, shoveling cold leftovers from a glass bowl straight into his mouth. "You didn't come home to make lunch."

"I'm not talking about lunch, and I have a good reason not to have been here for lunch," she said. Her talk with Vanessa and news about no investigation at the Bluet Café ate at her. But there was a bigger problem to deal with now. "Why did you put those campaign signs out on the road?"

"Les is our friend," Rick said. "He brought the signs over, asked if I could put them out." Rick shrugged. "Just doing a favor for him. We're gonna vote for him anyway."

"Okay, *you* are going to vote for him, Rick," Stacey said. "How do you know that *I* am going to vote for him?"

"We're just doing what we've always done," Rick said. He slurped a noodle, which meant this was the turkey tetrazzini she'd been thawing out for dinner. So much for that, then. "Gonna vote Les."

"You're going to vote for him."

"You're not?"

"I haven't decided," Stacey said. She could feel herself balling up, backing down. Les had been their friend, of sorts, in the past. Lots of folks voted that way, based on relationships, even if the elected official wasn't exactly doing a bang-up job.

"I didn't know anyone else was running," Rick said with a shrug. He took another forkful of spaghetti and turkey from the casserole dish.

Stacey shook her head. "Of course there is. Josie Neuenschwander. Why do you think Les Williams has been campaigning so hard, spending so much money on this?"

"People like to see he's trying to reach out to them,"

Rick said.

"Meanwhile, he's so busy reaching out, he's not investigating the fact that two towers have collapsed in less than a week?" Stacey tried not to shout. Would Rick hear her? Or just the rats in the attic?

"Wait, what?" Rick swallowed. "Another tower came down?"

Stacey explained. "I would have thought it had gotten around by now."

"I was out in the fields," Rick said. "Another ham tower?"

"No," she said. "It's weird, but I can't think of a connection between them. Harold Dutton's ham tower—he was climbing on the thing, unwisely, by himself, and down it fell. But Stephanie's new tower at the café? That one was professionally installed and maintained. The only thing that could have pushed it was the wind, and really, the wind wasn't that strong. Not strong enough to blow a hole in the kitchen of the Bluet Café."

"Might not have been the wind," Rick said. "Or maybe it was. You know these crews they bring in from out of town, they don't know what goes on with the weather around here."

"I'm pretty sure they were from Houston," Stacey said. "Which means, I'm also pretty sure they're kind of familiar with strong winds. They've had a hurricane or two there in recent years."

"So, a ham tower, and a cell tower." Rick took one last forkful and put the casserole dish down. Stacey didn't want to think how bad the casserole, that was still a bit frozen, must taste, but when he was hungry, Rick was never exactly picky. As long as it was a dish he knew, and not something weird and fancy like

Stephanie's quiche.

"You got it," Stacey said. "I can't see the connection, though." She took a deep breath. "I think there must be one. Can you help me puzzle this one out?"

"Sorry, babe," Rick said. He smoothed out the ripped foil and left the casserole dish on the table. "Gotta get back to it."

"Tonight, maybe?"

He shook his head. "Told Les I'd meet him for trivia night at The Jackrabbit."

Maybe that was for the better. Rick hadn't even mentioned the bandage on her head. How much help would he be puzzling out the connection between the two towers?

Stacey needed to figure this out, for Stephanie's sake as much as for her memories of Mrs. Dutton. But her best help had come from Stephanie, who was now in the middle of getting the café back together. Amy was out to sea, her parents were off somewhere in their RV. There was Vanessa, but she wasn't about to open up to her. If Tyler were home, or Caleb or even Ethan, she'd use them as a sounding board. But they weren't. She needed to talk this out with someone, and now.

And then, Addie sent her a text.

****

Addie had found something in the hallway of her school, slipped under a bench against a wall. Stacey told her that she should have taken the box of fliers to the principal, but at this point, Stacey was beginning to wonder whether anyone in authority was going to take this seriously. Addie had, carefully, slipped the box into a plastic grocery bag she had at the bottom of her backpack, one she was going to use to clean out her locker. Except she hadn't. The only one they had touched was a flier that had fallen off to the side. Which was how the box came to be sitting on their dining table with a flier beside, once Stacey had removed the very last of the tetrazzini sauce that had been stuck to the bottom of the casserole dish Rick had left on the table for her to clear away.

"Mom, look," Addie said the next morning. They hadn't been able to make heads or tails of it the night before. Stacey's head was also much clearer in the morning light. "Don't you think it's weird that they don't have a website or an email address or anything?"

"Or a phone number?"

"And what are these?" Addie pointed to a long string of numbers followed by a comma and another long string with a decimal in both.

"Coordinates?"

"Let's pull them up," Addie said. She grabbed Stacey's laptop off the small desk in the kitchen. Stacey pulled up her maps program and entered the coordinates. "Looks like the middle of a field? I don't know about this. This is the Kellers' farm, the middle of their bean field."

"Are they hams?"

Stacey shook her head. "Can't say for sure, but I've never seen them at a meeting, and they're getting up there. Thinking about selling the place, from what I've heard around church."

"Wait, can you zoom in on that?" Addie pointed to the satellite view of the field. Sure enough, in the middle, there was a box that could have been the beginnings of a high-tech irrigation system. "Are these controlled by radio?"

"Sure, they can be," Stacey said. "They can give you telemetry, that sort of thing. But they're not going to help you with your radio or your phone."

"But does everyone know that," Addie said. "Some people think they know everything, and they just assume and make other people miserable."

Stacey knew this was Addie expressing her unhappiness at her parents' decision to keep her home for her junior year of high school, instead of letting her go abroad. But now was not the time to argue. "They do, but I don't know what giving the coordinates but not a time would do. If they were going to, I don't know, all descend on the Kellers' bean field and smash the irrigation system. What good would that do?"

"Then, maybe it's not just the coordinates," Addie said. "What if we looked all over their property?" She pulled the map around with her fingertip. "What's that?"

Stacey zoomed in. "That is the remains of The Belt. Old FM radio station that went off the air before you were born. The antenna tower was halfway blown down in a spring storm not long after they went off the air. The studio is still there, but I doubt anything is hooked up. It's not a threat to anyone."

"But it's a radio thing, which makes it a target—" Addie started.

"We need to get you to school, sugar," Stacey said. She looked up at the green apple clock, ticking away on their wall. They didn't need to leave just yet, but who knows what they'd have to wait for out there. "I'd love to keep you here and mull this over, but math class awaits."

"Math I already know how to do, thank you very much," Addie said.

"Well, you'll just ace the test, then," Stacey said. She did want to keep her daughter here, get her help solving the problem. But she was, after all, just a teenager.

Addie shrugged, shoved the last of her sausage roll into her mouth, and grabbed her backpack. "Maybe we'll take the long way, just in case the protesters are back at it this morning?"

"Good idea," Stacey said. "We can swing by the Kellers' property and you can take a quick peek."

Chapter Twelve

The morning was cool. A slight wind ruffled the leaves on what grew in the ditches and along the fence lines. As they curved along the roads that accommodated the old property lines, Stacey watched for towers as much as she did for the deer who could sometimes leap out previously unseen.

"Mom, slow down," Addie said. She pulled on Stacey's sleeve and pointed out her window to the empty field.

"There's nothing in there," Stacey said. "No towers." A truck pulled up behind them and honked. Stacey sped up a bit.

"Mom, what are you doing?"

"Holding up traffic."

"No, Mom, stop."

Stacey shook her head and then pulled off onto the shoulder, or the small slope toward the ditch that served as one. The truck rattled the SUV as it passed.

"You're going to be late to school," Stacey said.

"Just give me a minute to show you," Addie said.

Stacey sighed. "One minute. Do you actually see anything, or are you trying to get out of school this morning."

"I see something," Addie said. "Promise." She jumped out of the passenger side. Stacey lost sight of her for a moment, but then her head bobbed back into view.

She waved her out.

Another truck rumbled by just as Stacey opened the door, nearly pushing her back into her seat. She wasn't watching as carefully as she should, was she? "Okay, let's take a look."

Addie walked back toward the entrance to the Kellers' farm. "Look," she said as she pointed over the barbed wire fence at the property's edge. A row of small flags, blue and orange, ran through the dirt.

"So, what, they're building something? In the middle of a cow pasture?"

"Mom, remember when you were putting up the new garage, and the gas company and the phone people had to mark where their stuff was so you wouldn't dig it up." Addie looked at Stacey with her big hazel eyes wide. "You don't think the protesters have heard about it, and they think?"

"I'll ask them what they're putting in," Stacey said. "It's in a cow pasture. It could be anything."

"Like a 5G tower?"

Stacey sighed again. "Like a 5G tower." She made a mental note to call the Kellers as soon as she got home.

Which was yet another thing she had to add to her already mounting to-do list.

"So, now you have three things to try to make a pattern with," Addie said. "The more instances you have, maybe the easier it is to see the connection between them?"

"Honestly, baby, this has me more confused than before," Stacey said. They got back in the SUV and pulled back onto the road. "I can sort of see what connects Harold Dutton's tower and Stephanie's. They're both radio towers, even if they're very different.

And we don't even know what the Kellers are putting in out here. If anything. Those flags could have been from something they'd planned years ago that fell through." Stacey felt a pang at projects she'd had to give up. "That happens all the time."

"Okay, so no jumping to conclusions until we know what's going on there," Addie agreed.

"That's very sensible of you," Stacey said.

Addie made her smug noise. "Mom, you see? I can be sensible. I am sensible. You just don't trust me. Not as much as you trusted Tyler and Caleb."

"Not Ethan?"

"I don't know," Addie said. She went quiet for a moment. "I guess you thought he was more like me than like Tyler and Caleb. We're your babies, even if we're not babies anymore."

"I know, sweetheart," Stacey said. "I know."

****

Stacey did know that, but she didn't believe it. She didn't feel it, not when Addie talked about going all the way to Europe. Her boys had been, at most, a six hour drive away when they went to camp. Now, they were only a couple hours away.

At the high school, she'd dropped off Addie, who was still working on her list of possible projects the Kellers were building in their pasture. Stacey went around the long way. So much to do at home, but the long way around gave her time to think. If there was a link between the protesters and whatever the Kellers were building, then that would be the clue to where she would need to look next. But it made no sense. Stacy stopped at a red light. Her cut hurt under the bandage that she needed to change. Had she taken her antibiotic this morning? Getting Addie to school was more urgent than that. Maybe she could take ibuprofen along with it too.

The light turned green. The connections between Harold Dutton and Judy, Jenna (or her committee, anyway), and Tess Clarke were pretty clear. The connections between Stephanie's tower were less clear between Judy and Tess Clarke. But maybe Jenna had said it best. Stephanie should have waited to put up the tower. For the good of Daw County's Wine and Pecan Festival, and, more importantly, for the good of the Bluet Café, which now had a gaping hole in its roof.

Stacey turned on the radio, and, just hoping, she tuned to the frequency the pirate had been broadcasting on. She thought of the station as a pirate station, operating illegally, but she'd just never heard the DJ announce the call sign of the station. Which wasn't legal either, but if he had a license, that would be slightly better, wouldn't it? Music washed over her. Her music, hers and Rick's. They'd danced to Garth Brooks, maybe even this song, homecoming dances, and then their senior prom. She remembered Rick in his tuxedo, the first time he wore one, for prom, and the second time at their wedding. Which was the last time. Rick was best man at his older brother's wedding, but he and his bride wanted something less formal than all that. Then, not long after, she left him, or he left her; no one could ever get the story out of them. And after that, he left Daw County altogether.

There was always too much leaving, wasn't there?

Stacey made her way back home. Just as she was about to pull into her driveway, she saw the figure of Sheriff Les Williams leaning against his Daw County Camaro.

"Morning, sheriff," Stacey said. She slammed the door on her SUV, hoping he wouldn't see how much she didn't want him here. "Trouble out this way?"

The sheriff shook his head. "Naw, came to see Rick. He around?"

Rick wasn't around. She told him that he'd be out in the fields until around lunchtime. After which he'd probably dig in to the lasagna she was thawing out for dinner. "I can pass along a message."

"Wanted to talk to him myself." Les spit into the dirt of her driveway. Stacey grimaced. "Like those signs you got out front."

"Was that a statement or a question?"

The sheriff laughed. "You know I like them."

"Well, good for you, and good for your designer, then." Stacey turned toward her house. "Look, I've got a thousand things I've got to do this morning. Wine and Pecan Festival will be here before we know it. And Ethan's coming back for homecoming this weekend."

Sheriff Williams laughed. "Something about your boy isn't quite right, is it? You should have sent him off to the army, not to that sissy college in Austin."

Stacey felt the sudden urge to drag her keys through the paint job on the sheriff's Camaro. "We all have our faults," she said. "And I'm glad Rick's not around to hear your comment about the army. You know what happened to his oldest brother."

"It's what you sign up for," the sheriff said. He put on his sunglasses. The glare off the Camaro made Stacey wince.

"Are you saying—" Stacey cut herself off. She had the sheriff on her property, and he had information. She smiled. "How's the investigation going at the Dutton place? I haven't been able to see Harold yet, but I've visited with Judy a couple times in the hospital."

"Case closed, little lady." The sheriff slapped his hands together. Stacey would have jumped if she hadn't been holding herself together so tensely. "Harold Dutton was a crap technician, and he should have had someone go up there with him. I don't see any reason to investigate stupid."

"Well, you must know why he went up there, right?" Stacey felt every muscle in her body tightening, though she didn't know whether it was to scream at the sheriff or punch a hole in his car's hood.

Sheriff Williams shrugged. "None of my business. You can ask him when he wakes up. If he does. You know where to find him."

"You must be busy. I won't keep you anymore," Stacey said. "I'm sure you've got a lot going on, with the tower collapse at the Bluet Café."

"I ain't investigating the wind, sweetheart." He adjusted his belt. "Besides, the thing was bothering some folks. I can't investigate the weather. Shoddy construction is all. Maybe if she'd used Daw County boys to build the thing, it wouldn't have fallen down."

Stacey decided it was screaming she wanted to do. She held herself together, though, to get this man off her driveway. "Will you tell me what you want from Rick, please, so I can get on with my morning? So we both can?" she asked, as calmly and slowly as she could.

"No need to get your panties in a wad, honey," he said. "Rick was supposed to talk to the boys in the ham club about putting signs out. You can pass that along for me."

Stacey wanted to argue about everything he'd just

said, but that would mean hearing more of the sheriff's nasty talk. "I'll pass that along. Goodbye."

Once inside, Stacey watched the Camaro pull out of their driveway a little too fast, engine rumbling, dust clouds kicked up either side of the car. That must make him feel like a big man, she thought.

If she forgot to tell Rick about convincing the ham club boys to put out signs, well, no one could fault her, could they? The cut on her forehead, the stress of the festival preparations, the worry for her best friend. All that would be enough to make anyone lose a detail or two.

Maybe, she hoped, not telling the hams would be enough to make a certain sheriff lose a race, too.

****

Stacey spent the morning finishing up the slide show pictures for the festival, updating the farm's books, and putting fresh sheets on Ethan's bed. His room was never tidy. Somehow, even after he'd left for college, his room still managed to get messy. Stacey straightened a picture, dusted a few shelves, and picked up a sock that must have fallen behind Ethan's bed when he was packing. The sheriff was wrong. There wasn't anything wrong with Ethan, or no more so than anyone else. Everyone has their faults. Ethan was a good kid, quick to stick up for Addie, clever, and better with power tools than the whole lot of them. She thought of all the blue bird houses he'd made with Rick, and a thousand other things.

Something rustled under the bed. Stacey held her breath. She leaned down and peeked underneath. Something with small eyes and a tail darted between a couple boxes and looked out at her. Something grayish. Stacey shrieked and slapped the top of the bed. The

171

something moved again, this time toward her. She lost her balance and knocked her head on the bed frame, right on her open wound. That stung. That more than stung. She grunted. The something dashed out again, running past her and stopping at the wall. Stacey stared at it for a moment before she realized what it was.

A good sized spiny lizard.

Slowly, Stacey approached it and grabbed it in a cage of her hands. She picked up the lizard as quickly and gently as she could and went to the kitchen. She nudged the screen door open with her foot and set the panicking reptile on the ground. "Go on, scoot, go eat some bugs," Stacey said. Her heart settled a bit. "And don't even think about coming back inside. You're lucky you're not a rat. I'm lucky you're not a rat."

She wiped her forehead with the back of her hand.

Blood smeared the back of her hand. The lizard watched her for a moment and ran off.

Stacey went back inside, patched up the gushing wound as best as she could, then drove off to the hospital.

****

Melinda caught her arm as Stacey weaved through the emergency room door. "Don't tell me something else fell down. Are you okay?"

Stacey nodded. Blood bobbed down her nose. "Chasing a rat that turned out not to be a rat."

"Well, thank goodness for that," Melinda said. She led Stacey to the window to sign in. An elderly couple and their son were in line in front of them, and they were apparently arguing over insurance cards. Melinda caught the eye of the nurse working the desk and pointed to Stacey. The nurse nodded back. "Let's sit down. They'll be a while."

"Frequent fliers?"

"Stacey, you know I can't give out information about patients," Melinda said. "Look, I'm glad I caught you. First off, because you're looking kind of pale."

"I'm fine," Stacey said. "Aside from pulling out my stitches when I banged my head on the bed frame. You said first off?"

Melinda sighed. "Okay, I did some more snooping."

"And?"

"I could use your radio expertise here." Melinda twirled her ID badge on its lanyard. "What do you know about the defunct station?"

"Defunct FM?" Stacey sang their jingle and laughed. "You mean 89.1? Used to be The Belt. Said they had our names all over them. That was the style then," she said with another laugh, this time cringing a little at her teenage fashion sense.

"So you know it?"

Stacey nodded. "Best hometown radio station in the county. Okay, one of two hometown stations in the county. It was huge when I was in high school. My sister Amy and I would listen with the volume turned up way too loud whenever we went anywhere together. That felt like freedom. Anyway, they were good to Daw County. They always sent their DJs to any event, homecoming parades, Oktoberfest, Christmas parades. Fourth of July. If there was even the slightest hint of a party, they'd be there. I think I might even have a coffee mug with their logo on it."

"Sounds like they were invested in the community."

"Yeah, didn't mean to stroll so long down memory lane, there," Stacey said. They'd even come to prom, taking care of the music and handing out just about anything they could put their logo on. The coffee mug must have come from prom night, when Rick had proposed to her. "You probably didn't ask me this to hear me reminisce, though."

"I would like to know more about them," Melinda said. The son in line shouted something. His voice echoed off the walls of the waiting room. "I read something about them in a Daw County newspaper."

"Where'd you find a copy of the paper from that far back?" Stacey asked. She pressed her hand against the bandage. Her head hurt, though she wasn't sure if it was the cut or thinking about things long gone. "The station shut down in 2004, if I remember right."

"You do," Melinda said. "Tiffany at the library is a whiz at microfiche."

"So why are you asking me about the radio station?" Stacey asked. "I don't have any commercial radio experience. Just crisis communication on my ham station."

Melinda's face fell. "I thought you might be able to help me."

"With?"

"Why the station shut down," Melinda said. "If there were technical problems. Equipment problems. I know it was bought out in 1999 by a huge corporation, they fired their local staff and no one was happy. It limped along for another few years or so, got sold again to someone who tried to sell airtime to whoever would buy it, then closed for good a couple years after that."

"I think that's the story," Stacey said. "Nothing wrong with the transmitters or the towers that I know of. There just aren't enough businesses around here to buy ads to support the station."

"Weren't," Melinda said. "But the economy has changed around here." She sighed and rolled her eyes.

"Someone's starting up the station again?"

"Someone is considering it."

"You?"

"Oh no," Melinda said. She leaned toward Stacey. "Someone I'm married to. Someone with enough engineering know-how to get the place back up and running. Or so he says. And a voice for job too. Or so he says."

Stacey could just about hear Dale's voice announcing news. Dale's voice that had almost talked her into doing things she knew she'd regret, only because she'd still loved Rick. If Rick hadn't been in the picture, who knows. "Well, congratulations, then."

"What do you mean? I think this is a terrible idea," Melinda said. "I need your help talking him out of it. There has to be some, I don't know, technical reason this is a bad idea. Goodness knows, I've tried the economic angle a thousand times, and that hasn't worked."

"Let me think about it," Stacey said. "When I don't have a head wound."

"Of course," Melinda said. The elderly couple and their son cleared away from the window, and Melinda guided Stacey up to the nurse to get checked in. "Our secret? For now, anyway."

"My lips are sealed," Stacey said. "I just need to keep this cut sealed too."

Melinda gave her arm a squeeze, and Stacey checked in.

****

Not long after, the emergency room doctor who'd stitched her up the day before tried to make her feel better. "Coming back for more a day later, eh," he said. "My record is less than an hour. Teenage superhero fell off his skateboard one morning, cut himself so bad he had to come in for stitches. I guess the pain meds made him feel invincible, because he tried some tricky maneuver on the stairs out to the parking lot. Stitches again. At least nothing was broken but skin. That heals."

"And leaves a scar," Stacey said, thinking about her own forehead.

"Less so with my handiwork," he said.

"There's always the inner scar," Stacey said. "The one folks don't see. How bad you feel for doing something stupid in the first place."

The doctor agreed. "No plastic surgery for that," he said.

****

Stacey was making her way down the hallway when she saw Judy in the coffee shop again. Stacey didn't want to think about Dale, and hearing some awful truths from Judy might drown out the sound. She didn't want to think about herself either, listening to the DJ when he came on that pirate station. It was him, wasn't it? It must have been him. No, think about Judy, she told herself.

Judy sat next to an impossibly tall whipped topping concoction. She looked slightly embarrassed, but she nodded hello and went back to her phone, that she was tapping at furiously.

"Judy, can we talk?"

"Not now, I'm busy."

"No, Judy, this is important," Stacey said.

"Look, I'm not interested in whatever project you've got going on with the ham wives or the Lutheran Ladies. I'm busy." Judy pinched the straw between her lips, and the whipped topping descended.

Stacey sat down. Her stitches pinched, but it wasn't time yet to take more pain medicine. "I'm sorry to have to do this, but was Harold planning on putting a 5G antenna on his tower?"

Judy looked up at Stacey over her glasses. "I said I'm busy."

Stacey leaned over her arms on the table. She was tired, she needed to get back to the house, she had a thousand things to do. But this was dropped on her like so much else was. She was going to see it through. She took a deep breath in, and stared straight at the overly made up woman in front of her. This was for her own good, wasn't it? "Look, Judy," she said. "You're busy, I get that. But a tower came down at the Bluet Café yesterday. You must know that by now. The sheriff's too busy shaking hands and putting out yard signs to see straight, and we're all worried about whose tower is next. You said yourself that you wanted the sheriff to do more. He's not doing it. I might not be much, but you've got me instead."

"Thank you, dear," Judy said. "But I'm busy."

"And I'm trying to keep us all safe," Stacey said. She thought briefly of Harold, his spiteful words at the last ham meeting he'd been to, and then swallowed hard. "I'm sorry this happened to Harold. He didn't deserve this. He was just a guy with a tower in his field, like lots of us are, and I'm worried." She felt a wave of nausea coming over her. Probably the antibiotic or the fact that she needed to eat lunch. "Harold didn't deserve this. I want to figure this out. For Daw County, but mostly because he's a good person. You know how much his momma meant to me, and I saw how good he was to her.

Harold has his moments, but he didn't deserve this. I don't want you both to walk out of this hospital wondering what's next. I want to help you both."

Judy pushed her glasses up and sniffled. She grabbed Stacey's hand and squeezed it. "Thank you."

"Oh, I didn't mean to make you cry," Stacey said. She grabbed a napkin out of the dispenser and handed it to Judy.

Judy held the crumpled napkin in her shaking hand for a moment before dabbing at the tears running down beneath her big sunglasses. "It's fine," she said. "You know, you're the first person to say a kind thing about Harold. Got a few flowers, that sort of thing, but anyone can do that. You know how Harold was good to his mother, and you know he's more than just a prickly old thing."

"Of course," Stacey said. The part about Harold being good to his momma was true, anyway, and no one deserved a tower collapsing underneath them. "Will you help me?"

Judy nodded. She sniffled once then took a deep breath in between her coral lips. "I think this was all my fault," she said. "Harold wasn't the one who thought of the idea to rent out space on the tower to the phone company. I had to do a lot of convincing, and I'll tell you, Harold wasn't pleased with me for bringing it up. The money was good. The last few years have not been the best in the books. We needed the money. And besides, after I told Tess Clarke about the 5G antenna going in soon, she was happy. That solved one problem for her, since cell phone reception isn't the best in that corner of the county. She'd have fast data well before the lines could be laid for her internet access."

"Do you know what she's doing out there?"

"No idea, other than bringing some much needed style to Daw County," Judy said. "If Bluet's closed for a while, I don't know what excuse I'll have to visit with her again soon."

The elderly couple and their son shuffled into the café and took a seat. She watched them, the man's attention to his parents, shepherding them around. Stacey was touched. With Amy gone, anything having to do with their parents fell on her. They were healthy and active still, but for how long? She filed this thought away for later, adding another item to her long to do list—to do for other people. A sudden worry hit her. "How many people knew about the 5G antenna going in? On that tower, particularly?"

Judy pinched her coral lips and ran a hand through her blonde bob. "Oh, well, Tess, of course. I may have made mention of it to the Daw County Women's Club." Just how Judy had finagled an invitation to the county's most elite organization had eluded her. Stacey had no interest in having tea with what passed for the upper crust of Daw County's more established families herself.

"Do you know who was there?"

"Well, all the usuals. Mrs. Williams, of course, our chairwoman. We were celebrating the induction of that lovely Jenna Bailey into our group. Her committee put her name in. She's not Daw County old blood, but she's what we need." Not that Judy was Daw County old blood either, but Stacey kept her mouth shut. Judy rattled off a list of two dozen names. "Oh, and Minty Sanders was there, too, giving a little welcome speech to Jenna. It was elegant. She knows Jenna so well from serving on the festival committee." She lowered her voice. "We're angling for Tess next. I don't know how we'll manage to do it, but won't she be a jewel in our crown."

Stacey tried to ignore the smug look on Judy's face and instead wondered whether she'd be able to remember half the names Judy just said. "Do you have a membership directory?"

"Our roster? Not the whole membership, but we list our chairwomen for projects on our website."

"You have a website?"

"Lovely thing," Judy said, perking up. "We use it to show off our hall, for rentals. Weddings, things like that. Elegant place, you should look at the pictures online."

"I'll have to check that out," Stacey said. "I need to get going before the day gets away from me. Thank you. And I meant what I said. I don't want you or Harold to have to worry."

Judy gave her another smile. Her phone pinged, and she picked it up, the plastic crystals on the back of her phone case glowing dimly in the fluorescent light of the café. "You're welcome."

****

Driving home, Stacey played with the idea of Judy and Tess working together to bring Harold's tower down. On one hand that made sense—if Harold wasn't going to go along with the phone company sticking a 5G antenna on his tower, then Judy might have taken the tower down out of spite. But Judy needed the tower up. Especially if she was trying to get on Tess Clarke's good side. And Tess needed the tower up too. None of it made sense. Well, none of it made sense when her head was throbbing and a thousand things were tugging at her at the same time she was trying to solve a mystery.

That was it, wasn't it? She needed to solve this

mystery.

And she needed to do it before any more towers came down on anyone else in Daw County.

Chapter Thirteen

Stacey pulled into the pick-up line at the high school. The medication dulled the pain in her head, but what she'd needed most was the strong cup of pecan coffee and the bacon and eggs she made for a late lunch. Rick came in just as she was finishing up. "Hey, babe, you read my mind," he said.

"It's my head injury," she said. "Or injuries. Opened up a portal between our brains."

"Nah, I'm simple. You always know what I want." Rick scooped her up in his strong arms, still smelling of diesel fuel, sweat, and the sweet tea he drank gallons of while out working. It was a combination she'd always adored on him. She felt safe in his arms, protected, loved. How long had it been since they'd just stood there, not worrying about the world, just knowing that the other was there? "And I want coffee, bacon, and eggs."

"If we stay here too long, the egg yolks are going to set," she said with a laugh.

"Aw, that's a risk I'm willing to take."

He gave her another squeeze and sat down at the table. She brought out the bacon, eggs, toast, and some sliced tomatoes and bell peppers. The eggs were runny, perfect for the buttered toast. If she let herself, she might have imagined this life, a late breakfast, just the two of them lingering over coffee, instead of a late lunch they rushed through.

"Bean fields coming along?" she asked.

Rick nodded. He took the last slice of toast, slathered it with her homemade blackberry jam, and stuck it in his mouth. He stood up and made for the door, giving her a detailed update as he chewed.

"I'll take that as a yes," she said.

Her phone buzzed. Vanessa's name popped up on the screen with the text message.

—*Can you come with me to see TC this evening?*—

Wednesday nights weren't ones she was used to going out on, but for Stephanie, and, she supposed, for Harold, she'd go see the woman. There was, after all, no time to waste. The thought of dealing with both Vanessa Dumont and Tess Clarke together after the events of the day was a bit much for her to contemplate, but there it was.

****

Stacey wondered whether they'd ever get the truck fixed. Monday, the shop had said. She'd be patient. In the meantime, she could easily go get Addie herself.

Addie emerged from the crowd of students pushing their way out of the glass doors in front of the high school. An energy buzzed in the students, but wasn't that always the case just before homecoming? Students asking each other on dates to go to the big game on Friday and to the dance on Saturday night. The school gym would be decorated in whatever theme the student council chose. Stephanie's daughter had always volunteered her mother, and by extension, Stacey and her kids, to decorate for the dance. But then Stephanie's daughter graduated, and Stacey couldn't get Addie or her brothers interested in the task themselves. Ethan had shrugged at her when she asked him if he'd asked a girl to the dance. He never went to the homecoming games or dances, declaring them not worth his time. Tyler and Caleb had asked a series of girls to homecoming dances, winter formals, spring banquets, and finally proms. When Ethan asked for money to buy a prom ticket last year, Stacey could hardly contain herself. "Who are you taking? This is going to be so amazing, you'll never forget it," Stacey said. "We need to rent you a tux."

"Going with friends, no date."

"No special girl, then?"

Ethan shrugged. "Just need the money by Friday," he said. "And I'll wear my suit."

"You sure you don't want a tux?"

Stacey had happily handed over the cash, which should have been the first red flag. Ticket sales, according to the school email, were online. Maybe he'd missed a deadline or something, she'd thought.

The second red flag came the night of the prom. "You're not wearing your suit," Stacey said.

"Not really." Ethan wasn't wearing the suit pants or his dress shirt and tie, but he was looking dressed up, sort of. Dark blue jeans, dress shoes, and a t-shirt with a logo of some sort under his blazer. Kids. Fashion. Stacey laughed when she remembered how she curled and sprayed and moussed and gelled and heated her hair into its late 80s to early 90s glory.

"Gotta go," Ethan said. He drove off into the darkening evening.

The third red flag happened during the dance. The air conditioner at the Daw County Women's Society's Banquet Hall went out, sending the senior class and their dates out into the gracious old gardens around the gracious old building. Many wandered back early, and

Stacey watched social media as parents posted pictures of their kids coming home to change before wandering off to the after party. She looked for Ethan, camera shy as he'd become, but never saw him. Finally, she went to bed. How would she have felt if she'd known her parents were watching her in the same way?

When Ethan emerged from his room the next morning, Stacey asked him about the power outage. For a moment, he looked stricken, then nodded, grabbed a breakfast plate, and ran for his phone. "It was hot," he mumbled. "Had a good time." A sky blue feather held tentatively to the back of his hair.

Later, all the red flags came together, and Stacey felt terrible. Ethan had asked her for months to go to the band Zvezda, who were, as far as Stacey could find on the internet, an esoteric mixture of electric eastern European folk instrumentalists headed by waifish twin sisters, and who were having a rare show at the Woodlands Pavilion, which wasn't that far away. "No, you're not missing your prom for some concert. The band will come through again. That's what they do. Senior prom is once in a lifetime."

"How do you know this won't be Zvezda's last appearance here?"

"Ethan," Rick said. "Listen to your mom." Which was Rick's way of helping. Which wasn't much help, but he tried.

"The show was amazing." Ethan was sitting at Addie's desk. She was on her bed, cross legged, painting her nails a deep purple. "They're even better live. And they're so cool. Jane talked us all into going backstage after, and she got Inese and Ilze to sign her wings."

Which probably explained the feather. And

explained where the money went. Stacey started to go into Addie's room and demand an explanation. But she saw Ethan, tilted back in Addie's chair, glowing, laughing at Jane's wings not quite fitting in the back of Eduardo's car. Names of people she'd never met: Jane, Eduardo, Juan, Skye. Names of his friends, when he seemed to have fewer and fewer these days. Ethan was okay. Sure, he'd skipped his senior prom, but he was okay. This seemed to be more important, right?

"Mom," Addie groaned as she threw her bag in the car. "Let's get out of here. Please."

"You okay?"

"I am never coming back to this place after I graduate," Addie said.

"What happened, baby?"

Addie shook her head, her purple hair falling down over her face. "Don't want to talk about it."

"Okay," Stacey said. The advice was that parenting tended to get easier with the younger ones, or at least parents tended to care less about the less important things. Not so for Stacey. Tyler and Caleb were not complicated kids, not in comparison to their younger two siblings. Ethan was a mystery sometimes. Addie? She was a mystery all the time. "Do you want to stop at—" Stacey stopped herself.

"The Bluet?"

"Oh, Addie, is that what's bothering you?"

"Mom, why do you have a new bandage?"

"I'm supposed to change them, thank you. But it's a new one from the hospital." She recounted the morning's events.

Addie nodded. "You need to put traps in the attic. Or else we will have rats in the rest of the house."

"Me?"

"You want me to do it?"

Stacey laughed. "We need a cat or three in the house is what we need."

"Good luck convincing Dad," Addie said. She tucked a lock of purple hair behind her ear. Stacey could see the red blotches on her cheeks that were fading but still there.

"You want to talk about it?"

"About what? Dad not letting us have pets?" She fished a pair of sunglasses out of her backpack and jammed them on her face.

"About anything." A long line ahead of them inched forward. No one, it seemed, wanted to go home, not yet. No one wanted to leave the buzz of homecoming. No one except Addie. "Are you sad about a homecoming date? Or a mum?"

"Mom," Addie said flatly. "I am not interested in homecoming. And I am not dating boys from Daw County."

"Or," Stacey hesitated. "Or girls?"

"Or girls," Addie said just as flatly. "I am not interested in dating anyone from Daw County."

"So this is not about homecoming?"

"That is correct, Mom," Addie said throwing her hands up. "I am not upset about homecoming."

"So what are you upset about?"

"Nothing."

Stacey hesitated again. "We can get you a mum, if you'd like. For Friday at school. So you won't feel left out."

Addie made her smug noise. Almost as soon as she'd said it, Stacey felt bad. If she knew anything about her daughter, it would be that Addie would be the last one in the high school to worry about being left out over something as tradition-based as a homecoming mum with its fake flowers, glittery ribbons, and charms dangling down. Which made her a bit sad. Somewhere in the now rat-infested attic were the four homecoming mums Rick's mom had made for her, starting with their first date, the homecoming dance their freshman year in high school. Stacey hadn't even tried to make mums for the girls Tyler and Caleb took to the dances. That was a cottage industry around here, and she knew of at least two women for whom the homecoming season paid their rent for the rest of the year. "Okay, you are not interested in homecoming mums, got it."

A phone buzzed. Stacey started to reach for hers, but they were still in the school zone, and one of the sheriff's office SUVs sat parked visibly just outside the school parking lot, waiting for folks to grab their phones or drive over the twenty mile per hour speed limit. Didn't matter—it wasn't hers. Addie grabbed her phone and began typing quickly.

"Good," Stacey said. "Catching up with a friend?"

"Yes."

"Not about homecoming, though," Stacey ventured.

"Okay, you need to drop your obsession with homecoming, Mom," Addie said. She paused for a moment to type. "Just because high school was yours and Dad's glory days doesn't mean they're mine."

"I understand." Stacey wished she did. "I just want you to be able to experience some of the good things in high school. Dances, which you've never been to. Football games that you refuse to go to. That kind of thing."

"My priorities are different from yours, Mom," Addie said. She sounded so adult, which Stacey hated to admit. "Unless you want Vanessa to ask me to the homecoming dance, which I think would horrify you, right?"

"You're texting Vanessa now? I mean, Dr. Dumont?" Stacey slammed on her breaks. The car behind them stopped short and honked. "What is Vanessa Dumont texting you about, exactly?"

"Do you want to read it?" Addie pushed her phone at her mom's face.

Stacey waved the phone away. "Do you want me to get pulled over?"

Addie took her phone back and cleared her throat dramatically. "Hi, Addie. I saw you looking upset in the hallway. I didn't want to stop you then because you looked like you were heading somewhere fast, but I did want to make sure you're okay."

"And your reply."

"I'm fine, thank you for checking in on me?"

"Are you?"

"I'm fine."

At last, Stacey cleared the driveway, and they pulled out onto the street. Twenty miles per hour seemed fast in comparison to the near-idling they'd done for the last ten minutes trying to get out of the lot. Addie was quiet. Stacey was at a loss for what to say.

Except she wasn't. "Okay, look. You're not talking to me. Because I'm your mom. So do you want to come see Vanessa with me?"

"What?"

Stacey explained. Addie nodded. "So that's a yes?"

"That's a yes."

They went home and rushed through dinner, which Rick was late for. They left him a plate in the refrigerator and a note on the table explaining where his food was and how to heat it up.

****

"This brings back memories," Addie said as they took the access road Harold Dutton had put in not long after his mother moved to her cottage.

"Good memories, but it's okay to be sad."

Addie shrugged. "Do you think Tess did it?"

"I don't know whether Ms. Clarke was involved," Stacey said. "But it's looking less and less likely. Judy Dutton had worked out a deal with the cell phone company where they'd put 5G on Harold's tower, so it wouldn't make sense for Tess to bring the tower down."

"She's driven by beauty though, right?"

"Who? Mrs. Dutton?" Stacey thought of all the beautiful things that had been in Mrs. Dutton's cottage, so many of them hand-made and sentimental.

"No, Tess Clarke. She moves out here because she thinks it's beautiful, except, oh no, there's this big ugly tower you can see from the kitchen window." Addie was quiet for a moment. "I remember seeing it from Mrs. Dutton's kitchen window. Eating blackberry cobbler and drinking milk from their old cow. Funny what you remember."

"Mrs. Dutton's blackberry cobbler was famous," Stacey said. "But from what I've seen from the inside of Tess Clarke's new home, she'd be way more likely to think the tower was beautiful than the mesquite trees."

"I'm trying here, Mom."

"You are." Stacey smiled. "And I appreciate that."

They pulled into the driveway. Vanessa's car was

already there, a subcompact that was very out of place among the work trucks and SUVs that most people around here drove. As soon as the SUV pulled to a stop, Vanessa got out. In a dark suit with a pencil skirt, her hair pulled back in a neat chignon, and wearing makeup, Vanessa looked like a picture out of one of Tess Clarke's art books. She was elegant, beautiful, not of Daw County. Or at least not of the older parts of Daw County anyway. She waved to Stacey and Addie.

"You just come back from seeing Cowboy?" Stacey nodded toward the suit. "No school spirit hair?"

"No, just cleaned up a bit for our meeting," Vanessa said. "With Tess." In the fading light of the evening, Stacey caught the hint of a blush as Vanessa turned her eyes toward the trim heels she wore. Not stilettos, but definitely not the clunky heels Stacey wore to church. "Are you ready?"

Stacey nodded. As they entered the cottage, Stacey suddenly felt unprepared, under-dressed, and overwhelmed. A few finishing touches had been made to the cottage since her last visit, though what had changed exactly, Stacey couldn't quite tell. On the coffee table, replacing the heavy photography books were two binders laid out beside a few brochures.

Tess had welcomed them in and asked if they'd wanted coffee, or at least Stacey thought she had. Before she knew it, she was in an uncomfortable black leather chair, sitting next to her daughter, who was looking more at ease in her chair's angular twin. Addie brought a cup of coffee up to her lips. She must have seen Stacey staring, since Addie stopped. "It's okay, Mom," Addie said. "Tess said it's decaf. Swiss water processed. Tanzanian single-origin." She took a sip.

On the table before Stacey, Tess set a cup of coffee. White porcelain ringed with silver. Or who knows, it might have been platinum. "Thank you all for coming this evening. I know it's an inconvenient time, a school night, but Vanessa and I thought this couldn't wait."

"What couldn't wait?" Stacey asked.

Tess sat on the black leather sofa. No, not sat. Stacey thought of those long-legged egrets that followed the cows around, looking for bugs they stirred up as they grazed. That, but more elegant. "First, let me fill you in on what we're doing here."

"We?" Stacey asked. The coffee steamed. She should have asked for milk, but no one else had reached for the little metal creamer that sat on the table under the lamp, so she didn't know if she should either.

"The Brazos Valley Artists and Writers Retreat," Tess said. She smiled broadly and pointed down to the binders and brochures on the coffee table. "We've kept our project quiet, though it's not a secret. We bought the land from the Duttons, Mrs. Dutton's acreage, and we're putting in a central meeting space along with seven small cabins to host writers and artists working on specific projects." She explained the process by which the creatives were selected and drifted off into a discussion with Vanessa about the kinds of art and literature they hoped to nurture out here. Addie watched, wide-eyed. Stacey hoped it was the coffee and not the talk about museums and books that had her so awed.

Stacey picked up her coffee cup, looked into it, and set it down again. "I'm sorry, go back," she said, interrupting Vanessa. "Tess, you said you bought the land from the Duttons?"

"Yes," Tess said.

"So you met them before you bought the land, before you signed anything?"

Tess inhaled sharply. "Mr. Dutton and I became acquainted after the purchase of the land. He made some idle threats. You saw him disturbing the construction workers yourself, Stacey. Mrs. Dutton introduced herself after I moved in. But everything before that was handled by our attorneys."

"Is it possible that Mrs. Dutton sold the land without Mr. Dutton's permission?" Stacey wondered aloud. Addie suddenly looked at her mother. Maybe that was admiration on her face?

"Why would she do that?" Vanessa asked.

"They need money," Addie said. "That's why they were putting in the 5G antenna, right, Mom?"

"That's right," Stacey said.

Tess nodded. "And we needed the 5G out here. Much of the point of coming out here is to get writers and artists away from distractions, but when the internet company informed us that it would be months before they could lay the lines for us to get reliable service out here, we were disappointed. Such a shame the tower came down." She took a sip of coffee. "Mr. Dutton is a rather disagreeable figure, but he didn't deserve to be toppled off the tower. And according to our attorneys, everything was set, for our sale and for the others that might be pending."

Suddenly, a thought came to Stacey. She thanked Tess for having them and Vanessa for arranging the meeting. As they were leaving, Tess handed Addie a copy of the brochure. "We'll be looking for interns next summer. Keep us in mind. Vanessa tells us you're quite astute."

Addie beamed.

Stacey did not. Instead, she was struck with the fact that Daw County was changing around her in ways that she couldn't stomach. And that someone needed Daw County to look the quaint part, not like the urbanized place it was too quickly becoming.

****

Stacey knew Jenna would be in her office. She was always in her office this early. After Stacey dropped Addie at school, she'd explain to Addie why she'd need to do this, to gather more information. Stacey resolved to go do this now. Because who knew how many more towers—and whatever else was deemed too ugly or dangerous for Daw County—would have to come down to satisfy the committee.

Rick glanced at her sideways for a moment as they were leaving the house. No, she hadn't told him where she was going and why. She'd put on her best pants suit, the one she'd been saving for the festival, the one with the good pockets and the flattering jacket. Makeup and hair done. If she was going to do this, she needed to look the part. Confident. Professional. Determined. Rick squinted for a moment. Last minute preparations for the festival were as good an excuse as any. "Truck still in the shop?" he asked.

"Should be able to pick it up Friday," Stacey said. She slipped out the door.

"What was that all about, Mom?" Addie slung her backpack into the SUV.

"I was hoping your father wouldn't ask me why I'm dressed up to drop you off at school." The SUV shuddered for a moment then started up.

"Since when has Dad noticed what you wear?"

Stacey laughed. "That's fair."

"It's a good thing I've never been one of those girls who wears crop tops and short shorts," Addie said with a laugh.

"Thank you," Stacey said. She'd wished for a moment for Addie to go back to being the little girl who was as happy mucking around in jeans and a t-shirt as she was in a pretty dress, but maybe it was time for her to have a style of her own. Experiment a bit, not fall into line with the other girls like Stacey had uncomfortably done. "What do you call your style, anyway?"

Addie made her smug noise. "Um, gothic granny?"

Stacey glanced over at her daughter. Long black skirt with a gauzy layer over the top, black boots, and a purple t-shirt over the top, a shade darker than her hair. A string of fake pearls and a pale pink cardigan worn, ironically Stacey assumed, over the top. "I think you're right."

They took the long way, glancing in the Kellers' field for a clue, but finding none. She'd called them and left a message, but hadn't received a call in return. One more thing for later.

****

This, however, this was for now. Stacey stood in the lobby of the Daw County Winery Association's building, looking up at the ornate light fixture in the ceiling. A winding staircase came down to meet her. She inhaled deeply and went up to Jenna's suite.

Chapter Fourteen

Confronting Jenna meant risking the Hengesbachs' participation in the Wine and Pecan Festival. It meant risking Stacey's connection to so many people in the community. But if Sheriff Williams still refused to investigate, then it was up to her to figure it out, to prevent anymore towers from falling and hurting anyone else.

Jenna's assistant Camille was on the phone as Stacey walked into the office. She glanced at Stacey in much the same way Minty Sanders had when she'd confronted Stacey days ago. The assistant was fresh out of college, ambitious, and with roots that go back about as far as you can go in Daw County. Her blonde hair was set just so, and she'd incorporated the headphones and mic she was always on the phone through as a sort of fashionable headband. Her manicured nails clicked on the keyboard. She lifted one hand for a moment at Stacey then returned to typing as she spoke. Much as Stacey hated to admit that there was a divide between the classes of the older families in Daw County, there was, so much so that Stacey could never have imagined herself sitting at a desk like this right out of college. This elegance wasn't something new to the assistant, though. She'd grown up in it.

Camille hung up and smiled at Stacey. "I don't have you on Ms. Bailey's calendar."

"No, I was just hoping to talk with her for a few minutes, if she has the time," Stacey half-mumbled. Her hands were sweaty, and she knew she'd have to steam clean the jacket herself before she wore it again, as a bead of sweat trickled down the back of her neck in spite of how cold it was in the office building.

"About the festival?"

Stacey nodded and tried to smile, her eyes unwilling to cooperate.

"I'll go check," Camille said. "One moment, please."

Her pencil skirt showed no wrinkles in spite of how long she must have sat at the chair. Like Addie, she had on a pale pink cardigan and pearls, but hers were matched with a pale pink shell under her sweater, hose, and heels, which she managed not to clack on the tile floor.

Jenna emerged a moment later. "Stacey, what a nice surprise, I needed to talk with you anyway. The photographer says you need to reschedule the appointment Rick missed."

"We're getting to that," Stacey said. She'd asked Rick for a free morning, but he'd just shrugged. She'd have to make the time for him, instead.

"Come in," Jenna said.

"May I bring you some tea?" the assistant asked, her mic flipped up.

"Thank you," Jenna said. "That would be lovely."

Camille left, leaving the door open just a bit. Stacey sat down in the chair she'd become accustomed to during all their meetings.

"What brings you here this morning, Stacey?"

Stacey inhaled. It was now or never. "You know

about Harold Dutton's tower coming down?"

"Yes," Jenna said. Her hands were folded on her desk, as if she were a teacher waiting for Stacey to show a crack in the story she'd told about why her homework was late.

"And about Stephanie's tower at the Bluet Café?"

"Yes." Jenna nodded again. "Strange coincidence."

"Well," Stacey said. Now or never. "It looks like a coincidence, yes. But what's the one thing that connects them?"

"They're both towers?"

"Yes," Stacey said.

"Can we get to the point here? I have a meeting in fifteen minutes," Jenna said. "Minty Sanders is coming in personally to ask about the state of our sponsorships."

"Towers, yes, and the point is, who can see them?"

A shuffling sound outside the door caught Stacey's attention for a moment, but then it stopped.

"We can all see them? Stacey, please don't make me play a guessing game here," Jenna said. "I'm really busy today."

Okay, now or never. "We can all see them, that's the point. The festival is here in two weeks, and Daw County is looking less and less like, well, the Daw County of the recent past. I saw on the brochures Tess Clarke showed me, Daw County before the tower at the Bluet Café, without the protests at the new intersection and all the traffic lights in here now. The new bridge over the railroad crossing, all that—"

"Yes, signs of progress. Get to your point, please."

A heel clacked just outside the office, Camille's, or maybe it was the air conditioner clicking on. "I think someone is bringing down towers because what is more industrial and big city than a bunch of big metal towers sticking up everywhere, right? I think someone is bringing down the towers to make Daw County look more like Daw County and less like, say, Houston."

"And what does that have to do with the festival or the committee?"

"Well, the committee, or someone on it—"

The clacking outside was definitely heels now, someone trying to get somewhere fast.

"Are you saying what I think you're saying?"

Camille rushed in with two cups of tea. The assistant whose parents were both on the committee. "Do you take cream or sugar?" she asked brightly as she handed a hot cup to Stacey, cup first, keeping her own fingers on the handle. Stacey should have closed the door.

"I don't," Stacey stammered. "No, thank you."

"Mrs. Hengesbach was just leaving," Jenna said. "Will you excuse us for a moment, Camille?"

She left, leaving the door open a crack. Jenna walked over and closed the door fully. "Are you saying someone on the committee is bringing the towers down? And hurt two people in the process? And temporarily closed one of the most successful long-running and visible businesses in the county? Because towers are ugly?"

"You said it yourself, that Stephanie's tower is an eyesore." She set the teacup on a side table and rubbed her hand where it was starting to burn.

"Yes, but thinking something is an eyesore and committing a crime to bring it down is another thing completely," Jenna said. "Stacey, how could you accuse us of something like this?"

"I don't think you're involved, not personally."

"Oh, thank you," Jenna said. "I just work for a corrupt organization, is that it?"

"It makes sense, doesn't it?"

"No, it doesn't." Jenna held tight to the door handle. "For one, yes, people will be going to tour the new artist and writers retreat Ms. Clarke is spearheading, but that's not a main feature of our events. And besides, getting their work crew was her idea, not mine, I'm a little peeved to report. So that's Harold Dutton for you. And as far as the café tower goes, I don't think anyone would have noticed it. I hate to admit it, but you were right about that one. Having 5G there as well as at the retreat center would have benefited the community at the small cost of a couple towers that admittedly don't fit into the landscape very well."

"People have done far worse for far smaller slights, Jenna. Especially for appearances." Stacey looked down at her own shoes, not knowing where to look, really.

"I have a meeting to prepare for. Stacey, please leave the criminal investigations to the proper authorities. Especially about the towers." Jenna squeezed her eyes shut for a moment.

"I would," Stacey said. "But Sheriff Williams thinks nothing criminal happened. Just negligence and weather in Stephanie's case and plain stupidity in Harold's. No one is looking into what happened, and I thought someone should."

Jenna sat down again. "You thought that should be you?"

"Who else was stepping up?"

Jenna sighed and leaned back behind her desk. "Stacey, please, just stick to farming."

****

Stacey left it at that. She wanted so much to go sit at the Bluet with a cup of coffee licking her wounds with Stephanie. She wanted to call Amy and tell her all about it and ask her to come up with a clever solution the way she always seemed to do, but Amy was somewhere in the middle of the Atlantic. Stacey even thought about calling Vanessa, of all people, but she'd be teaching a literature class at the college or the senior English dual-credit class at the high school. Stacey had to leave it at that for now.

Instead, she drove to the parking lot of the Bluet Café. The café itself was taped off still, waiting for the insurance adjusters to come out—Stephanie had, thankfully, been giving Stacey a detailed report on the long and arduous process of getting her café back up and running. There were other places she could go and think, but none of them seemed right. So, she turned off the engine, rolled down the window to let in some of the cooling October air in, and turned on the radio. There it was again, the pirate station on the end of the dial.

It had all seemed so clear to her.

But now? No, Jenna was right. It didn't make sense that the committee would take out the tower. Okay, maybe it would make sense that they'd take out the tower, but it made no sense that they would blow a hole in one of the most iconic locations in Daw County. Especially right before the Wine and Pecan Festival, a time when so many of the festival goers would stop in to take their pictures in front of Stephanie's notable pastry case before ordering something that tasted like belonging.

Stacey had been wrong.

Maybe she could drive to Stephanie's house, see how she was doing. Stacey should go home and make the final preparations for the festival. Or at least make a nice dinner to put in the freezer for Friday night, when Ethan would be home.

Home, that was a good idea. That was a complicated idea, Stacey realized. But a good idea.

She started the SUV, still listening to the pirate station.

Then, her phone rang. Jenna. Here was an earful she didn't need right now. She let the phone ring until it went to voicemail. The way home was long from here, as she avoided the intersection with its promise of protesters. The phone buzzed, first to let her know that she had missed a call, a second time to let her know that she had a voicemail. And a third for a text. Addie? She parked just before the exit, picked up the phone, and gasped.

Jenna—*Please call me now. I think we can help each other.*—

Stacey's hand shook as she hit the dial button by Jenna's name. "Oh, good," Jenna said. "Listen."

"I'm listening. It's loud where you are, though."

"I'm in my car. I told Camille that I needed to go run a personal errand," Jenna said. "Minty was not happy with my lack of success in finding another sponsor. By the way, Camille heard everything. I need to tell you that first."

"And that's a problem."

Jenna explained, "Camille is a second cousin of some sort to Minty's family, and I'm pretty sure she's going to end up on the Wine and Pecan Festival committee herself, along with getting invites to the Daw County Women's Society, and the League of Wealthy Ladies with Too Much Time on their Hands."

Stacey stifled a laugh at that last one. "I know, but

what does that have to do with the towers?"

Jenna inhaled sharply. "With Stephanie's tower, I don't know for sure. But Minty Sanders has been trying to get her husband to buy her a winery. They scouted out the Dutton place as the perfect location. Land, history, and right next to that chic new artist's retreat."

"But Harold wouldn't sell out?" Stacey heard a honk in the background.

"Oh, these protesters. They're too much." Jenna honked her own horn, causing Stacey's phone to distort. "Sorry. I'm, just, oh, I don't know. No, Harold said no. And, surprisingly, Judy said no. I don't know if she saw how badly Harold took the loss of his mother's place or what, but she said no, too. Or maybe it gave her some power over Minty Sanders. How do you think Judy Dutton got into the Women's Society in the first place, except to wrangle her invitation through the estimable Mrs. Sanders?"

"So you think the committee might have taken down Harold's tower to take out Harold?" Stacey shuddered at the thought of a group of people so dedicated to preserving Daw County's history trying to injure one of the longest residents of the area. Injure, or worse.

"I don't know what to think," Jenna said. A siren blared past. "I'd heard that Minty Sanders was trying to short change them, to get the land for less than it was worth, because the Duttons were just a couple yokel farmers."

"Judy must not have liked that," Stacey said.

"No, she wouldn't," Jenna said. "I'm sorry, Stacey. I can't talk more. I have to try to do some evasive maneuvers to get back to the office."

"Good luck."

"Thanks, I'll need it. Oh, and one more thing." Jenna sighed. "Much as I do not want to admit it, I think the committee is trying to get me bumped from my job with the Chamber of Commerce. I've only been here, what, twelve years, worked up to this job, headed seven—now eight—Wine and Pecan Festivals and how many other events? This job is so much to me, this community means so much to me. And Minty Sanders wants me replaced with her newly graduated second cousin, or whatever Camille is to her."

Replaced. The word sent a chill down Stacey's spine. Suddenly, her prime suspect became the next potential victim. "You be careful, Jenna." She meant that in more way than one.

****

Stacey pulled back out of the parking lot. She had no idea what to do with the information Jenna had just passed along to her. She had no idea what to do with the fact that she would be expected to attend the Wine and Pecan Festival the following weekend and pretend that all this was okay. And she really didn't have a clue what to do with the fact that she knew, for a fact, in her heart, who the electronically disguised voice of the radio pirate DJ belonged to.

Dale Hillegeist. New owner of the possibly unlicensed station, The Belt. Or whatever Dale would call the thing now.

Stacey should have gone home, but something pulled her toward the Kellers' farm. She'd have to go the long way around anyway, given the protests. Stacey took the rounded curves slowly, watching for animals. Something flew up out of the ditch and startled her. Her heart was racing. Maybe it was better to stop. She pulled over toward the ditch and got out of the car. The weather was still warm, but something about the year felt like it was winding down already. She looked out over the fields of the Kellers, then, squinting, just past them. "Oh," she said to herself. "Oh, okay." From the glove box, she pulled out a pair of old binoculars they took with them just in case. She rolled down her window. From her vantage point on the road, she could see, clearly, the top of what was left of the antenna tower from The Belt, and, between it and the Kellers' farm, the small building that had once housed the station's studios. "Yeah, this is not good." Just on the other side of the Kellers' fields was the real target, the one the GPS coordinates had just missed. The one Stacey and Addie had missed.

What it meant, though, she wasn't sure. It wasn't lunchtime yet, but she wanted to grab Addie from class, sit with her, and think this through.

Stacey put the binoculars up to her eyes again and peered down the road. A slight figure, blond and loping like a coyote, came up the road. Stacey knew who it was almost as soon as she saw his head hanging down. Was he limping? He'd come from a well-to-do family, but it was easy for Stacey to feel sorry for Bo Sanders, the one who'd never quite fit in anywhere in Daw County. Too rangy for his family and peers but at the same time too mannered to fit in among the farm kids he would have gone to school with had his parents not sent him and his siblings to private school two counties over.

He looked up and waved at her, his hands beefy and well suited to the trade he'd settled in, much to the chagrin of his mother. "Mrs. H," he called out.

"What are you doing out here, Bo," she said. She knew he was one of the protesters, though he'd probably joined them not out of any conviction or another, but just to be part of a group. "You need a ride?"

"Nah, I'm good," he said. He shifted to one foot, winced, then shifted back to the other. "What are you looking at?"

"Birds," Stacey said. "Something flew out at my car, and I was just curious. You know how we've got nest boxes running up and down our pastureland."

Bo nodded solemnly. "Nature must be protected," he said, almost mechanically.

"You out here on a nature walk, too?"

"You could say that," Bo said. "I like coming out here. It's peaceful." His face was red, though with wind or sun or something else, she couldn't figure out.

"It is," Stacey said. She smiled. Here was Bo Sanders, the youngest son of the same Minty Sanders who was threatening to pull Jenna's job out from under her and who, she shuddered at the thought, wanted to bring down Harold's tower and him along with it. Just what Minty Sanders had against Stephanie, she didn't know, but here was her chance to find out. "Listen, Bo, how about I take you somewhere, get that foot looked at?"

"What foot?"

"Oh, Bo, I've been a mom too long not to know when young folks are hiding injuries so they don't have to come inside," Stacey said. "Tyler once fractured his elbow falling out of a tree and wouldn't let me take a look because he said he didn't want to come in."

Bo shook his head. "I'm fine."

"That's nothing," Stacey said. "Ethan once took a nail in his foot, doing who knows what. I had to pull him out of the shop just about."

"Do you like being a mom?"

The question shook her. Not because she didn't know the answer—she liked being a mom. She loved it to the core of her being. What shook her was him asking it. "Oh, more than anything."

Bo looked down at his foot then back up at her. "Yeah, I wasn't watching where I was going and stepped into a low spot. I think I twisted my ankle."

Stacey opened the passenger door, and Bo pulled himself up into the seat. He looked over at her and smiled. Would he ever look his age? Or would he always be caught in this youthful waywardness? "Do you want to go to the doctor, or just home to ice it?"

"Home," he said, turning to look out the window.

"You'll have to remind me how to get to the estate," she said starting up the SUV.

"No," he said. "I don't live there anymore. I found a trailer in Mesquite Park. It's not much, but I had more than enough saved to buy it outright and get it fixed up. I redid all the electrical myself."

"Congratulations on your new home then," Stacey said. Mesquite Park had been where Stephanie had moved with her new husband all those years ago, where she'd brought her newborn daughter. She'd sold the trailer after the business took off, but she and Stacey sometimes went back to visit the families who'd helped her out in her time of need.

They drove in silence until they'd passed the Kellers' farm, Bo watching out the window and Stacey glancing over at Bo when she could.

"Did you walk all this way?" Stacey asked after they crossed the intersection that ended the Kellers' property line. "From home?"

Bo shook his head. His hair was thinning, and there were wrinkles around his eyes. "I was doing a job," he said. "Boss picked me up, but he left without me when we were done."

"Abandoned you?"

"Not really," Bo said. "I think people don't notice me. Or they try not to." He looked over at her and smiled sheepishly.

Suddenly, his smile dropped away. Stacey, stopped at a stop sign, followed Bo's gaze out her window, over to the station. It would add at least twenty minutes to their trip, but she wanted to find out more about his mother, didn't she? "You been out there?"

"A couple times," Bo said. "I remember The Belt going off the air."

"You can't," Stacey said with a laugh. "You're not that old." A couple pickups were coming down the road crossing with no stop sign. She could have made it across easily, but she waited.

"I'm thirty one," Bo said. "My parents, however, treat me like I'm twelve."

"Why's that?"

"Because I'm the youngest, I guess." Bo nodded again. "If I could figure it out, I would. If I could go somewhere that isn't Dawville, maybe. I'm smart, got good grades, had a lot of friends in that stuck-up private school I went to. A couple girlfriends too. I used to be popular, kind of a jerk, but I know how to play people. I didn't like that, but I did it to fit in. When I'd come home from school, though, then everyone would baby me. Belittle me. Mom especially. Like she wanted to keep me a kid. I didn't know how to fight against that. Fight against it and win, anyway."

"That must have been hard," Stacey said.

"Still is."

The trucks pulled past her, and the road was clear. "If you have a few extra minutes, want to drive by the old station? I'm curious about something."

Bo looked panicked for a moment, then agreed. "Why do you want to go out here? Isn't it dangerous?" He pointed at the big antenna tower, which had survived more than a few windstorms.

"Dangerous?"

"I don't know," Bo said. "Dangerous. Like microwaves."

Stacey shook her head. "Well, you don't want to be right under the tower when the radio station is transmitting, that's true. But as long as you stay away from the tower, far enough, it's not going to hurt you. And the frequency they used to broadcast on was not in the microwave range. So you don't have to worry about getting cooked."

"Used to, huh."

"Bo, do you think someone is broadcasting from the tower now?"

He stared off into the distance, silently. Stacey turned the radio on. There he was again, Dale's voice, slightly modified so you wouldn't be able to say it was him for sure. But she'd known Dale so well long ago that she could hear something in the way he said Daw County that she would swear it was him. Melinda was right to be worried.

"Do you?" Bo asked her. Stacey felt her face flushing red. "I don't think we need a radio station in Dawville. Isn't that dangerous?"

"Bo Sanders," Stacey said with a sigh. "Are you

actually listening to those 5G protesters you've been hanging out with?"

"Sure," Bo said. "They researched stuff, and they told me what the big companies, the rich people running them, want to do. How they want to control people with the microwaves coming off the 5G antennas." He looked sincere.

"Well, let me tell you, don't listen to them, Bo. They don't know the first thing about how the antennas work. And they're making a mess of the highway and keeping us from getting something the community sure could use right now." Stacey wanted to grab his hand, but she didn't. "Look, you told me yourself that you're smart, and you know how people work. Don't you think the protesters are getting something out of this? Think of the community, Bo."

"The community," Bo said. He snorted. "Sorry, Mom says that all the time. She doesn't know the people of Daw County like I do. She's got the staff at the estate, as she calls them. Maids, gardeners, people like that who live here and work hard. And she doesn't treat them well, either."

"So she must not be a fan of the 5G or the antennas around here?"

Bo shook his head. "She won't have to worry about that."

"How do you know that?"

They circled around the land on which the little studio shack stood with its tower in the distance. Bo shook his head, his lank blond hair getting in his eyes. "I just heard things. I like talking to people, real people, not just Mom and Dad's rich friends. I heard things from real people. After Friday, no one's going to have to worry about the protesters anymore. Or anything else."

"Well," Stacey said. "That's good to hear."

If the protesters were cleared out on Friday, that meant the homecoming parade would go on as planned, that no one would be caught in traffic heading to the high school stadium for the big game. Bo's eyes wrinkled up as he smiled. Maybe he was older than she realized. Maybe they all were.

And maybe he knew what he was talking about.

Chapter Fifteen

They drove past the Kellers' field. Stacey talked Bo into going to the hospital to get his ankle checked out. How many times was she going to have to see this place this week? Bo hopped until a nurse came out to the lot with a wheelchair. "You going to be okay?" Stacey walked him to the entrance, its big glass doors calling her inside. "You call me if you need a ride home, okay?"

"Thank you, Mrs. H," he said, looking small inside the wheelchair. "I'll get Dad to pick me up after he's done at the office."

Stacey patted him on the shoulder, and he looked up at her with a big grin. A son's goofy grin.

She turned to go, but a figure waved at her from just inside the glass. "Stacey!"

Well, in spite of her plans, the hospital was going to get her inside today too. Judy met her at the door and grabbed her arm. She was beaming, her coral lipstick bleeding into the skin around her mouth as if her smile couldn't be contained. "Stacey, he's awake and talking and so much better today!"

"Oh, Judy, that's wonderful."

"Sorry for making such a fuss, but I'm so happy. I've never been so happy to be grumbled at by that grumpy old man," she said with a laugh. Some of her fragrant latte splashed on Stacey's sleeve, the jacket she was still wearing from her meeting with Jenna. "The doctor was giving him a good once over, so I went out to get a cup of coffee. I'm so glad I saw you. It just meant the world to me that you kept me company in the café. Why don't you come back with me to say hi?"

"I'd like to," Stacey said. "But I don't want to tire him out."

"Please?"

"Maybe I'll come back tomorrow? I need to get home," Stacey said. Her stomach rumbled. She could swing by Gertie's on the way there.

Judy's face fell. "I need you to come talk to him," she said. "I've told him all about what happened. He's not talking too much yet, since he took a line on the jaw. Just a nasty bruise, he's lucky. But I told him about the sheriff's office thinking it was an accident, and I told him too that you were looking into things, especially after what happened to your friend and the Bluet."

"Okay, then," Stacey said. "Let's go."

****

Even under the bandages and with all the wires sticking out of him, Harold Dutton was plainly Harold Dutton. His grizzled short hair was covered in a bandage, and his scowl was swollen from the nasty bruise on his jaw, but that was definitely Harold.

Judy kissed him gently on the cheek and squeezed his hand. "Harold, look who I found."

Stacey sat down in a chair next to the bed. "Hey, Harold. Everyone will be so glad to hear you're getting better."

"Not all," he mumbled. "Tired." Harold closed his eyes. This was a bad idea, and Stacey felt guilty for being here at all when Harold was in no shape to be chatting when he needed rest.

"Oh, Harold," Judy said. "Stacey can't stay too long anyway, so just tell her what you were telling me, and then you can take a nap."

Harold grunted. "Don't remember much. Blond man by my tower that morning."

"Blond?" Stacey asked. "And you're sure it was a man?"

Again, Harold grunted. "Don't remember much else."

"Dark blond? Light blond? How tall was he?" Stacey stood up.

Harold's eyes closed. "Hmm."

"I should go, let Harold get some rest," Stacey said. "Will you call me if he remembers anything else?"

Judy agreed, and they parted ways at Harold's door.

****

That was love between them, that Stacey saw as she pulled the door closed when she left. Judy holding on to Harold's hand with one hand, her other palm pressed against his cheek. The one that wasn't bruised. That was love. Judy couldn't have done it, could she?

Halfway down the hall, Judy popped her head out of the door and called for her in a half-whisper. "Wait up!"

Stacey stopped. Judy's kitten heels clacked on the tile floor. "Harold's asleep?"

"Getting there," Judy said. "Look, we need to talk. I have a confession to make." She tapped the down arrow to call and elevator.

"A confession?"

The elevator door dinged to signal its arrival. Stacey examined the sliver of darkness between the elevator and the floor they were safely on for a moment. "Come on, then." Judy grabbed Stacey's arm and pulled her into the elevator just before the doors began to close again.

Stacey rubbed her arm where Judy had grabbed her with those long coral nails. "That hurt."

"I'm sorry, I'm in a hurry," Judy said though Stacey couldn't find any contrition on her face. "You're willing to help Harold. Do you know that you're the only person who came to visit him besides Pastor Muller and the nice police officers? Deputy Valdez and Deputy Muller. Harold's kids didn't even come. My daughter lives in New York, so she can't come now. It's her busy season."

"Well, with the shape Harold is in, maybe they didn't want to bother him," Stacey said. She wondered for a moment whether she would have visited him at all either if she hadn't been tasked with bringing him flowers. "Or you."

"I wanted to be bothered," Judy said. "Or, not bothered. Visited. You know what I mean." The elevator opened. Judy ushered Stacey, more gently this time, back to the little café.

Stacey looked at the clock sticking out of the wall, its red blocky numbers warning her that the day was slipping away. "You said you have a confession to make."

"Hush," Judy said, but there was no one else in the café, as the workers were out on their lunch break and the silver mesh had been pulled down over the line.

"Judy, I'm willing to help. I want to know more about this blond man Harold saw," Stacey said. "But I need more to go on."

"That was the first time he said he saw anyone out there messing with the tower," Judy said. "Blond man isn't much to go on, not around here. That could be any number of men. That could be your Ethan, couldn't it?"

215

"Ethan is in Austin," Stacey said. "And thanks to Addie, he's not blond anymore. It's more, I don't know, sky blue?"

Judy nodded. "Let's leave that for now. Here's my confession. I love Harold Dutton more than anything in the world. But the past ten years have been hard on me. I don't love living on a farm, and I don't love living in Daw County. I'm sorry, I know it's where you're from. But there's a lack of panache here. And Harold kept telling me that one day, we'd sell up and move to Dallas. Then, all of a sudden, he says, no, we're not. He's staying on the land until he dies, and his kids and I can deal with the land after that."

"What brought than on?"

"5G," Judy said. She groaned. "Harold had this preposterous idea that we could put in a bunch of towers and rent them out to the cell phone companies. The land goes quite a ways down the highway, so we'd stand a good chance of making some money off the scheme."

"So, how did he end up deciding to sell his momma's place?" Stacey wished she could will the line to open so that she could at least grab a cup of coffee. Caffeine was in order if she wanted to make sense of what Judy was telling her.

"He didn't," Judy said. She took out her big sunglasses and set them on her face. "I did, through our lawyer. I thought that if the piece of land that he loved most was put to a better purpose than just letting that darling little cottage fall to pieces on the acreage it was on, then he'd see that it wouldn't be that hard to move on from the farm. And then Tess Clarke came along, and I knew she'd be perfect for it."

"But Harold grew up on that land. He saved the land

from being taken from his family by the bank," Stacey said. "That's a hard thing to let go of."

"I know," Judy said. "I didn't grow up here. I only came here thinking I could bring my sense of style to a boutique, that I could live here and there at the same time. But my business failed, and I moved on. Life is about moving on, not getting stuck. Harold is stuck."

"Harold is a good caretaker of something he finds a lot of value in," Stacey said.

"True, but no one in Daw County likes Harold," Judy said. She tapped her coral nails on the plastic table. "Sometimes, I don't know if I even like him, even though I love the old thing. I thought if we could start over in Dallas, then we could make a life where people did like Harold. If they actually got to know him. The part I do like. The man I love."

"I like him," Stacey said. "I like you both. And I'm glad you're here in Daw County. And I think you can help me. Do you know Minty Sanders from your women's society pretty well?"

Judy gushed about the doyenne of decor in Daw County. Her enthusiasm fell, though, when Stacey explained her plan and about her suspicions. "Look, if you like the people here in Daw County, if you want to get to the bottom of what happened to Harold and why Stephanie's tower came down on the Bluet Café, then you'll help me."

Judy agreed.

"Good," Stacey said. Even though she herself wasn't convinced it would be good for either of them.

****

The plan was simple enough. Go get evidence that Minty Sanders's distaste for the towers—Stephanie's,

Harold's, and who knows what other ones—would be strong enough to motivate her to bring them down. No one would mistake Minty Sanders for a blond man. Her auburn hair and pageant queen swish in heels precluded that possibility. But that's not to say that she couldn't have hired a blond man to do the work for her. She was used to delegating, wasn't she? Living on the largest estate in the Brazos Valley region, she had to be.

The blond man could have been any number of construction workers, but it could also have been the former Judge Sanders. Minty's husband was less prominent a figure than she was in some way, but the power had been in his family, as had some of the money. She'd brought a finishing school sensibility to the political family, and that combination had proved even more powerful. But did that make them dangerous?

She sat in the drive through line at Gertie's, grateful to have a few minutes to gather her thoughts. Which were, admittedly, scattered. She turned on the radio to help her think, which she'd left on the pirate station. Dale Hillegeist was blond. Dale Hillegeist was also operating a low-powered FM radio station without, as far as Stacey and perhaps Melinda knew, without a license. So that made sense. And he could have easily brought down Stephanie's tower to throw the police off the trail, making it look like whoever wanted to hurt Harold was really just after the 5G antennas in Daw County. But then the police weren't investigating either.

Behind her, a car honked. Stacey pulled forward to the ordering window and made her choices. Plates for her and Rick, plus an extra since Addie would smell the scent in the SUV when Stacey came to pick her up. "What do you want on the third plate?" came the cheerful voice out of the speaker.

Stacey paused for a moment. "Oh, let's do the vegan special."

"One vegan special it is."

She pulled her car forward to pay and get the food.

****

Addie made face at the Styrofoam box she'd just hungrily opened. "Ew, Mom."

"What's ew? You ordered this yourself last time we went to Gertie's," Stacey said. "It'll be better once you warm it up." Addie had been quiet on their way home. Nothing unusual, but Stacey's attempts at conversation during their twenty minute trip home proved unsuccessful.

"No, thanks," Addie said. She closed the box and put it back in the refrigerator.

"I'm going to ask one more time," Stacey said. She took out the pecan cake she'd baked for Sunday and set it on the table. "What's going on?"

Addie shrugged and turned to go toward her room. "It's nothing, Mom."

"Sit," Stacey said. "There's cake."

"Fine," Addie said. "I'll eat cake."

Stacey cut her daughter a slice and put it at her place at the table. Addie grabbed the plate, but Stacey gently guided her to her chair. Addie had something going on, something teenaged and dramatic for sure, but something that was weighing on her. Addie wasn't going to talk now, though. Stacey had miscalculated at Gertie's. She didn't have time to miscalculate again. "We're having an emergency family meeting."

"With our emergency family?"

Stacey laughed. "You're telling Ethan's jokes

now?"

Addie blanched, her fork halfway up to her open mouth. "Is this about Ethan? No, Mom, I don't want to talk about Ethan."

"It's okay, we're not talking about Ethan," Stacey said. "This has nothing to do with Ethan. Or Tyler or Caleb."

Addie sighed then shoved the forkful of cake in her mouth. "Where's Dad?" she asked, her mouth half-full of cake. "You, me, and Dad, that's an emergency family meeting, right?"

"Uh, no, not just," Stacey said. "Emergency family meeting, plus friends."

Addie shrugged and finished her cake.

****

Stacey made a few phone calls, wrangled Addie to do some of the cooking, and at 6:30 on the dot, the meeting began over dinner. Rick looked tired and was stained with some kind of grease on his shirt. Stephanie was used to it, having had dinner with the farm family on more occasions than they could count.

The only one looking out of place and slightly uncomfortable was Vanessa. But she needed to be there, didn't she?

"First off, thank y'all for coming at short notice," Stacey said, setting out dressing for the salad. "I think we need to work fast on this, before something else gets damaged. Or someone else gets hurt."

Addie had her notebook open, her green pen at the ready.

"Thank you for asking," Stephanie said. She looked sallow, quiet, and not exactly like she'd start eating the scant food she'd put on her plate anytime soon. "I've had the Bluet on my mind, and I can't puzzle it out. Especially not why someone would take out a tower with an explosive device."

"That," Stacey said, "is what we're here for."

"Speak for yourself," Rick said. "I'm here for the food." He laughed, but no one else did.

"You think someone else is in danger?" Vanessa asked. Stacey had been careful with her dinner plans, confirming that Vanessa wasn't in fact vegan but vegetarian who did eat dairy. Cheese lasagna it was then, with homegrown salad and the buttery garlic bread Stephanie had given her the recipe for. "They're going to bring another one down?"

"Who, Harold?" Rick snorted. "Yeah, he's not going anywhere anytime soon."

Stacey glared at her husband.

"No, Dad," Addie jumped in. "There's a connection between Harold's tower and Stephanie's. We just need to figure it out."

"Well," Stacey said. "We need all the information first." She looked at her daughter's face, at the smallest smear of tomato sauce at the corner of her mouth.

"My insurance company isn't being helpful," Stephanie said. She pushed a leaf of lettuce from her salad around with her fork. "I asked them if I could hire someone to do a private investigation. But they wouldn't cover it. Not when the sheriff concluded it was an accident caused by the weather."

"What's there to investigate? Wind?" Rick asked, his mouth half-full of garlic bread.

"A lot," Addie said firmly. Stacey had filled them in on what she'd learned from Jenna and Judy as they'd brought the food out to the table. "Okay, so, there's the possibility that someone is taking down towers because they're an eyesore."

Vanessa nodded. "True, but a lot of things in Daw County could be considered eyesores that might drive away tourists or affluent property buyers. The oil pumps, Jerry Kurtz's wall of rusted trucks, the abandoned radio station and its towers—"

"Wait," Addie said. "Let me write all this down."

"I doubt anyone wants Jerry Kurtz to take down his wall of rusted trucks. You can't see them unless you're on his property or you're flying over it anyway," Stephanie said. "Besides, he's a good guy in town, comes in every Sunday after church to treat the pastor and his wife to lunch."

"You're one of the good ones, too," Stacey said. She squeezed her friend's hand. "Don't forget that."

"Flying," Vanessa said, as if it were something strange and new. "Stacey, didn't you tell me that Harold had turned in one of his fellow hams for having a tower too high?"

"That was years ago," Rick said. "And no one was upset at him then. Some newcomer, bought up land for a weekend cabin. Guy sold up after he decided we wouldn't play ball with his fast and loose ideas about the law."

"That's not the only time he's turned someone in," Stephanie said. "You remember that guy who had a pirate station around here, not too long after The Belt closed down?"

"That wasn't exactly a pirate station," Rick said. "He was operating at a low power. Sort of legal. And we liked his talk."

"Sort of legal isn't *legal* legal, Dad," Addie said.

"Even if it is to broadcast some wanna-be talk show celebrity."

"What happened?" Vanessa looked elegant, her hair up, makeup done, a silver bracelet at her slender wrist. Stacey wanted to ask if she'd just come from Tess Clarke's, or whether she was going there right after dinner. "With the pirate or not-so-pirate?"

"He was just a kid," Rick said. "FCC investigated, kid turned in his equipment and paid a fine. Came from one of the new families around here, the richer ones. Kid said he was bored."

"Bored enough to spend a chunk of money on equipment and set it up decently," Stacey said. "I think folks would have been fine if he'd just played some music or something his friends had written and performed, like he said he was going to. But instead, he spouted—" She groaned and waved her hands in resignation.

Stephanie turned to Vanessa. "Hate speech," she said. "I know we seem pretty backward around here, but we won't put up with folks inciting violence. I suppose the rest of us were more than bothered by the kid, but Harold knew how to stop him."

"So, Harold Dutton turned out to be a good guy in this case?" Vanessa asked.

Stacey nodded. "I think that's why we tolerate him, even if he's a grouchy old bag of moldy potatoes to the rest of us."

"Wait, Mom," Addie said. She put down her fork and grabbed her pen. "So, Harold Dutton twice turns in people who are breaking the law? Don't you see what this means?"

They all looked at each other and then back at

Addie.

"What?" Stacey asked her daughter.

"It means we aren't asking the right question. We don't need to ask why those towers. Well, we do need to ask those. But the bigger question is who's afraid of Harold Dutton? Who was he gathering information on to turn in to whatever authorities next?" Addie looked pleased, happier than she had in weeks.

"You're right," Vanessa said. "We still need to get to Harold's connection to the Bluet Café, but we need to ask who's involved with both."

"Naw," Rick said. He scooped more lasagna onto his plate. "Why can't y'all see that Harold had an accident, because he's not the most careful guy in the world. And that windstorm that brought down yours, Stephanie. We don't have some guy wanting to take down towers going around Daw County making trouble."

"Are you saying that because you believe it Rick? Or are you saying it because you want to defend your friend, who has decided that there's nothing to investigate?" Stacey stared at her husband, waiting for an answer that she knew wouldn't come. An answer she most likely already knew.

"Who's afraid of Harold Dutton?" Addie asked again.

"The committee?" Vanessa suggested. "Stacey, you told me yourself that they're scheming to get Jenna out and put in Mrs. Sanders' relative. What if they're doing something that Harold found out about?"

"What's my connection to Harold that the committee was so afraid of?" Stephanie asked.

"Tess said Judy had bought cakes from the Bluet

Café a few times to bring over," Vanessa said. "And she mentioned that Judy was planning to ask you, Stephanie, about catering a party she wanted to have to celebrate her induction into the Daw County Women's Society."

"She hadn't asked yet," Stephanie said.

"Maybe she wasn't going to ask," Addie said. "Look, Mom, you said the Duttons were having money problems, right? So Judy spreads the word about having a lavish party, even though she can't afford it and won't. But the women in her ladies group don't know that for sure, and it looks like she's going to have it at the Bluet."

Vanessa nodded. "To get to Judy, even if tangentially, take out the Bluet's tower?"

Stacey's stomach dropped. She felt even more sorry for Judy now.

"That's one idea," Addie said. "Then there's this pirate, right? If he's worried that Harold caught on to what he's doing and where he is, then he might take down the tower to get rid of Harold."

The pirate. Stacey's stomach tried to pick itself up from where it dropped, but instead, it crashed against the side of her rib cage, taking her heart along with it. "That doesn't make sense," she said quietly. "What does Stephanie's tower have to do with the pirate radio station?"

"You, Mom," Addie said.

Stacey's lungs had lurched over with her stomach, and she reminded herself to breathe.

"And you, too, Dad." Addie twirled her pen. "What did Harold have on his tower? A ham radio antenna. Before it fell over, Stephanie had leased space to the cell phone company. Y'all were looking for a new place for another repeater antenna, right, Dad?"

Rick nodded. He looked confused for a moment, then looked over at Stacey. "You were so busy bringing cake to the ladies, you might not have heard it, but that was the plan. We were supposed to ask you to bring it up with Stephanie."

"And you forgot to ask me?" Stacey asked her husband.

"I'd asked Addie to remind me to ask you," Rick said.

"You asked me after Stephanie's tower fell down, Dad," Addie said. She wrote down a few notes on her notepad.

Vanessa set her fork down elegantly. "So, let's get this straight. The pirate is afraid Harold will inform the authorities about his illegal operation, so he takes out Harold's tower. He then brings down Stephanie's tower—but why?"

"Hams can locate pirates by direction finding," Rick explained, looking like something in his world had just broken into two pieces that wouldn't fit back together. "You wouldn't use a repeater for that, though. Repeaters just take low-powered signals and repeat them at a higher power and from a taller height so more people can hear them. Direction finding you'd do with different equipment."

"Maybe the pirate doesn't know that?" Vanessa asked.

"It's a possibility," he said. "But point is, we can do it. We could go out there and figure out where the pirate signal is coming from."

"Okay, Rick, you on board with us now?" Stacey asked. Rick nodded and took a bite of garlic bread. "Then call in the troops, honey. We're going to find that signal."

And, she hoped with all her heart (and her stomach and her lungs), that the pirate wasn't the one behind the fallen antenna towers.

Chapter Sixteen

Stacey's alarm went off, jolting her out of some dream she couldn't remember moments after she'd left it. A bad dream. She sat up in bed, hesitating for a moment before turning on the light. Her head hurt, and she groaned as she touched the bandage. Rick could sleep through her alarm, her light, her noisy getting ready, the kids running through the house. Only thing that ever seemed to wake him was the cup of coffee she'd bring him fifteen minutes after she got up.

The house was quiet. Addie's alarm would go off in a few minutes. Stacey padded in her slippers to the kitchen, past the dining table where they'd met last night. Was that all part of the bad dream, or just her brain not wanting to think it was something she had to deal with? Could she blame it on the cuts on her forehead?

The plan was simple enough. Vanessa and Stephanie would get in touch with their contacts at the Daw County Women's Society and find out what they could about the antennas, obliquely as they could. Stephanie had a contract to cater their fall festival, which she could do from the grand kitchen in the Society's building. She'd lost a fair bit of her supplies and equipment in her café kitchen, but she could make do with what they had there. Stephanie could always make do with what she had, and that was just one of the many things that Stacey admired about her best friend.

Vanessa, however, Stacey wasn't as confident about. The Daw County Women's Society had invited her, then nagged her, about joining ever since she moved to Dawville years ago. Stacey hadn't known this, and she could tell that Vanessa was loath to admit it. Seems they didn't want her as much as they wanted her position and her degree among their ranks. "I like the friends I have," Vanessa had explained. "I don't need friends I have to pay for." Apparently the society ladies had grossly overestimated Vanessa's income and interest in playing card games while gossiping about the gauche over gin. "I suppose I could ask, though, what I'd need to do to join," she'd said. For the first time that night, the Vanessa Stacey was used to, frazzled and frumpy, showed through the elegant one. Stacey wondered which was the real Vanessa, or if she was just both and good at compartmentalizing. "And there's Tess," she'd said. "I know they've been excited over the prospect of getting her to join."

"Would she?" Stacey asked, bringing out dessert.

Vanessa looked uncomfortable and amused at the same time. "Let's say they'd have a harder time wrangling her than me."

In her head, Stacey thanked whoever invented the coffee maker that automatically turned itself on and got to its job early in the morning. She poured cups for herself and Rick, added cream to hers, and walked back to the bedroom. It was Thursday morning, and if Bo Sanders was right, they'd only have to deal with the protesters one more day. Good that was coming to an end. She'd have to get Addie going early again today, get herself going early today, since, chances were they were out with their placards and guitars singing and yelling in the intersection until the sheriff's office sent deputies down to clear them out. Like rats, like the ones up in the attic, they kept coming back. She hadn't seen a rat, though, just heard a shuffling and assumed. They'll be there tomorrow, and she could take care of setting traps then. Too much to do before Friday, she reminded herself.

In the hallway, Addie almost bumped into her. "Good morning," Stacey said as she balanced the cups against herself. Nothing spilled onto her robe, which was a dark burgundy and already stained with countless drips of coffee already. "Didn't hear your alarm go off."

"It didn't," Addie said. She sounded sleepy. Not just waking up sleepy, but stayed up too late sleepy. Or woke up hours ago and couldn't fall back to sleep sleepy. "Is there coffee left in the pot?"

"Yes," Stacey said. She had Rick's cup by the handle, but it was still too hot against her hand. "But you sound like you don't need coffee. You need sleep."

"I got sleep," Addie said. "Some. Enough."

"What's going on?"

Addie shrugged and shuffled toward the kitchen.

Stacey looked down at her coffee. She went into her bedroom, set Rick's down on his nightstand and stubbed her toe on the bed coming back out. Coffee splashed up on her sleeve this time. At least the cream had cooled it off just enough so that it didn't burn her.

At the dining table, Addie slumped over a cup of coffee. Stacey looked at her daughter for clues, for something that would crack the shell of the teenage worry that covered her. Maybe there was a boy. Or maybe there wasn't a boy, not one in Daw County worth bothering about homecoming over. Stacey almost laughed when she remembered Amy swearing that she'd never marry a boy from Daw County and that she was going to live somewhere big and exciting after college. Well, she didn't marry a man from Daw County. Instead, she married a Brit who wanted to live in Daw County, which they did. Sometimes, life surprised her. And then, they divorced and Amy finally got her wish to live somewhere big and exciting. A big, exciting ship, anyway. Stacey tried not to judge. She looked at Addie looking down into her coffee. If it was a boy, this phase would pass. She thought of Dale for a moment and then realized that maybe it wouldn't. Not totally.

"I'm making bacon and eggs," Stacey announced. She'd drop Addie at school, work on the farm's accounts for a while, and the finish up her preparations for the weekend. For Ethan. And she'd find time to figure out the towers. Somehow. "You want to start the toast, baby girl?"

Addie nodded. She pushed herself up and ambled over to the pantry. "Where's the bread?"

"Where the bread usually is," Stacey said. She pointed with a packet of bacon she'd just pulled from the fridge.

Addie nodded again, and fumbled with the loaf. She let out a short sob as she turned the twist tie on the plastic bag.

"How about you sit down, and I'll get the toast." Bacon popped on the hot frying pan. She'd do the bacon first, then cook the eggs in the grease. Best way to go about things.

"No, Mom, I can handle toast this morning," Addie said. "I'm just tired."

"Because you didn't sleep?" Stacey asked. She took

the bread bag from her daughter and led her to a chair. "Sit. Tell me what's going on."

"It's fine," Addie said. "It will be fine. I'm fine."

"It's not fine," Stacey said. She put in four slices of toast into the toaster. Their big toaster from when there had been six of them eating breakfast at the now too big dining table. "You don't have to tell me what's going on, but I think it would be a good idea."

Addie was quiet. The bacon popped and sizzled. Stacey took the eggs out of the fridge, the homemade blackberry jam, the butter, the orange juice. She set the table, waiting for her daughter to say something, anything.

"I'm worried," Stacey said, breaking the silence. She turned the bacon.

"Mom, why are you looking into the towers?" Addie asked. She got up, grabbed glasses, and poured three cups of orange juice. She moved one to Rick's place. "I get why you want to figure out what happened to Stephanie's tower, but why are you looking into what happened to Harold Dutton? And Judy too, I guess."

"Someone has to," Stacey said. "Sometimes, you have to stand up for people when they can't do it for themselves. Like the Duttons right now. Stephanie can stand up for herself, I'm sure. Sometimes you have to stand up with them."

"No, I get that," Addie said. She put a cup at Stacey's place. "But aren't you worried about what will happen? To you?"

Stacey pulled the bacon from the pan and set the browned strips onto the paper towel she'd laid on a plate. She watched the grease spread out for a moment, bubbles still popping off the meat. "What do you mean?"

"If you stand up for Harold, and it turns out he did just have an accident, then what? Do you get lumped in with him and his wife? It's not like they're exactly popular around here?" Addie said. She swirled juice around in her glass. "People say nasty things about them. You know that. And then Harold got hurt. He could have died."

"If it turns out I was wrong, I hope folks will just see me as a concerned neighbor, someone who cared enough about people and Daw County to go sticking my nose where it maybe didn't belong because no one else was going to do it," Stacey said. She broke eggs into the bacon grease. The whites became opaque as soon as they hit the pan. "And besides, you know how much Mrs. Dutton, old Mrs. Dutton that is, meant to me. And a lot of people. I think that's enough right there."

"Because you're a good person," Addie said. "And you're strong enough to tell them they're wrong. Even if you don't belong there in the first place."

"Who's wrong?"

"I don't know," Addie said. She was quiet for a moment. The toaster popped, and Addie got up, took the browned bread out and refilled it for herself. "The sheriff. I don't know. People at school. A lot of people at school. In Dawville. In the whole stupid county."

"People at school are wrong about what?" Stacey put the plate of bacon on the table.

Rick ambled in, holding his empty coffee cup.

"Nothing," Addie said. She picked up a piece of toast and lashed it with butter.

For the rest of the meal, Addie stayed quiet. Rick laid out his plans for the day, which included avoiding preparations for Ethan's arrival. "And then, the boys and

I are going hunting for that signal."

"You and the boys?" Stacey narrowed her eyes at him over her coffee cup.

"Yeah," Rick said. "The club has some equipment, and we're all going out this afternoon."

"You didn't think to ask if I would come along?"

"Nah," Rick said. "You just do radio for crisis communication. And to see the ladies at the meetings."

"You don't think this *is* a crisis?"

Rick shrugged. "It's important, but it's not a *crisis* crisis."

"Dad," Addie said with her mouth full of toast. "This whole thing was Mom's idea."

"I'm coming with you," Stacey said.

"I got a truck full coming with me already," Rick said. "And the rigs."

"I can drive myself, thank you," Stacey said.

"And me," Addie said with a mouthful of bacon.

"And Addie," Stacey agreed.

Addie looked at her mother wide-eyed.

"Suit yourself," Rick said. He grabbed another slice of bacon and left.

"Mom, do you have the equipment for this?" Addie asked. She refilled her juice cup.

Stacey shook her head. "No, but I don't think we'll need it."

****

Addie took the conversation to the list of suspects and wouldn't let go of it, talking louder and faster about the possibilities the closer they got to school. At least the girl looked awake now. She gave her mom a quick kiss on the cheek, then slid out the passenger door when they got to the drop off lane at the high school.

Back home, Stacey finished cleaning up the kitchen from breakfast. She looked down at the cleared table, at where she should be setting up her laptop and going through the accounts. Instead, the possibilities whirled. She texted Stephanie, who probably had begun her part of the plan, and Vanessa, who probably hadn't, because of the school day. This afternoon, they'd figure it out, or at least part of it. And tomorrow? She could put all this behind her and focus on Ethan.

The phone lay quietly on the table. She should text Ethan too, make sure he was still coming out this way right after his morning classes. The drive wasn't long, and he'd done it before, coming back from freshman orientation. He'd just have to do what he'd done before, right?

Stacey picked up the phone. There was one person she should loop in, one person who was in more danger than anyone else she could think of right now.

The line trilled the ring tone once. She wondered if her kids even remembered what a dial tone sounded like. "Hello?"

"Jenna," Stacey said into the phone flat on the table. "Are you okay?"

A long sigh washed over the speaker. "They're threatening to boot me."

"Why?"

"Because I haven't been able to replace the sponsor."

"You've had what, a few days?" Stacey tried to remember but the week was a blur.

"A few whole days," Jenna confirmed. "If I can't do it, then I'm out."

"Oh, I'm sorry," Stacey said.

"I don't think this was just because of the sponsor," she said quietly.

"Oh, I am sorry," Stacey said. She should have closed that door, or at least met Jenna somewhere other than her office. Like the Bluet Café. But meeting her at the Bluet wasn't a possibility at that point.

"Truth is, I'm afraid," Jenna said. "Something like this has been possible for a long time, and I didn't want to see that. There's a lot of power in that committee, more than I'd like to admit."

"Oh?" Stacey ran a paper towel over the ring Rick's orange juice glass had left on the table.

"I'm going to resign," Jenna said. "I'll be fine. My family will be fine. I can't find another job like this one in Daw County, but my husband can work anywhere, and the girls will make new friends at their new school."

"No, Jenna, please don't," Stacey said. "Look, I'm going to help you."

"Please, don't try to help any more than you already have," Jenna pleaded.

"Well, okay, I'll say it this way," Stacey said. It was risky, but if it worked, Jenna could keep her job, and Stacey would be able to meet with the committee and ask about the towers. "I'm about to do something I'll probably regret, but it's for the good of the community. You're good for the community, Jenna, and I need your backing on this."

"Fine," Jenna said, sounding resigned already.

"You're going to tell the committee that you spoke with me," Stacey said, trying to keep her voice from shaking. "In my capacity as vice-president of the Daw County Pecan Growers Association. If they pull you from the project because of one lousy sponsor who did a lousy thing, then we're going, too."

"What?"

"Okay, make it sound better than I just said it," Stacey said. "You're good at this committee communications stuff. I'm not."

"No," Jenna said. "You explain it to me. Did you just say what I think you just said?'

Stacey swallowed hard. "Daw County's wineries need the tourism. If they don't have things like the Wine and Pecan Festival to bring folks in, then their business takes a hit. There are how many winery owners on the committee? Us pecan farmers, well, we sell out our crops every year whether or not there's a festival going on with our name on it. If the committee gets rid of you, then you can tell them that the pecan farmers are out too."

Jenna sighed again. "So the Daw County Wine and Pecan Festival?"

"Becomes the Daw County Wine Festival. No pecans."

"No pecans," Jenna repeated. "This is dangerous, Stacey. People love the pecans. The pecans bring in the families and the people who aren't into wine."

"Pulling out last minute is far less dangerous than towers coming down on farmers, and local businesses," Stacey said, her confidence coming back. "And friends."

"I'll give it a try," Jenna said.

"You'll succeed," Stacey said. And she trusted that her friend would do just that.

****

"You sure I'm not going to get into any trouble with this?" Stephanie held up the small radio to which Stacey had attached a cumbersome antenna. They were driving down the one road Stacey didn't want to be on, down near the Kellers' farm, by the old antenna tower and studio for The Belt. Stephanie sat uncomfortably under the equipment she held in the passenger seat. "I don't have a ham radio license."

"Well, first off," Stacey said pulling the SUV as gently as she could onto the dirt road so that Stephanie didn't jab one or the other of them with the antenna, "this is just a listening device. We're sure the pirate isn't transmitting from the old antenna, because the signal would be a lot clearer, and I'm sure the power co-op would be squawking about it to the sheriff's office. And second of all," she picked up the rarely used ham radio rig that she'd brought to the SUV but rarely used, "see this PTT button? Stands for Push to Talk. Just don't follow those instructions, and you'll be fine. You don't need a license just to listen."

Stephanie laughed that short quick laugh of hers that meant she'd seen more of the world from behind the pastry case of her café than most folks would give her credit for. "I think they do need to hand out licenses for listening. And training manuals."

"Oh, an exam would be good," Stacey said. Under them, the tires rumbled, but Stephanie held everything stable. "'Are you listening to me?' 'Yep, got my license right here, ma'am.'"

"Would be nice if the sheriff's office listened," Stephanie said, suddenly serious.

"Any luck with your insurance company listening?"

Stephanie shook her head. "Sheriff said it was the wind, so insurance said it was the wind. At least they'll pay for the repairs."

Stacey patted her friend's arm, mostly to try to comfort her, but also to aim the antenna out of her face.

"Okay, let's go ahead and turn on the radio," she said. She parked the SUV just off the side road that went between the Keller farm's property line and the land on which the old studio sat. "I'm coordinating with Rick and the others. We'll report what we find." Stacey knew what she would find, but she wasn't ready to admit it.

"Hand me the binoculars," Stephanie said after they'd gotten out of the SUV. She handed the radio equipment over to Stacey. "At least I know what I'm doing with those."

"We won't need those," Stacey said. "That won't help us listen any better." She realized that she'd had the binoculars around her neck again, the ones that she'd used when she'd picked up Bo yesterday. Stacey had her suspicions, but there was no evidence that anyone was in the old studio anyway, and whether Bo had seen anything useful or not.

"Is that a truck over there?"

Stacey turned around sharply. She realized too late that the makeshift antenna was headed straight for the door of the SUV. It crumpled and snapped. "Oh," she said. "We weren't getting anything anyway, were we?"

"You're the expert," Stephanie said. She bent down to pick up the broken off piece of metal, then stood up quickly. "Look, over there. Isn't that a silver truck parked just around the corner? I can just make out the edge of the tailgate."

Stacey held up the binoculars. "No," she said quietly.

"No, what?"

"No, I don't think that's a truck," Stacey said. "I think it's just a piece of radio equipment."

"That looks like a truck?"

In the distance, Stacey saw the flash of sunlight off the tailgate as it pulled forward, out of sight. "It's gone now, whatever it was." She put up the binoculars, verifying what she'd seen. Another movement, but just discernible, like a snake moving through a wood pile.

"We're not very good detectives, are we?" Stephanie sighed. "I need to go get back on the phone with the builders to schedule the repair work."

"You do that," Stacey said. "I'll drop you back at your house and head back out with the rest of the hams."

"Sure," Stephanie said. "But you never said why you wanted to come out all this way."

"Just a hunch," Stacey said. "I doubt anyone would be in the studios of The Belt, though." She sang the old jingle for the station, and Stephanie joined in.

"We had that station on when my husband proposed," Stephanie said with an expression Stacey could read in a hundred different ways. "Our song came on the radio, and he pulled over, and there it was, the most beautiful little ring. He said he wanted to take me out by the lake, but the weather was chilly and he decided since they were playing our song while we were warm in the car, he'd just do it then and there."

"I'm sorry if I brought up something you didn't want to think about today," Stacey said. "Not with everything else going on."

"No," Stephanie said. "I like remembering him. I like remembering those days. I think he'd be proud of me, everything I've done for our daughter and myself. I hadn't thought about the station in a long time." She looked down at the broken antenna she'd picked up out of the gravel. "Let's go. Take me home."

"Country roads?"

"Do not sing," Stephanie said, shaking the antenna at Stacey and laughing.

"I promise," Stacey said.

Chapter Seventeen

Truth was, Stacey didn't expect to find any signals coming from the old studios. Who would be caught that aware that folks wouldn't want to look for him? Sure, there had been pirates out here before, but it was sort of a game that the hams played, going out and finding them. One turned off his gear for good after a talking to from the hams. Another had bought the parts from a shady website that made false claims about the legality of them. He turned his off for good too after replacing them with a legal transmitter that let him pick up FM radio signals he transmitted around his house. The third one? He must have done something to get on Harold Dutton's bad side, for as soon as Harold had tracked him down, he'd tossed the pirate to the FCC. The fines, as Stacey remembered them, were astronomical.

Stacey pulled past the Les Williams for Sheriff signs that waved the man's gloating face around her driveway and drove back to her house after dropping Stephanie at hers. Rick's pickup was there, along with two others.

"Can't believe the guy was cavalier enough to put a transmitter there," one of the hams said with a laugh. The others joined in. "Like he was teasing us."

"Where?" Stacey asked.

"Honey, can you bring us some coffee?" Rick smiled up from the couch like he was a cat who'd caught a mouse. Or rat. Not the ones in the attic, though. She'd have to do that herself. "We sure had an interesting ride."

"Interesting, huh," she said. "You going to fill me in?"

"Sure could use some coffee," another one of the men said. "After all that."

She looked at the half-dozen men chatting in her living room. This would, she realized, take more finesse than she'd thought, getting Rick to tell her anything.

"Wait until the sheriff finds out." Rick's voice followed her from the living room to the kitchen. The thing about catching rats is that they were smarter than you'd expect. Always more than one way to get inside. Into attics or, in this case, into radio station studios.

The coffee maker chugged and burbled.

"How'd y'all figure it out?" Stacey said with a smile as she brought the mugs to the living room.

"How do we ever figure it out?" another ham said. "Some luck and a lot of skill."

"It's not magic," Stacey said. "How did you pin it down?"

They looked at each other. Stacey went back to the kitchen for cream and sugar and the boiling hot carafe full of coffee.

She returned to the men arguing over what they'd found. "One we found was outside the high school," one ham said, picking up a cup of coffee.

"Another one on top of the Ford dealer," another ham said.

Rick leaned back with his coffee perilously perched on his paunch. "Well, me and Jerry can confirm that there's a third on the library."

Stacey set the creamer and sugar bowl down. Then she sat down herself. On her phone, she opened up the maps program. "Hey, slow down, y'all," she said. "One by one, tell me where you found the sources of the signal."

One by one, she marked the sources on the signals they'd found, dropping pins on her online map. Going back and forth between them, the pins made a line right through Daw County.

"Amateurs," the oldest ham said, dumping another spoon of sugar into his coffee. "I found the hardest to locate, but that comes with doing direction finding since long before you were licensed."

"Since before we were born, you mean?" another ham said with a laugh.

"Okay, okay," Stacey asked calmly. "Where did you locate the signal?"

"At the old Keller farm," he said. "Or right near there. Something on his property line, and old man Keller doesn't like it when you go poking around his place. Came out with his rifle. Not pointed at me, mind you, but holding it like he could at any moment. Shouted at me like he'd seen someone poking around not long before."

Stacey suddenly felt bad for Bo Sanders, having wandered so near to the danger. "I think you're all right," she said. "Look."

Rick nodded. "Guys, we are not done."

"What do you mean?"

"Look," he said. "At Stacey's map. She's put it together. If we found these, we probably found just a few of a bunch of weak signal transmitters."

"That's just strange," the oldest ham said. "Why would he do that?"

"Y'all go find the rest of the transmitters," Stacey

said. "I've heard the station over near the Bluet Café, and none of the ones you located are near there. There would have to be one over that direction to get a signal out that way."

The hams finished their coffee quickly and left. Stacey saved the map and sent it to herself on her laptop. She opened the map there and looked at the trail using the map satellite images. The roads she had driven this week were all on the trail of transmitters, the roads she had taken to get to the protesters and to get around them. Everything would be over on Friday, Bo had said. Which was today. This probably had nothing to do with the protesters anyway. She picked up her phone again, hesitated, then called Rick.

There was one place they hadn't covered, one place that they would need to cover if her hunch was right. Rick picked up on the third ring, which meant he was driving and probably fumbling with his phone while doing so. "Baby, I need you to do me a favor," she said. She clicked on the map and hoped it wouldn't come to this.

****

Stacey shouldn't have come alone. She'd left before she would have needed to pick Addie up, and she'd texted her to call her dad just in case she wasn't in the pickup line on time. Ethan had a key to the house with him, so she hadn't worried about him. The SUV bumped down the gravel road that led to the Kellers' farm, then down the dirt path that led to The Belt's abandoned radio studio. Or the heretofore abandoned studio.

The silver truck wasn't where it had been earlier in the day. Was this what she'd been looking for? The blond man. Other than that, everything she was working on was hunches, assumptions, fears. If she was going to solve this before Friday, this Friday, the day of the homecoming game, the day her youngest son would come home for a visit from college for the first time, she had to do it now. She had to get in, get what she needed, then get out as soon as she could.

She shouldn't have come alone. She parked under an overgrown mesquite tree, hoping the inadequate cover would protect her somehow.

From the glove box, Stacey grabbed the heavy flashlight. She put her phone and keys in her pocket, breathed in, then got out of her SUV. She went back, grabbed her handheld ham radio, and then closed the door as quietly as she could. If she'd had decent pockets, then she could have put that in one of those in her jeans. But women's jeans being what they were, her pockets were already stuffed full with her keys and her phone. She slid the belt clip over her waist band, just behind her left hip and grumbled at the long history of bad storage in women's pants. A chill blew through her, and she tied her flannel shirt around her waist over the top of the radio, just in case.

The door was locked but propped open. She held her breath as the door hinge creaked a bit. Quietly, quickly, she made her way to where she'd remembered the studio being, a memory from decades ago. Inside, away from all the windows. Rather than the dimness and the dust floating around in the few shafts of light coming in, Stacey tried to focus on the tour her senior class had taken of the studio, holding Rick's hand as the piped in music played their song, singing along with Stephanie when they played a song the girls had chosen as their anthem for breaking free from childhood and embracing the young women they'd soon become. How it would all work out for her and Rick. How life surprised her. How life gave so much to Stephanie and then kept taking it away. She'd get the Bluet back up and running. They'd all rally around her, all of Daw County if need be, to get her back up and running and where she needed to be.

Her phone buzzed. She balanced the flashlight under her arm and put the phone on silent with one hand. Rick had texted her. Two more hits, heading away from where she was. With any luck, they'd be at Tess Clarke's place soon. When had she begun to think of Mrs. Dutton's cottage as Tess Clarke's place? Not something for her to think about right now. She slid the phone back into her pocket, took a deep breath, and went to find the heart of the station.

Around the corner hung dusty pictures she could just make out. Images of Daw County's past, when the radio station sent its DJs and staff to reach out to folks in real life just as they'd reached out on the air. A whole line of parades moved around the wall, like the Christmas parade she'd been to every year since she was born, coming back from college just in time each year, and later, bundling up babies to bring them out, covering their ears when the marching band came thundering by. All the many celebrations of Oktoberfest and Halloween and the Fourth of July. Every back to school day she and her sister had gone to, and every last day of school too. Stacey's graduation, and Amy's. But not Tyler's or Caleb's or Ethan's. And not what would be Addie's. The Belt had shut down long before then. Stacey fought back her tears. She had to focus on the moment, this moment. Her footsteps in the shadows.

And someone else's.

The footfalls were heavy. Someone big, someone who might have known she was there.

Stacey leaned against the wall holding her breath. There was no place to hide, not without alerting whoever was there that she was also there.

And then the sound coming from her pocket. Her reminder to go pick up Addie.

The tune from when Addie was a little girl, dancing across the kitchen floor in her white ruffled socks.

The footsteps grew louder, closer. And then she saw him. The big blond man in front of her. He held a piece of curved metal with sharp ends in his hand, which he pocketed before he reached for her.

Stacey gasped.

She didn't have time to catch hold of her heavy flashlight before he'd grabbed her and swung her toward the office door. He kicked the door open and pushed her toward a rolling office chair. Swiftly, he tied her hands behind her.

"What are you doing here?" he breathed into her face.

"What are *you* doing here?" she managed to squeak out.

He stood upright, his full height impressing her. Didn't it always? "I'm taking care of what should have been taken care of when this place closed down."

"Wait," Stacey said. She needed to stall him, stall for time, whatever it was he was about to do.

"I can't wait," he said. He swiveled her chair so that she could just barely see out the window. He'd pulled the curved metal piece out of his pocket and pointed with it. "You see that out there?"

"The antenna?"

"It's a threat," he grumbled.

"The antenna hasn't transmitted anything in ages," Stacey said as calmly as she could. "The tower was damaged in a storm over a decade ago. I doubt anything is still connected to it."

"That antenna has been a threat to the area since it was put up here," he said. "Leaking out radiation all over the spectrum."

"You're scared of it?" Stacey asked softly.

"Do you know who built that antenna?"

"The station's original owners," Stacey said. It was getting harder to do, but she tried to keep her voice calm, trying to soothe as much as she could the frightened child she saw in front of her now. "They put it up in the 1950s."

"Before a lot of research had been done on the harmful effects of radiation." He grabbed something in his other hand, a remote from the looks of it. A remote to what, though?

Stacey smiled her "it's all going to be okay" smile. "Bo, sweetie, as long as you're not right underneath the antennas when they're transmitting, they're not going to hurt you, okay? The kind of radiation that can hurt you from a long ways away, they don't put out, okay? There are lots of different kinds of electromagnetic radiation. You know that. You said you did the electrical on your new home yourself."

"That was before I knew the real dangers." Bo swung around. "I knew you were with the radio people," he said. He pointed the curved metal at her. "But I didn't know they'd brainwashed you too. Sorry."

"No need to be sorry, Bo," she said. "Come untie me. We'll talk, okay?"

"I didn't think you'd be one of them, Mrs. H."

"One of who?"

Bo looked down at the remote. He pocketed the metal piece then ran his finger over the top of the remote, just barely touching it. "One of the ones trying to do mind control with the antennas. When they're turned back on."

"What do you mean?"

"You're brainwashed. Wake up, Mrs. H. The 5G antennas put up all around Daw County? Someone buying the old station and getting the antenna refurbished? The pirate station? It's all a little too much to be a coincidence. Think for yourself." Bo looked out the window.

Antenna refurbished? Stacey filed that away for later. "There's a good explanation for all of those, nothing to do with each other." Stacey writhed against the rope. She felt the tip of the handheld radio's antenna. "Technology changes, and we want faster and better cell service, especially out here in the middle of nowhere, right? So that's the 5G. And whoever the pirate is, that's just some kid who doesn't know better, right? Sheriff Williams will be on that before too long. The hams are out looking for the pirate now."

Bo looked at the window and squinted out. He looked down at the thin gray remote, his fingers playing over the back of it where a long cord trailed out of it. "You're wrong."

"Am I?"

"You're wrong," Bo said. "Just wrong." Something creaked. "Someone in the government is planning on using all these antennas for mind control, you know. Or you don't know. I didn't figure you for a sheep, Mrs. H.

You were always so nice to me." He looked out the window again. "I'm sorry to have to do this. When we found out, the protesters and me, we started up our campaign. It started with all the antennas going up, then someone buying the station. We figured it out. But no one listened to us. Not even the sheriff. If he'd done anything about the antennas like we asked, then it wouldn't have come to this."

"Okay, first, Sheriff Williams isn't doing anything right now except trying to win reelection," Stacey said. Her handheld slid off its clip, and she held the radio tight in her sweating hand. "And second, all this came to what?"

"Someone bought the radio station. This one. It's a cover for the black ops that are about to take place," Bo said.

"Who bought it?" Stacey had one chance to do this, and if she messed it up, she knew she wouldn't be able to see her daughter's graduation. She tried to picture Addie's class in their gowns and mortarboards and the photo of the ceremony that might hang on the wall of this station, maybe near the photo of her own graduation. What she hoped Dale would do with The Belt, once he had it up and running again.

"We don't know," Bo said. "There's a name on the license, Orion Audio of Daw County, but we know that's just a cover."

Orion's Belt? "Bo, maybe I can help."

"You can't," Bo said. "We've rigged the station with explosives. They should be strong enough to take out the building and the antennas. I didn't want to hurt anyone, but you left me with no choice."

"Explosives?" Stacey shuddered, but she gripped

the radio tight. "Did you blow up the Bluet Café?"

Bo was silent for a moment. Then he nodded solemnly.

"Okay. No one got hurt, so that's okay. But let's focus on right now." She breathed in as deeply as she could. "Bo, were you going to stay in here while the building blew up?" Stacey fought back tears, not only for herself and her family, but for Bo, broken as he was.

He nodded again, his long blond bangs covering his face. "We didn't want to use a radio remote and endanger anyone else. So we rigged it up with a cord. See?" He held up the slack cord.

"Bo, you don't have to do this," Stacey said as softly and calmly as she could manage. She thought of all the times she'd talked her children away from choices that would have made things harder, though none of those choices came close to what Bo was about to do. "Think about it. You're smart, you've always been smart. Look at you. You have a career now. Think about that, think about all your coworkers you'll leave behind. And I'm sure there's someone out there who loves you. Think about everyone who loves you."

"Mom." Bo looked down at the remote again.

"Did your Mom have something to do with this?"

Bo nodded. "Might as well tell you, since we're not going anywhere after I—" He held up the remote. "Mom was the one who told me about all this in the first place. The antennas and stuff. I got together with some other people who were against cell phone radiation, and it went from there." He looked down at Stacey with a sincerity that broke her heart.

"Your Mom was wrong. A lot of people are wrong about things like this," Stacey said. "And it's okay. You don't have to do this."

"You're wrong," Bo said, suddenly straightening up and looking around. Was someone else here? Someone else Bo and his conspiracies would kill too? "We don't know what the radiation will do to all of us."

Stacey sighed. "Radio has been in use for over a hundred years, Bo. If something was going to be discovered about it, I'm sure someone would have discovered it by now."

Bo looked genuinely scared. "Your kind of radio, maybe. But not cell phones."

Behind her. Stacey grabbed the handheld radio more tightly. She wriggled against the rope as hard as she could while Bo looked around. "Listen to me, Bo. Let's think about this. Who bought this radio station?"

"I did." Dale Hillegeist swung the door open. "Bo, listen to Mrs. H. She's telling the truth about radio. And look, I'm not black ops anything. I'm just a guy who loves music and engineering. I got this because I wanted my daughters to have the same experience with music and community as I had when I was growing up." Dale looked down at Stacey. She wanted to think he was looking at her in their shared danger, but she knew he was instead assessing the ropes around her, the cord the remote was attached to, the whole thing with the bravado that must be in him somewhere still. "Stacey and I."

"Orion's Belt?" Stacey asked with a shaking voice.

Dale smiled. "My daughters love outer space. It just seemed to fit. I had to do that for them."

The way Bo looked at Dale nearly broke Stacey's heart. Would have done if he hadn't been threatening to blow them all up. Had Judge Sanders been as bad as Minty to the kid?

Dale pulled his cell phone slowly from his pocket. "Bo, I'm going to call someone who can help us. Who can take apart the explosives safely. Get us out of here without getting anyone hurt."

Bo laughed nervously. "Look at your phone. No reception."

Dale looked down at his phone in alarm.

"A bunch of us took down all the cell phone antennas all around here," Bo said with a sneer. "You're not going to hurt us anymore. Mr. Keller shook his rifle at us, but he didn't see what we'd done. And if we'd been hurt, then it was for a good cause. Protecting Daw County. He's going to hurt us." Bo glared at Dale.

"But you don't understand how—" Dale started to say, but Stacey cut him off.

"Hurt who?" Stacey shouted. "Who is going to get hurt? Besides the three of us?" Dale looked down at her. Stacey caught his eye and looked down at the large metal flashlight that half stuck out of her pocket. She looked back up at Bo. "Who is going to get hurt, Bo?"

"We're already hurting," Bo said. "All of us."

With a swift motion, Dale pulled the metal flashlight from her pocket, nudging the pocket knife up to her hip. Stacey grabbed the knife and started sawing at the rope. Dale swung the flashlight at Bo and missed.

"What are you doing, Dale?" Bo looked in horror at the other lanky blond man. They were both the same height, same build, but they couldn't have been more different in character. "You are part of black ops after all. You tried to trick me."

The rope fell from Stacey's arms. She grabbed the handheld radio and pushed the antenna as hard as she could into Bo's ribs. "That's right," she said. "We're both black ops. And if you don't hand Dale that remote right now, I'm going to hit the transmit button on this thing, and you'll be sorry."

"No, don't," Bo said. He looked down at the remote. "You wouldn't."

"Think about all the things you feared," she said. She pushed the antenna harder. "You blow up this place, black ops will come back ten times harder on Daw County. You're just going to make it worse. And get yourself radiation poisoning in the deal."

"No, don't," Bo said. He looked at the remote one more time and then passed it to Dale.

Just then, sirens announced the arrival of two sheriff's office SUVs and Les Williams's Camaro.

Deputy Valdez announced their presence and ran into the building followed by Deputy Muller. Sheriff Williams inched backward behind his sports car.

"We've just picked up the rest of the protesters," Deputy Valdez said. "Bo Sanders, you're under arrest." Bo sank to his feet and started sobbing.

"I tried." From Bo's pocket fell the curved metal piece that he'd clutched earlier. Stacey could finally see the thing in its entirety. A horseshoe meant for a goat. Just like the one that had punctured Stacey's tire and the one Addie had picked up out of the ditch near the protests.

Deputy Valdez picked up the metal piece to keep Bo from trying to grab it again.

Deputy Muller arrested Bo Sanders, and Dale set the remote down as carefully as he could. "We've got folks coming to take care of the devices," Deputy Valdez said. "But just in case, let's all get out of here. Dale, Stacey, we need you to follow right behind us so none of us sets off any explosives. We'll all meet back at the station."

As he was ushered into the SUV, Bo looked back at her.

"Bo, I'm sorry," Stacey said. "I said what I said there at the end to keep us all safe. I wasn't lying to you about there being nothing to this. Your mom was wrong about the conspiracies."

"Is that a guy wire thimble?" Dale asked pointing at the metal in Deputy Valdez's hand.

"I have no idea," she said. "It's evidence though." She held her hand out flat.

A guy wire thimble. That's what it was. Which made sense. They went over the guy wires to protect the wires from abrasion and keep them from wearing out. They were meant to protect the guy wires which kept the antenna towers stable and safe. Which kept those around the towers safe. Except when they were used as threats.

Stacey wanted to rush over to Dale, to thank him for saving her, to be near him, in his arms, until her heart had shaken the fear from her core. But he was already halfway into his truck. She looked for a while at his hair, graying, thinning, lank over his still charming smile. He was going to the station to give his statement, then he'd probably rush home to Melinda and their daughters. Right where he should be. And she was going home too, after she spoke to the deputies. Right where she belonged too.

Chapter Eighteen

In the football stadium, the Daw County high school band played a fanfare. Above them, dozens of tiny lights sparkled in the dimming sky, first spelling out the name of the school, then forming a giant heart in maroon and white. "They're not fireworks," Rick opined, "but these drone shows are pretty neat." Drone show. Where had Stacey heard that?

Fireworks at the homecoming game never failed to thrill Stacey, but in the aftermath of Bo's threats to blow up the radio station with her and Dale in it, she relished the lights and music instead. Something about not knowing what was coming next, what combinations, what colors. And it gave her something to focus on that wasn't Bo and what he and his friends and family had done. Fireworks meant celebration to Stacey, always had and always would. But sometimes new ways to mark what's good in life were needed too. Rick still held her hand, though. He'd grabbed it as soon as she came home from the police station and had held it pretty much ever since. Stacey held on tight to Rick, thinking about the lights, the colors, the music, and everyone around them that she loved, everything that made Daw County their home.

Home. Addie had sat at the dining table with Vanessa earlier that evening, both of them looking down at a box under the table. Just beside it sat Ethan, like a light out of the darkness.

"I kept texting you, Mom," Addie said. "Where were you?"

"I was—" She would have time to tell the story later. "Well, we'll talk about that later. How did you get home?"

"I knew Vanessa would be on campus still, so I asked her," Addie said. Stacey tried not to roll her eyes. Vanessa. Of course. "And then Ethan texted me and asked where everyone was."

"I even looked for y'all in the attic," Ethan said.

"I hope you were careful," Stacey said. "There are rats in there now."

"No, Mom, not rats." Ethan moved away from the box. "Cats. Or one cat and four kittens. Momma cat made a nest in an empty box, and I brought it downstairs. They'll probably be happier down here."

Nestled inside the box was one of the young barn cats, licking her nursing babies. "Look, Mom," Addie cooed. "Pfeffernuss had her kittens in the attic. And we almost, ugh."

"I know, sweetheart. I'm sorry." Stacey kissed the top of her daughter's head.

Addie looked admiringly into the box at the young calico she'd been taming and her newborn family. Pfeffernuss couldn't go back out with the other cats in the damp, cold barn now, could she? Not with babies. Not with babies Stacey had mistakenly thought were rats. Somehow, in some way, Stacey would convince Rick that his long-standing "no pets" policy had to come to an end. They'd keep Pfeffernuss inside, if the cat was happy with that plan, along with any of the kittens they couldn't adopt out when they were old enough.

Especially if that meant their daughter would happily stay home until she graduated from high school. "You're a good momma, aren't you Pfeffernuss?"

"She's a great momma," Stacey added.

"How about Gertie's and then the big game?" Rick suggested. He squeezed Stacey's hand. The green apple clock on the wall ticked loudly at her.

"How about Gertie's at the big game?" Ethan suggested. "It's late already."

"Are you coming, too, Vanessa?" Addie asked with a note of hope in her voice. Addie almost never went to football games, but if it took Vanessa Dumont to get her there, then Stacey wouldn't complain too much.

Vanessa pointed to the maroon lock of hair that had slipped down. "Wouldn't miss it. I'm going to pick up a friend, though, and I'll meet you there?"

"Cowboy Jenkins ain't gonna sit with us," Rick grumbled.

"Oh, no," Vanessa said with a slight blush. "Tess. You'll like her. Or better than you like Cowboy, anyway."

Ethan whistled. "That's a low bar, there."

"Ethan!" Stacey shot her son a look.

Her child, she corrected herself, looking up at the tiny points of maroon and white light in the sky now. He, no, they told Rick and Stacey on the ride over. This would take some getting used to, using the language Ethan wanted them to use now. Genderqueer. Nonbinary. They, them. Not their son, but their child. Their beloved child.

Addie had asked if she could ride over with Vanessa and Tess. Stacey reluctantly agreed. She thought of Bo, of how controlling his mother had been. It wasn't simple, not that simple. Every interaction was one that could go wrong. With Bo, a lot had, it must have. With Addie, she still had a chance to make things good, to give her daughter space to find her own way. Not to push. Not to cling. Addie had given Ethan a tight hug, and Stacey thought she'd heard her say "good luck" before she left. Now she knew why.

This could have exploded. Stacey knew that. She and Rick hadn't thought much about identities before. Her sons were her sons, and Addie was her daughter. And then, on the way over, Ethan told them. Genderqueer. Nonbinary. The words swam around her head before she realized Rick was asking Ethan a question.

"No, Dad, it doesn't change anything at home," Ethan said. They. "This is just who I am. I wanted to tell you that."

Rick was silent for the rest of the trip. Stacey had a thousand questions, not only for Ethan, but also for Addie, who must have been carrying the weight of this with her for the last week. Ethan who went to one of the most liberal universities in the country saw things so much differently than Addie, who still went to one of the most conservative high schools around.

After they stopped, Stacey got out. She looked at Ethan. Her child. She didn't know what to say about identities and pronouns, so she didn't. She just said what was in her heart. "I love you," she said. And she hugged them.

"Yeah," Ethan said, squeezing her back. "I know, Mom. I love you too."

Rick took a deep breath. "Two things. Are you still helping rebuild the shed this weekend? And you'll stand in line for Gertie's?"

Ethan said yes to both. Rick handed over cash for dinner, and Ethan went to stand in the line that wrapped around the parking lot. Addie scuttled out of Vanessa's car and ran over to stand next to her brother. No, her sibling, Stacey corrected herself. Addie jumped onto Ethan's back, just as she had done when they were younger, both laughing and shouting.

"You okay with this?" Stacey asked him.

Rick squeezed her hand. "I don't know," he said. "Honestly, I don't even know what it means."

"Neither do I," Stacey admitted. "Not really. Ethan's still, I don't know, Ethan, right?"

Rick nodded. They were, if nothing else, practical people. And as a family, they'd find a way to figure it out.

Stacey and Rick found a long bleacher empty, just about at the top row. Too high up to see the game well, really, but it gave them room. Ethan and Addie found them, and they brought up the plastic boxes filled with what Stacey had been craving since she'd left the sheriff's department. Vanessa, back in her frumpy long skirts and a sweater waved when she saw them. The maroon lock in her hair clung to her sweater. Tess, looking elegant even in her jeans and a black long sleeved t-shirt, followed her up.

"It's been years since I went to a football game," Tess said. She pulled a vegan sausage from her box, but at least she'd chosen the coleslaw and potato salad to go with it.

"You went to football games?" Stacey asked, hoping the question wasn't too gauche.

Tess nodded, chewing a bite of sausage. "Marching

band in high school," she said. "I played the clarinet."

"So you've been involved in the arts for a while," Ethan asked.

"Music was short-lived for me, but I started writing about the visual arts in college, and I never stopped," Tess said. "I worked in the tech industry for thirty years, sold out my share of the latest successful startup, then invested in the retreat. I still do quite a bit of tech consulting work, but I wanted to make a more meaningful life here. Get away from industry and big city pressures."

Stacey thought about Mrs. Dutton's cottage and how the big city imposed itself on the walls and floor of the small house. "You wouldn't happen to know what became of all of Mrs. Dutton's belongings, do you?"

Tess swallowed a forkful of potato salad. "I do, in fact. Judy went through everything before I moved in. Boxed up a lot of things she wanted to save for Harold and his children and grandchildren. I think there were some things she didn't know what to do with, like the bigger pieces of furniture. I had my crew wrap those up and take them to a climate-controlled storage unit in Dawville." She scooped up another forkful of potato salad. "This is amazing, by the way."

Stacey wanted to ask about all the tiny things, the needles, the thimbles, the unused yards of embroidery thread. But the announcer's voice boomed over the loudspeaker. "Ladies and gentlemen, welcome to Daw County High School's Homecoming Weekend." A flock of drones shot up into the sky, looking like a white hot spray of sparks followed by the maroon of the school's colors. "Before we begin the show, please rise for the national anthem."

They set their boxes down on the bleachers as they stood up. Rick gave Stacey's hand another squeeze before putting his hand over his heart. Addie and Ethan stood with their arms linked, right hands over their hearts too, swaying to the slightly off-key rendition of the tune they were all singing together. Stacey looked over at Tess and Vanessa, smiling at each other, Tess giving a slight shrug as she nodded toward the band. This was a song about home, wasn't it?

Home. Daw County, but also the Hengesbach farm.

Between the notes of the song, Stacey heard footsteps coming toward them. She looked down to see Tyler and Caleb walking up, their girlfriends between them, all making their way up the stands. Behind them were Stephanie and her daughter. People around them made room for them to slide in beside their family. Home.

And applause after the impossibly high notes at the end. Tess cheered for the band, and they all took their seats, sliding in uncomfortably close to each other but all the happier for it. And the lights dancing above them all.

****

Stacey had hardly watched the game, which was a decisive victory for the home team. Stephanie had filled her in on the sheriff's office's newly reopened investigation in light of the arrests, and the insurance company's willingness to go to court against the Sanders family should Bo be found guilty. Which meant Minty might be implicated too. "The Women's Association bent over backward to distance themselves from her," Stephanie added. "And they've let me rent out their kitchen cheap so I can make pies and cakes for the festival. I'll need some of your fresh harvest."

After the game ended, half a dozen hams who had their handheld radios clipped to their belts came over as they were filtering out. "We did it," the oldest of the bunch said. Stacey remembered his call sign, but she couldn't recall his name. "You figured it out, but we did it together. Saw Bo's truck over there after the protests and figured something wasn't right and called the sheriff's office."

"Thank you," Stacey said.

"Just part of crisis communication, ma'am," he said, tipping his cap.

"What did you think of the drone show?" another one of the hams asked her.

Drone show. Stacey remembered now. "Just beautiful. Just perfect. You did a great job."

"Well, we can't take all the credit," he said. "The drones were my daughter's idea. She's president of the high school robotics club. The kids in the club put the show together. We just helped out." He gave Stacey a long look, like he was about to volunteer her for something. "Say, do you think you'd be interested in—"

"I don't know, I'm pretty busy these days," Stacey said. "With the harvest."

The ham shrugged. "I get it. But if you ever have time, you might reach out to the girls at the high school. My daughter would like to start a radio club, but she's not interested when her old dad here offers to help out. You could show them that it's not just a club for the old men. I'd be willing to take over as secretary from you if that gave you more time."

She stood for a moment, hearing the words before nodding once to herself. "I could," she said. "I sure could. I'd like that, actually."

Dale, Melinda, Michelle, and Mae ran over to greet the hams too. Mae unzipped her jacket to show off the logo on her t-shirt. "Look what Daddy's doing!" she shouted excitedly.

"Orion's Belt," Stacey read. "Is this the radio station?"

Melinda nodded with a sigh. "Jenna found her last sponsor for the festival," she said. "And, coincidentally enough, we just found our first major advertiser. One of the Houston-based air charter companies just signed a contract for office space and hangars at Daw County Regional Airport, and the festival committee took it upon themselves to talk the charter company into joining the festival and maybe buying some airtime as soon as the studios at The Belt are ready to transmit again. Jack McGraw's flying for the air charter company now. Beats spraying crops, he tells me."

"Ah, good," Tess said. "Chartering flights for our featured authors will be much easier than flying them in to Houston and then driving them the rest of the way to Daw County. Especially with traffic as bad as it's been. That should make events at our new retreat all the more appealing."

Vanessa nodded. "Oh, and, Tess, maybe you can book time on The Belt so that your guests can read their poetry on the air?"

Dale scratched his head. "I don't know about poetry on The Belt. I mean, cowboy poets? Maybe? But we're mostly going for a hometown, feel-good, community vibe. Something people can, you know, get. Without trying too hard."

Tess started to protest, but Vanessa put a hand on her arm and laughed. "I know, Dale. You hear of anyone who does want to learn more about deciphering poetry, you can send them my way. I've got a class at the community college for that."

"Yes, ma'am," Dale said. "You can count on it."

"Well, maybe Jenna can think of a way to bring the featured authors out to the Wine and Pecan Festival next year for a reading and book signing, or whatever it is y'all do?" Stacey smiled at the thought of Jenna's negotiations working. At least the pecan growers would be part of the festival this year and for years to come. And Minty Sanders, if Bo's accusations could be trusted, might not.

"That's a lovely idea, Stacey." Tess took out her phone and made a note. Vanessa leaned in toward the screen, and Stacey noticed that she hadn't taken her hand off Tess's arm yet. "We should be off. Thank you for a lovely time, all. I think Vanessa and I have a few more ideas to discuss about featured authors?" Vanessa nodded at Tess then said her goodbyes.

Addie and Ethan followed the two older women to the parking lot.

"You're okay with this radio station business?" Stacey asked Melinda after she'd watched her two youngest children catch up with Tess and Vanessa.

Melinda laughed. "Okay is a strong word, but Dale showed me the books. The charter isn't the only company willing to buy airtime, and it's not like The Belt has much competition on the airwaves around here anyway."

"It'll be nice to see The Belt at events around town again," Stacey said.

"We certainly do have boxes of loot to hand out at the festival," Dale said. He wrapped one arm around

Melinda. Their daughters pulled on his other hand.

"Boxes and boxes," Michelle said. "T-shirts, water bottles, wrist bands—"

"And key chains and squishy things too," Mae added. "Best of all, we have these astronomy laser pointers. You can point out where different planets and stars are in the night sky. And they have The Belt's logo on them and everything."

"They're not really astronomy lasers, Mae." Michelle rolled her eyes at her sister. "That would be too dangerous. Green lasers can damage people's eyes. And they're a danger to anyone flying airplanes."

"I know, Michelle." Mae rolled her eyes more dramatically than her sister had.

"They're more cat toys than anything else," Melinda said. "And you two be nice to each other. Please."

"Sounds like that'll keep you busy," Stacey said with a smile. "And please do set aside one of the astronomy cat lasers for us. We might need it. Or five." She shook her head at the thought of five cats running through their house. "Anyway, be sure you save room for some of Stephanie's treats too."

"We wouldn't miss her booth," Dale said. "Can't keep me away."

"As long as you bring home some pie for me," Melinda said.

"How about we bring some over to the hospital if you have to miss the festival?" Stephanie said. "Which reminds me that I want to bring over a cake to Judy and Harold. He's supposed to be in for a while. I should go visit him now that he can have folks in with him."

"Let me know when you go. I'll come with you," Stacey said.

"Mom, Mom!" Addie ran over after saying goodbye to Tess and Vanessa. "Tess wants to adopt the kittens when they're old enough."

"She does realize that there are four of them, right?" Stacey asked.

Rick shrugged. "Wouldn't surprise me if she was the old cat lady type."

Stacey elbowed Rick. "Would be nice to have cats running around the retreat. Mrs. Dutton always had outdoor cats. Though I'd imagine any cats Tess would have would get pampered in her cottages and the meeting center."

Addie must have ignored her father's suppositions as she nodded at her mother. "And can we get Pfeffernuss fixed, and maybe keep her indoors?"

Rick was about to launch into his "no pets" speech, but Stacey cut him off. She'd convince Rick later about the errors of his previous "no pets" ways. And Rick, Stacey figured, would be more receptive now than he might otherwise have been before. "We'll talk about it," Stacey said. Rick squeezed her hand and nodded.

There was so much to talk about. Addie, for one. And Ethan's news. And there was Tyler and Caleb, too.

They'd all have a chance to talk out all of it soon enough.

For now, though, under the starry Daw County sky, Stacey just wanted to go home with her family.

Her beautiful, happy home.

A word about the author...

Tammy D. Walker writes cozy mysteries, poetry, and science fiction. When she's not writing, she's probably reading, trying to find far-away stations on her shortwave radios, making poetry programs, or enjoying tea and scones with her family. Find out more at https://www.tammydwalker.com

Thank you for purchasing
this publication of The Wild Rose Press, Inc.

For questions or more information
contact us at
info@thewildrosepress.com.

The Wild Rose Press, Inc.
www.thewildrosepress.com